THE LIGHT IS DIMMER

THE LIGHT IS DIMMER

SAMARA KATHARINE

BOW'S
BOOKSHELF

EBook ISBN: 979-8-88716-023-8

Trade Paperback ISBN: 979-8-88716-021-4

Hardcover ISBN: 979-8-88716-022-1

Cover design and artwork by Justin Scott

Published by Bow's Bookshelf, Inc.

Anna Stileski, Publisher

Join our Bow's Bookshelf Reader's Club for new projects, deals, and giveaways. Sign up at Bowsbookshelf.com.

To Terra, for inspiring me endlessly.

L ucky Barlowe stares at the colors swimming through the well water as he washes the rust off the small pendant in his hand. He pulls it out and holds it up to the light, studying it. It's not beautiful, very few things are, but even after all his years out on the streets he can still pick out spots of pure silver on the locket that haven't been scratched and scored with time. Lucas still thinks he almost misses the little clipped picture from inside the pendant when he was young, but in truth, he can't remember the names or faces of anyone or anything who would've been inside it.

He pats the chain dry and clasps the hook around his neck, hiding the silver under his thin shirt and pressing it close to his chest. He knows he had a life before this, and a family that loved him, but their faces are obscured in the fabric of time.

He must've had something—a father and a mother with golden hair, and a baby sister in a swaddle he feels so sure he used to hold. She doesn't have a name anymore—she never has. All he has left of them is the heart-shaped metal clasped around his neck, and even that, he's unsure the origins of.

He jumps as the bells in the tower of the temple behind him toll the time as high noon, signaling the beginning of service for the day. He turns around and stares up at the clock face up in the sky counting out the minutes. Doors open around him and children laugh as they clamber out of their houses and rush ahead of their parents. He sighs, walking forward and opening the temple doors. The wood creaks open on rusty hinges, and he winces at the sound. Footsteps sound behind him, and he looks back, holding open the door for a stranger in expensive-looking Saturday worship attire, her long chiffon dress brushing against the cobble pavement. She smiles and gives him a curt nod.

"Gods bless, Lucas," she says. He grimaces, but echoes the sentiment and follows her in before the worship crowds can force him to stand outside too long.

"I prefer Lucky," he says in his best impression of courteous formality. The woman's lip wrinkles, and she casts him a gaze of judgement down her nose.

"Nonsense," she insists, turning away. Her dress flutters out behind her in a display of Saturday perfection—groomed, prim, and proper in speech and appearance as Lucky could never dream to be.

While the woman in the dress saunters up to the front row and sits with her hands folded and legs crossed, Lucky relegates himself to the very back, and tries to appear as small as possible. It's not like he'd be wanted in the front anyway, with his dirty slacks and torn shirt that seems to attract grime like a moth to a flame. In these outskirt towns, most days he's an ordinary kid, but on Saturdays, he must find a way to hide. The people of the village pull out all the stops dressing up in their best clothing and donning fancy hats he knows must set them back a week's food supply, but they don't seem to care. It will all come back to them, they say, when they've paid their tithes to the gods.

The doors open and close in regular intervals as worshippers file in, greeting one another with warm smiles. The temple is filled with the sounds of neighbors catching up while Lucky sits with his shoulders hunched over a Book of the Triad, pretending to read.

He only manages to pick up jumbled nonsense about the Siren's birth. He's sure he's heard the story of the torrential rains and clouds of golden silk before, but he can't register the words on the page no matter how hard he tries. As he struggles to read the passage for a moment longer, the margrave approaches the front podium, and the people in the temple stand up to greet him with balled fists held close to their hearts. Lucas joins them.

The grave picks up his leather-bound Book off the podium, and in a fluid motion, turns to meet the kind faces of the statues of the Triad. The tall windows of the temple let in the bright, unobstructed sunlight of noon through red, yellow, and white stained-glass panes. Each window shines its light on its respective god of pure marble, staring out at the people of the temple.

The first stoic face of stone is the Angel of Dawn—the creature of the shadows. The creator of all life on earth, and the face which guides the kingdom's dead to what waits after death, if there is anything at all. Lucas casts his wistful gaze to the Angel's protective feathered wings, curled around the other gods like a shield. He wonders what it's like to have something familiar, soft, and warm wrapped around him. Hugging himself in the cold of the night couldn't possibly compare.

To the Angel's right, the adopted daughter Lady Retribution, the War Goddess. A tall woman in a long cloak with curly hair chopped at her shoulders, and a sharp crown resting atop her head, emanating strength and power. Every portrait of the goddess makes a point to show off her sharp canine teeth and collection of daggers all painted blood red. She's meant to look as fearsome in godhood as she was in mortality before her ascension, but Lucas finds flaws with the dangerous mask. Though every inch of the clear skin of her face is marred with dark scars, there's no denying it; everything about the goddess is beautiful. She's gorgeous in a grotesque sort of way, and in her eyes that are meant to swim with the blood spilled on the battlefield, he sees smaller, soft lines that speak of wisdom beyond her years, and compassion yet exhibited in war.

And to the Angel's left, the kind eyes and soft features of his son—Lord Siren, the Silver Tongued, god of all things artistic—human in a way none of his family could ever be. He always looked the nicest in every painting and every carving, a hard contrast to the ever-present sneer of his sister, and cold, commanding gaze of his father. The god of all things just and pure, the progenitor of all music, communication, and art with a thin smile carved onto his face and eyes wrinkled at the corners.

Though he appears warm and hospitable—and Lucky can almost imagine if he closes his eyes that the Siren smiles at him alone—he knows that nothing that cares for justice would ever care for him. Whatever the Siren really is, he would never spare Lucas even a glance.

The grave dips into a low bow before the sculpture of the Silver One before placing the opened Book of the Triad into his extended hand. He backs away, lowering his head and standing in silence. The crowd of worshippers in the temple do the same, looking to the ground and shutting their eyes, letting silence envelop the surroundings.

It's said that after a devout gives the Siren the book, the god takes this quiet moment to communicate with his speakers on earth. They're not supposed to be able to read during service—that's what the emperor says. If a grave has access to the book during his speech, he may be tempted not to speak from the heart.

No one in the temple raises their head until the margrave does himself, the sound of the fabric of his cloak brushing together as he folds his arms alerting them to the beginning of service.

"Good day, everyone," he says, his voice carrying through the grand hall of the temple. "I trust you all found your way well." Murmurs of agreement go through the temple, and he nods. "Excellent. Why, it's such a wonder to see so many familiar faces each week. True devotion can't be feigned."

Lucas looks down to try to avoid the grave's eyes, though he knows he wouldn't look at him anyway.

Truth be told, there's something to be said about the inviting atmosphere of the temple and the people's devotion to the gods, but that's not why Lucky's here. A sense of community is built here, but that is between the more well-off. Lucky gets no acknowledgement. Instead, he looks out the stained-glass windows and sees frost begin to settle upon blades of grass in the gardens. The autumn has only just begun, and still, the chill sets in without remorse. He's not sure he'd even be here if it weren't for the invisible hand of the cold.

"Friends, today we must begin with some saddening news," the grave says. Lucky looks up. "It will never stop being too soon when another is taken from us. The weeks have been too few to already feel the hole left behind in our community in her absence. On this sacred day we must not dwell on the consequences of the dead and remain fixated on them rather than our Triad who look upon us with their grace, and rather, we shall continue to live on as she would have wanted. Celia remains in our hearts for our service, and by our Angel's graces, shall not cloud our minds."

"Peace with her family," the people in the temple mutter to a practiced tune. Lucky doesn't join them.

"Margrave," a child closer to the front of the temple addresses. The grave smiles at her.

"Yes, dear?" he asks.

"Where will Celia go now?" she posits, and the temperature seems to drop. The people of the temple are silent, and the child's father shushes her with a hand, whispering things to her that Lucky can't hear. The margrave nods, and motions for the father to relax. He removes his hand, but not without some hesitation.

"We do not wonder where our friends go when they leave us behind," he says. "Rather, we put our trust into the judgement of our Angel. We do not think of what comes after we've left this world, for it is his to decide. Why would we shirk the beauty of this land we've been given by our Angel to spend time wondering what remains once we abandon it? Would that not make our Angel so very upset?" he questions. The child shrinks back and nods.

"He would be sad," she agrees. The margrave smiles.

"Fear not, Celia is in the Angel's hands. We put our faith into Him."

Lucky feels the convivial air return as the grave assumes his place before his podium and gives everyone a placating look.

Sometimes he does wonder what comes after death. He could never voice it outside his own mind, but he thinks about it sometimes. When he stares off the edges of the buildings as he hops from roof to roof, he wonders how simple it would be to take a step and find out.

He never does, because there's the Angel carved of marble staring at him with those commanding eyes and telling him not to fear.

The margrave continues his emphatic speaking as usual, and Lucky tunes the majority of it out. Instead, he digs through his tattered, worn bag, and takes out the remainder of a loaf of bread from the market. He earns himself some pointed glares from parents in the temple trying to set a good example for their children, but he ignores it all.

Before he knows it, the sun has dipped down lower into the sky, and the grave launches into the Triad's Oath for the day. Lucky tries to follow along as best he can with a mouth full of bread.

"And we thank our Triad for our lives, for the food we eat, and the homes we live in," he says.

"Gods bless us," the other people in the pews mutter, eyes trained on the floor.

"We thank the Triad for our prosperity, our happiness and the safety of our Kingdom."

"The Light we live under, such is Their work," Lucky

mutters along with the rest of the worshippers, already yearning for the safety of Saturday worship to return as it finishes. Each Saturday around this time he gets to live in the fantasy that he has somewhere to belong, and two hours later, gets it stripped away. He wonders, distantly, where he plans to sleep tonight.

"For our greenest pastures and sweetest fruits," the grave hums rhythmically, practiced and scripted.

"We thank our gods, for fertility and nourishment," he says, though he can't find it in him to concentrate now that his mind races with plans for the night. He's made it sixteen years this way, and he'll make it sixteen more.

"Blessed be the pious." People begin to collect their bags and brush off their clothes, standing up from the benches. Lucky stands and passes through the aisles between worshippers leaving the way they came, approaching the front as he always does. The margrave makes quick work with his own belongings, taking the Book of the Triad from the Siren's hand and bowing from the waist before him. When he turns and spots Lucas, he smiles.

"A wonderful and blessed evening to you," he says. Lucas bows his head.

"Thank you, Grave." The margrave scowls, and Lucky backtracks. "Margrave," he corrects.

"You ought to save that manner of speech for inside the home," he says, and Lucky bows once again.

"Apologies, margrave. It won't happen again." The grave gives a fake-looking smile and a stilted bow of the head to Lucky, and makes for the exit. The doors creak open and slam shut, and the boy is alone in the empty temple, keeping his gaze pinned just below the eyes of the statues of the Triad.

As the sound of the last few steps leaves the building, he sits down on his knees before the statue of the Angel and hangs his head.

"I know it's been a while since I talked to you," he says

quietly, ears open to listen for any sound of someone coming to intrude on his conversation. "I've been busy."

There's silence in the temple, because of course there is.

"I've uh—had a rough few weeks, you could say. I hope you don't mind that I haven't come to worship for a bit. Trying not to starve and what have you." He chuckles without humor and rubs his arm. "I suppose I've got to apologize to the Siren the most. I've lived a dishonest life—somehow even more than usual in the time since I've last seen you. I hope you guys are nice and that you'd forgive me for doing what it takes to survive. For some reason I feel like you would."

The temple doors open again, and Lucky turns his head. Across the aisle stands a tall man with curly brown hair, wearing a nice, tailored coat and slacks. He looks down and feels under-dressed. The stranger approaches the statues, and grins at Lucky as he kneels. His eyes are a deep, dark brown, and the light of the stained glass reveals flecks of gold and amber scattered throughout. It's somewhat unnerving, the way his eyes seem to glow in yellow light. Lucky gives him a curt nod, and hangs his head again, though he feels the stranger's gaze on him still.

He continues to whisper his conversation with the gods in his head. He always likes speaking aloud much better, but he supposes it's the best he can do.

"I always get interrupted," he continues in his mind. The stranger next to him breathes out through his nose in something that resembles a laugh. Lucky ignores it. "I suppose it's vain to expect I can have private conversations with the gods, but you'll forgive me for being a bit selfish this once."

There's shuffling to his side, and he opens his eyes to see the tall stranger's gaze already trained on him. He raises a brow, and the man continues to stare, seemingly not at all phased by having been caught.

"Is something wrong?" Lucky asks in his best imitation of formality, cringing at the words in his own voice.

"Not at all," comes the reply, laced with a sweet, entrancing accent. The man is a Northerner, Lucky notes, a bit out of place this far South. There's silence in the temple for a moment as he looks around uncomfortably, the stranger's eyes still on him.

"Can you stop lookin' at me then?" The man seems to finally come to terms with the fact he's been staring at the kid for so long and tears his gaze away.

"Apologies." Lucky looks back down and tries to shake the strange interaction away.

"This man in your temple keeps laughing," he says to the gods in his head. The stranger exhales again at the very same time, and Lucas stills. "Are his prayers usually this funny?" He looks to his side, but the man still sits with his head hung and eyes closed. "I'm sorry, I can't seem to remember where I was going. I'll be honest, I don't have much of interest to say, especially not to you. You're the epitome of perfection in every way possible, and me? I won't be surprised when you've had enough of listening to me."

A hand lands on his shoulder. He breaks out of his thoughts and looks up to see the stranger once again smiling at him.

"I'm sure the gods are accepting no matter our flaws," he says quietly, with a strange air of pure confidence. Lucky raises a brow and opens his mouth to speak, but the stranger's touch has already gone. The man is walking out of the temple, then out of his sight. He looks around in confusion, searching for an explanation he knows he won't find in the empty pews.

The colored light of the windows cast strange shadows, and Lucky can swear that the eyes of the Siren's statue shift downward to where he kneels.

L ucky would be lying if he said he wasn't fed up with this. Every single day, there's something new.
Like the morning he'd woken up in a cold alley he'd fallen asleep in the night before, his brown tunic feeling inexplicably damp. The humidity must've risen in the night, and it was incredibly uncomfortable.

As he sat up to rub his eyes and take in his surroundings, he noticed a strange feeling on his feet, tangling around something.

A soft, white, fur blanket was draped over his legs and torso. It was heavy and comforting, insulating as well—the rest of his body cold and damp, but his legs, perfectly warm and dry. He looked around the dark alley cautiously, looking for any sign of the person who must've left this behind—obviously it was a mistake.

There was no one. Not a retreating silhouette, nor a prying eye. It was just like the apples and loaves of bread left inexplicably all over the roofs he frequented, as if placed with the intention to fall in his path.

On top of it all, he'd found that over the past few weeks he'd been escaping capture from the market far less narrowly than before; his pursuers were slowed down for some unknown reason.

He wouldn't complain, but gods, was he confused.

So with his blanket stuffed in his satchel and his cloak still air-drying from its recent wash in the well, Lucky steps inside the temple once again. Today, there is no service.

The temple is quiet, and candles melt slowly, flames burning a dark orange. Light from the stained-glass panes cast a peaceful pastel glow over the empty pews.

Lucky moves to sit in a bench in the very front. The orange of the candle flames prick in the corners of his vision as he puts his head down. Even though the statues are unmoving as always, he feels the uncomfortable feeling of eyes on him again.

That's another weird thing that's been happening recently. The temple was a warm place to sleep when he could find a quiet, unexposed place, so he lingered here often. But as of late, no matter what he's doing, he can feel a gaze pinning him. He thought maybe he'd displeased the gods at first, and this was their way of telling him he was no longer welcome in their worship, but that was ridiculous. He had seen what happened to people who truly displeased the gods, and it wasn't pretty. They wouldn't simply stare at him, that's childish.

It was just Lucky's mind, he figured, conjuring a gaze that didn't exist to make himself feel less alone.

He keeps his eyes open as he begins talking.

"Hey guys." Most often, the margraves' voices would carry through the grand building effortlessly, but the incredible acoustics of the temple can't pick up the low decibels of Lucky's nonexistent voice today, and there's no echo to be heard. "Uh— you wouldn't believe it. There's been this weird thing. The other day I woke up with like... a really expensive blanket. It was kinda weird. It's nice too. Wait—" He fishes through his bag quickly to pull it out, like a child presenting to his class for show and tell. "Look at it! It's cool, right?"

No one answers. Lucky sighs, and drapes the blanket over his legs. The temple is warm enough, but the weight of the blanket makes him feel safe.

"That's honestly all the news I've got. I'm sorry I'm boring, but hey, you guys aren't listening anyway." In the corner of his vision, he sees the candles flicker. He trains his gaze on them and catches the moment the vibrant orange switches to a bright yellow flame, rising higher and blazing bright. He raises his brows at it and opens his mouth. "Okay, nevermind," he says, his voice small and surprised. The yellows flick back to orange, and Lucky smiles and laughs. He hasn't laughed for real in a while. "Now then funny guy, too much of a coward to talk for real?"

It might not be a good idea to call the gods cowards, he considers. He doesn't know whether he should cower in fear or cackle when the fire shifts to bright red, but he chooses the former, backtracking without hesitance. "Wait, I'm sorry," he amends. The light stays red, but the flames burn lower, and less bright. What does that mean? "Hey, if you've waited *this long* to get mad at me, that's your problem." Orange again. Lucky smiles.

He lays back on the bench, digging into his bag and pulling out an apple that he'd been saving. He takes a bite, and swallows it down before speaking again. He has manners enough to not speak with his mouth full in front of the gods.

He looks up to the marble statues and frowns.

"So, uh... candle guy. I've been talking to you guys for a while. You're a little late." Not exactly red, but a darker shade of orange for sure. "Uh, I don't know what to make of that color." It shifts back to pure orange and Lucky raises a brow, shrinking back on himself. "It's amazing you've decided to speak to me, but I don't know what this means." Lucky realizes something, and shrinks in on himself, mentally backtracking. "Or—you know, it's an honor and all, to be communicating with the Triad. I feel blessed?" It comes out sounding more like a question than a statement and Lucky cringes.

He doesn't know what to say. Clearly he can't be the same delinquent teen that swears at merchants on the street when he's getting the honor of talking to the gods, but what is he supposed to think of this? Instantly, he feels a faraway sense of something resembling guilt. He leans back against the pew and lowers his head, the confidence and cockiness he once exuded now called back into his body as he rubs his arm and looks away.

"No offense, but... you're kinda wasting your time, candle guy." The light stays orange and he takes it as his cue to continue. "I'm not really worth the effort. I'm sure there are plenty of people better to talk to, right?" He glances at the candles, and they stay orange for a long moment before erupting into an angry bright red flame growing taller and higher. Lucky presses his back against the pew, something between shocked and afraid. All around him, candles that previously had remained orange throughout the entirety of his conversation burst into beacons of dark crimson light and grow towards the ceiling.

This is it, Lucky thinks. He should've accepted it for what it was and waxed philosophical about how honored he was. Instead, he's offended his gods, and the temple will go up in flames with him in it.

Lucky shrinks into the pew, begging it to take him in and accept him as a part of the wood fiber so he can escape imminent doom. The red glows brighter around the room, and smoke begins to form a haze in the air.

He closes his eyes tightly, and braces for impact, ready for the heat to grow closer and the flames to lick at his blanket, but it never comes. Slowly, carefully, he opens his eyes back up to see the once raging fires calming to a mellow white, and shrinking back down closer to the candles, no longer brushing the high ceiling.

He opens his eyes wider, and sits back up, looking around. Every candle has shrunk, and its color calmed. He lets out a relieved breath and lets the tension leave his shoulders in waves.

He stares into the flames a moment longer, and hugs his blanket a little bit closer in spite of himself.

"That was a bit intense," he mutters. The white remains, and

Lucky can't think of anything else to say. The sunbeams come in through the windows, and Lucky gets a piece of bread out of his bag. If the measurement of the sun that the margrave was so proud of was to be believed, it's getting close to high noon. These days he could afford the luxury of eating lunch. Three meals a day were starting to come naturally.

He leans back in the pew, and the candles do nothing. Hesitantly, he bites down on the bread, and nothing happens, so he swallows it down. The gods have never been concerned with someone eating in their temple before, but there's a first time for everything. And especially with that pyrotechnic display of red flame, Lucky doesn't want to risk angering anyone more than he apparently already has.

And there's silence in the temple. The candles continue to burn cool yellow, and the smell of incense float in the air as Lucky eats quietly, avoiding the eyes of the statues. It's not often he has true free time in his day, so he doesn't exactly know what to do with himself.

Minutes tick by quietly, and the next time Lucky looks up, the light from the colored glass shines perfectly onto each of its respective statues. Lucky smiles. Noon.

Pastel-hued yellow hits the marble of the Siren, red on Lady Retribution, and the faintest of calm greys paint the Angel's cloak.

And there's a crack.

Lucky gets out of his seat and approaches the statue of the Siren. Standing at seven feet tall, there's no way Lucky could look the Triad eye-to-eye, but he can see it clearly—a small crack in the pristine marble on the Siren's face, filled with yellow light. Lucky runs his finger over the crack, and it runs deep.

Then a sound reaches his ears, and he takes pause, eyes shifting from the small gouge on the Siren's cheek, to his kind eyes, where another fissure forms. Then, again, on the next eye, the stone breaks. He backs up away from the statue with wild eyes, looking around as the air is filled with small popping sounds. Chips of marble break away from the statue, clinking onto the ground.

Lucky should leave. He should pick up his things and run away before someone comes, blaming the imperfections on the first street rat they can find. But as he turns on his heel to grab his bag, the candles shift again, captivating him. They burn orange once again, drawing his attention, and he has no choice but to stand there watching as chips clatter to the floor.

The breaking gets faster. Lucky covers his ears, shutting his eyes tight and trying to ignore the sound. He bites down on his lips to keep himself from screaming and pulls away with a little piece of skin. The cracking surrounds him, and even with his ears covered, it worms its way into his mind as if clawing into the very fibers of his being.

A weight lands on his shoulder, and he opens his eyes cautiously, looking up, light green meet dark brown, with flecks of shining amber.

A tall brunet man stands before him, smiling down at him softly with a kindness in his eyes Lucky has never seen in his life on the run. He has a long white cloak, and Lucky can pick out windings of thread of pure gold stitched on each seam. His curly hair is windswept, falling in a curtain over his eye, and atop his head rests a circlet Lucky could only begin to imagine the value of—shining silver with sharp peaks, and metal so polished and bright Lucky has to avert his eyes. There's a shape behind the man, too—tendrils of golden light sweeping behind him in a feathered cloak, extending such that the light touched the walls of the temple on either side of the figure, just transparent enough that Lucky could see through them back to the statues.

Wings. Seraph wings.

Lucky realizes with a start that he recognizes this man. It's the stranger from the temple those days ago that interrupted his prayers. Through his wings Lucky can see the statue of the Siren completely broken down into dilapidated relics of its former self, and finally, he makes the connection. The strong cheekbones and sharp jawline, and the kind smile and soft features...

"It's nice to finally meet you."

... and when he speaks the dark intonation, the downwards inflection, and the posh far-North accent are so startlingly, unnervingly familiar. His voice carries the same eerie weight it did the last time Lucky had seen him.

Having put the pieces together, Lucky stares, pupils dilating as he takes a step backwards with his mouth agape.

"What?" he squeaks in fear, and the man—the god—cringes away, the golden cirrus wings retracting in on themselves sharply. What once reached the walls on both sides in a wingspan that had to have been five meters or more now folding against his back. He reaches out with his palms facing Lucky in a placating gesture.

"Hey, hey, calm—"

"Calm?" Lucky asks indignantly. "What just happened—who are you?" The man seems genuinely confused as his face wrinkles up and he tilts his head, brown locks falling over his face. Lucky swears he can see flecks of gold dancing in his hair from the stained glass light. The man is glowing. "This isn't real," Lucky breathes.

"I feel pretty real," the god says. Lucky doesn't know what to do, think, or say, so he just laughs.

The Siren raises a brow at him, but says nothing as he continues to laugh to himself. It feels far less like genuine laughter and more a nervous breakdown of sorts, but what is he supposed to do?

"Did I say something?" The Siren asks. Lucky looks back up, and doubles down again, because good gods—that's the Siren right in front of him, and good gods, he's laughing at him, and *good gods*, he's going to get himself killed.

But Death doesn't come for him in that moment—that would be one too many gods to meet in a day. Instead, Lucky takes a moment to assess his situation, and scrambles to find his footing in front of the god.

"I am so sorry," he lets out swiftly, dropping down to the floor to bow to the deity. "I'm so sorry, I don't know what..." He can't finish his sentence, as the Siren's hand lands on his shoulder again, and he looks up to meet his eyes.

That doesn't feel right. He should be looking down.

"Be not afraid. And please, don't bow, Child," the Siren assures. Lucky hesitates, but stands up, and when he speaks his voice is shaky.

"I'm not a child." The Siren only smiles crookedly at Lucky, and he feels something strange bloom in his chest, a warm feeling spreading through him. There's something in the expression he can't place—fondness, for sure, but something else; something like pride.

No one's ever been proud of Lucky before.

"Right. Very strong man, Lucas." He stops dead in his tracks and widens his eyes at the Siren in disbelief.

"You—ha, you know my name. That's—wow." The Siren laughs, the sound carrying in the temple effortlessly, and for a second, Lucky feels he lives up to his name truly. He briefly feels nearly weightless, lost in the sound like church bells and rustling leaves. It's disorienting.

"And you'd know mine, I hope?" he asks. Lucky wastes no time nodding and agreeing.

"It's a true honor to be speaking to one of the Triad. Your reputation precedes you. I'm humbled by your presence, Lord Siren of the Silver Tongued," Lucky says, stumbling over his words and trying to sound as genuine as he can, but he can't help the anxiety coating his every thought.

The way the Siren raises his brow at Lucky makes him take pause—like he's finally made a mistake and this conversation is over.

It's not the first time Lucky's been wrong when the Siren simply waves his hand and grins. "I'll have none of that. I believe

THE LIGHT IS DIMMER

a proper introduction is in order, instead of whatever it is these people," he gestures vaguely to the temple at large, "make you read. Please, just call me Siren for now." He holds out his hand towards Lucky, and the teen simply stares at it in confusion.

"You want me to shake your hand?" he asks. The god retracts, and seems somewhat confused.

"Oh, do people not do that anymore?" Lucky looks at the god, searching his face, not quite sure what he's looking for.

"I mean, they do, I just... am I allowed to touch you?" The god only chuckles at Lucky and shakes his head.

"Lucas, there aren't rules. I'm simply speaking to you. As equals." That word shakes Lucky to his very core, and he lets his mouth drop open slightly.

Equals. With the Triad? Not a chance. No, that is not right by any definition.

"Are you sure you have the right person here?" Lucky asks before thinking. At the Siren's confused expression, he continues, somewhat breathlessly. "I mean, I'm honored, this is amazing, I never would've in my life guessed I'd meet you, but, you know, there are more important people. I'm not even close to your equal. I think you've got the wrong guy, I'm just a—"

"*Silence.*" And Lucky shuts up. There must've been something in that word, because no matter how Lucky tries to apologize, or open up his vocal cords to let out a simple affirmation, nothing comes out.

Lucky nods and looks back into the Siren's eyes, and recoils. His dark brown irises have shifted to a blinding gold, swirling like the shining liquid of the tonics Lucky has seen the clergy craft from time to time. The shifting cirri of light-borne seraph wings extend back out again, and the presence of the god in the room, somehow more than before, is commanding. Lucky breathes weakly, waiting for him to speak again.

The swirling gold contains no pupil, only staring down at Lucky with a gaze like the very sun beating down into him. "Are you questioning Our will?" His voice is now darker, and echoes through the temple, hostility dripping off it. Lucky shakes his head. His eyes dance with fear, and he twists his countenance into strained terror unwillingly. The god before him notices, and his wings retract. Lucky relaxes his shoulders, but only slightly. *"You may speak."*

"I'm sorry," Lucky says immediately. "I didn't mean to, I'm sorry, I'm sure you know what you're doing." The golden fluid in place of the Siren's eyes clears up, revealing the kind dark brown irises underneath, and he nods.

"I do, and I am sure it is you I'm looking for," he says. Lucky nods tersely.

"Right. Right, of course. What can I do for you, Lord Siren?" he asks. The god raises a brow at Lucky, prompting. "Siren," he tries again. The Siren smiles.

"Lucas," he says, and the dark tone dissipates, "I wish to bestow upon you the blessing of the Triad." Lucky gawks at him.

"You what?" he says, voice small. The god smiles once again, and Lucky notes for the first time how incredibly white and *sharp* his teeth are. The image is not comforting.

"The blessing of the Triad, Lucas. For your prosperity and well-being, so that you should not be made to sleep in the cold ever again." Lucky lets out a strained breath through his teeth. "Give me your hand, Lucas." He's not going to question the god again. He gives him his hand.

For a moment that feels like an eternity, his hand is warm—it feels like he's been lit on fire from the inside out, blood in his veins carrying the heat from his hand up his arteries and into his heart. A bright light encases the two hands, and the feeling of full-body cauterization leaves him. When the god speaks again, it takes on a rounded melodic form like orchestral music worming its way into Lucky's senses.

"I bless you with the regards of the Triad. Let no mortal means within your control bring harm to you, should your bones never break, flesh untorn with the power of the Bleeding One in heart." A sharp pain sticks itself into Lucky's chest, and he doubles down, but the god keeps an iron grip on his hand as he clutches at his skin in pain as if it could ease the ache. "Should your dreams be not plagued by the creatures of night, as granted by the Angel in protection of the mind."

A gripping headache rips into Lucky, and he clenches his teeth, shutting his eyes tightly. The Siren doesn't let go. "And should you seek to persuade, blood leave no stain, the weight of mediation lain heavy upon your tongue, the gifts of the Silver One." The metallic taste of blood fills Lucky's mouth, and he opens it to spill the liquid, but none comes out. The taste remains. He gags, earning a sympathetic look, but The god doesn't stop.

The Siren speaks a few phrases in a language Lucky can't understand—a sound archaic and grating to his ears with sharp vowels and rounded consonants creating a deathly symphony of eldritch knowledge swimming around in his brain, digging claws into the tissue and burrowing a home in the depths. Distantly, he wishes he'd have been warned about how horribly painful earning the gods' favor was. If he didn't know better, he'd think blood came out of his ears.

As if it were never there, the bright light shrouding Lucky's hand disappears, as does the sharp pain shredding across his body. He opens his eyes to see not irises of churning gold and a kind smile waiting, but rather, pastel light from stained glass windows painting the floor in front of him, and three pristine statues, with not a crack in sight.

☙ 3 ❧

Lucky wakes up on a bench in the temple with the bitter taste of metal in his mouth. When he sits up and stretches, he lets himself yawn, and a drop of warm red falls onto his pants. He stares at it in disgust before racing out of the temple into the gardens. With the scent of wildflowers and falling leaves surrounding him, he spits out the contents of his mouth—a mess of dark red fluid and saliva that makes him gag. Not the best start to his day.

Lucky tends to chew his lips and cheeks as he sleeps—a life on the run would fill anyone with unfiltered anxiety. Even without consciousness, he tends to be mildly self-destructive, and though waking up with the taste of iron isn't unusual for him, the sheer amount today catches him by surprise.

He approaches the well in the courtyard to wash his face, and as he opens his mouth catches sight of the second distressing sign that something is very wrong—canine teeth, long and sharp, and practically shining pearly white. Curious, he raises his hand and runs a finger over the points as if to assure himself, but catches a long tip protruding away from the rest of his teeth that tells him he's not seeing things. When he pulls his finger away, beads of blood drip down. So sharp he didn't even feel the cut.

Lucky dips his hands into the well and splashes the cold water over his face with urgency, shocking himself awake.

When the water settles, he looks into it again, the sharp canines still remaining. He backs away in fear. He faces a window pane of the temple, viewing his reflection yet again, and picking out another peculiarity—his dull freckles seem darker, and marks that the villagers would call "angel kisses" that he'd never had before mar his complexion. One on his cheek, another below the right corner of his eye, and a final one to the left of his top lip.

Panicking, he traces the marks and freckles with a finger, rubbing at them slightly as if they could be removed with pure willpower. Upon the realization that the angel kisses are there to stay, Lucky clenches his teeth—his breathing becoming hollow and staggered.

His vision clouds. The world seems to bleed into a textile of greyscale tones and contours, he blinks rapidly to clear it. The black and white color scheme stays. He turns back to the window pane and stares into his own eyes, and can't seem to recognize himself. If not only because his color vision seems to have faded, but because his green eyes have gone as well— replaced with a rippling flow of sparkling silver, hit by the light of the morning sun and shining. He blinks his eyes over and over, each time studying his face, breathing becoming faster and shallower as the grey metallic irises remain. He holds himself back from screaming.

Mind racing, he rushes back into the warmth of the temple and falls onto the pew again, raising a hand to his chest to feel his pulse. All at once, the wind is knocked out of Lucky's lungs, and he feels like he is completely under water. He holds back the nervous reaction to bite at his lips again, and holds his mouth open slightly to avoid even touching the soft tissue with the weapons inside.

He gazes up to the statue of the Siren God and pleads inwardly for some sort of explanation, beginning to bite at his nails. As he brings his hand up to his mouth, he makes the distressing discovery that within mere minutes, the beads of blood bitten out from his sharpened teeth had disappeared, and any indication the cut ever existed healed over.

Bones never break, flesh untorn.

Lucky glances around the grand hall of the temple frantically, making a rash decision. Biting down hard on his index finger as a test, he feels the flesh tear away under his sharp teeth. However much he wants to scream in pain, he simply grits his teeth—pulling it back out to study. Coated in blood and buzzing with pain, he watches his skin reach out across the expanse of exposed muscle, pulling itself together before his very eyes until all that remains as evidence of his impulsivity is a dull red mark circling his finger. Scarred, but gone. In the blink of an eye.

Lucky grasps at his hand and wipes away the excess blood to get a better look at it. He feels the color drain from his face.

And with the light of the stained glass beating down on him from above, Lucky curls into himself, face in his hands, and yells. Something between anger and fear and devastation comes out of his throat, and tears begin to dampen his palms as he scrambles desperately for explanation and finds nothing.

His brain returns to images of the night before in the temple, holding the Siren's hand, fire surging through his veins, and pain singing every nerve—and he sobs. He bites down hard onto his lip, and though he can taste the blood, he can also feel his skin pull itself together under the fluid crimson cowl.

He lifts his head and has no reprieve from his revelations, as he watches tears of liquid mercury dry onto his hand.

In blinding panic, Lucky turns around, and is only slightly relieved when he sees no wings of silver reaching out behind him.

The eyes of the Triad's statues seem to stare into his very soul with intensity—recoiling, he presses his body into the pew.

"Stop looking at me!" he yells into the empty chapel, and the feeling of being watched stays with him. He directs his attention to the Siren with osmium tears sliding down his cheeks. It's only then he realizes how unnecessarily cold the liquid is. "What did you do?" And there's silence. Silence that breaks down to Lucky's bones and makes him shiver. Withering silence that seems to eat away at Lucky's already out-of-control psyche.

There's a crack. Lucky freezes.

He stands stiffly and points to the statue of the Siren—a fissure now marring its eye. His tears drip freely off his cheeks onto the floor, and when they land, they smoke and sizzle like dry ice before evaporating and disappearing. "Don't move!" he yells. He probably shouldn't—he knows he shouldn't shout at the gods, but the cracking stops, and that's all he needs. "What am I?" he questions indignantly, lip quivering despite his attempts to keep a calm facade.

A candle flickers into white, and Lucky groans.

"I don't know what that means, Siren!" he says. Lucky feels a splitting headache hit him without preamble.

"*Do not raise that tone with me, Lucky,*" a familiar voice mutters, his nickname like poison from the Siren's lips.

Lucky screams and closes his eyes. "How are you in my head?" He hears the god laugh—no, he *feels* the god laugh from inside his mind.

"*I'm everywhere.*"

Lucky looks around the grand hall and sees no sign of the deity.

"*Are you scared, Lucky?*" the Siren asks. Lucky shakes his head fiercely, even though it pains him to do so.

"I'm not afraid of you!" he yells out. The headache worsens momentarily.

"*I know when you lie, dear.*" Lucky lets out a fearful breath.

"You do?"

"*Of course I do.*"

Lucky wants to run and hide and avoid the Siren's voice, but he knows he can't. He wants to plug his ears—the whispers of the god only make his head hurt. More tears drop to the ground, and he whimpers.

"Please just talk to me normally," he says, dropping to his knees and clutching his head in his hands. "You're hurting me." A flash of light bursts out into the temple, searing Lucky's eyes, and for a moment he feels sure he might faint.

Lucky looks up to the god to see the Siren's eyes already shifting bright gold, and he cowers away, keeping distance between them.

"I won't hurt you," the Siren says as he steps closer to Lucky. Lucky shuffles back again in response.

"You have," he says, voice small and cowardly now that the god stands in front of him yet again, lustrous wings at their full span. The Siren scowls and approaches Lucky, who moves back more. The god sighs.

"*Stay,*" he commands, and Lucky freezes. The Siren kneels down next to him and studies him, his eyes returning to a warm brown. "Lucky, please calm," he says, reaching out to touch Lucky's face lightly, "then you can have your beautiful green eyes back." Lucky gawks at him, but he can't move away. "It's an emotional reaction. You can learn to control it. I know it's frighteni—"

"You don't know anything!" Lucky says. "Am I like... like you now?" The Siren smiles and laughs lightly.

"No, no. Better than you were before, but not like Us," the Siren says, and Lucky tries to laugh but comes out watery and drenched in terror.

"I was great before."

"But so terribly, humanly fallible." The Siren looks at him for a moment, before taking his hand and smiling. "And I see you've discovered Retribution's gift?" Lucky nods. In a much gentler, softer tone, the Siren speaks. "Let's try not to be so self-destructive, though. It heals, but if it can bleed, it can die."

"Siren, what am I?" Lucky asks, voice breaking on the last syllables. He tries to keep his veil of rage unfurled over the sense of overwhelming dread curling up in his stomach, but he can't help the tendrils of fear that creep out into his question.

"Like I said, better," is all the response Lucky gets, and his face twists into distaste. He doesn't have time for the Siren's bullshit.

"I'm serious!" Lucky's vision gets darker, and suddenly the brightest whites that crowned his vision fade into dark greys and angry black, and Lucky blinks, surprised. The sudden change catches him so off-guard he forgets he was about to yell at the god. The darkening waxes and wanes in an unsettling current and before he knows it, he's hyperventilating. He pinches his arm and clenches his fists to keep himself grounded as time begins to pass in a blur, and suddenly he's under water.

And in his mind he's falling. Falling, falling, and never hitting the ground. The sun-beaten concrete outside the temple catches his eyes from the window panes, and he can almost hear the sickening crunch of bones as he hits the ground. He's under water. He's in the sky. He never hits the stones under his feet. In his mind, he's falling.

The god before him seems to have the slightest resemblance of guilt or worry dancing in his eyes, and snaps his fingers before the teen. He's saying something Lucky can't understand. He sounds like a waterfall.

Lucky pinches himself harder as the world falls away, stealing hopeless, frantic glances around the temple for things that are real, like he taught himself. Statues are real, Lucky can see them. Benches, floor, window, god—god, the Siren is here. Is that real? Lucky is real, he knows that. He shakes his head and closes his eyes tightly, and when he opens them, all instances of white and light greys have vanished, leaving only the darkest shades and pure black clouding his vision.

The Siren's eyes which Lucky knows must be gold are entirely vantablack down to the core, and it sickens him. All at once Lucky feels like he might throw up, staring into the cold, unfeeling, unblinking abyss that is the Siren before him.

He can hear the Siren yelling, and he can hear the disorienting shattering of glass, and he clenches his eyes tight as vibrations carry through the floor like the feeling of heavy boots stomping towards him. He can hear two voices speaking frantically, but he can't tell what they're saying. When he opens his eyes to try to get a look at the second person, he's shocked to the realization that in the time between closing his eyes in fear of the glass, and opening them in fear of the world, his vision has gone dark. A completely black void. If he closes his eyes again tight enough, maybe he'll see the swirling synthetic patterns of his imagination.

When he feels a hand on his shoulder he screams, because it's not the hand of the Siren. The Siren's hands, he knows, are larger than this one, and they touch him as if he were made of porcelain, primed to be shattered with any force. When Lucky looks up to find the face of the new person, he can no longer tell if his eyes are open or closed.

He's being shaken, and it feels distantly like wind. And in his mind he's falling, but Lucky isn't scared of heights.

"Kid!" someone yells. This time Lucky can register the word. He pinches tighter onto his forearm, and can feel something warm drip onto his fingers—letting go. "Kid, come on, breathe." Okay. Okay, breathe. Lucky can do that. Lucky knows how to breathe, right? In and out.

In.

Out.

In. In. In.

Out, in one long breath.

Okay, Lucky knows how to breathe.

"That's it, Kid, come on, you got this." Lucky registers the words spoken by a new voice he doesn't recognize. It's melodic, crested with dark notes that rip Lucky out of his thoughts and back into the present.

"It's alright, I'm here," the Siren says. Lucky has never been more happy to hear the Siren's voice. It's warm and welcoming and feels like coming home, like the sound of tolling bells and peregrine calls.

"You idiot, shut up."

"He's panicking!" the Siren calls.

"You're not helping! Kid, can you hear me?" Lucky nods in response to the voice. "Can you see anything?" Lucky shakes his head. He can only see black, and when he closes his eyes, he sees falling. "Okay, more breathing, Kid."

Lucky nods. In, and out. In, out.

On the third breath, Lucky can see the black begin to lighten into tones of dark greys, and he lets himself hope. He keeps breathing, watching his surroundings come into focus as the dark fades away, and his heart rate steadies once again.

He can see the shape of a person with long hair, a cloak, and something like the shape of a poet's shirt. It's this person who has his hand on Lucky's shoulder. Lucky can't make out anything other than a vague silhouette.

He breathes, in and out, and looks around the temple. He puts a hand on his heart and focuses on nothing but the fast beating, feeling it slow infinitesimally, second by second. The weight leaves his shoulder as he begins to see white highlights in the world around him, vision lightening back down to what it was minutes ago.

"Take care of your kid, or I'm telling Elric what you've done," the sweet voice says again. Lucky turns his attention back to the Siren, and watches the cloaked silhouette disappear in a cloud of darkness.

The Siren is smiling kindly, and Lucky breathes out slowly one more time, letting the greys disappear and the colors he once knew in the world come into focus. Despite himself, he smiles. The pastel light on the floor from the stained-glass panes returns, and some sense of normalcy slows Lucky's racing heart.

"You really scared me there, Lucas," the Siren says. Lucky opens his mouth, but can't find it in him to say anything. He only nods. The Siren takes his hand, and the tension leaves his shoulders. "So, I'll take it you understand the—well, the eye thing." He gestures to his own face, eyes fading from bright gold back into dark brown. Lucky can't lie, he doesn't truly understand. He shakes his head no, and the god sighs. "Right, right. It's an emotional reaction. You got a bit panicky there and your eyes… stopped being green." Lucky cocks his head to the side.

"And they're green again now?" he asks. His voice is gravelly, and his tone is shaking. Still, the Siren understands him, somehow.

"Yes. Yes, they're normal again." It doesn't feel right at all, but for no reason, Lucky starts laughing.

He laughs as the Siren stares at him in confusion. He doubles over himself and looks at the floor, picking out every crack and every track worn into the stone from shoes and canes and daily goings-on. His laughing morphs very quickly into nervous crying, and silvery tears fall to the ground once again. He continues to laugh even as the liquid freezes his cheeks on the way out. gods, why is it so cold?

But soon he can't laugh anymore, and simply sobs into himself, staining his tunic grey with metallic tears, until he feels arms wrap around him. He looks up to meet the Siren's kind eyes. He swears he can see a small drop of gold clinging to the god's eyelash.

"What did you do to me?" he asks through tears. The Siren seems thrown off, and just shakes his head—looking away uneasily, seemingly avoiding Lucky's eyes with everything in him.

"I'm sorry," he says. "I'm sorry, it wasn't meant to be like this."

"Who was that?" Lucky asks.

"No one to worry about," the Siren responds, holding Lucky closer in his arms. Lucky can't help but melt in the god's embrace. He's had a long day already, and the sun has barely risen. He can't avoid it, he thinks, as he drops his head onto the god's shoulder and goes limp in his arms, finally letting his muscles relax.

"What did you do to me?" Lucky asks again. When the Siren backs away and holds him at an arm's length to look into his eyes, Lucky can see himself reflected in the most grotesque way.

It's still him, he can see himself, but his sharp teeth remain, his green eyes now seem too bright and eerie. It feels like looking into a broken mirror, pieces each reflecting another broken part of his synthetic visage; like if he shifts, the shattered vision of himself will disappear. He doesn't know what will remain after that.

He doesn't know what he wants the god to say. He doesn't know what he expects to achieve from asking the question, but he does know, he doesn't like the answer.

The god opens his mouth, searches Lucky's eyes and squeezes his hand lightly, before looking out the window as if it can provide him reprieve.

"I don't know."

4

Hope, they say, is the thing with feathers that perches in the soul. Lucky thinks it must be true, but not for the same reasons as they do.

When for others Hope is the thing with feathers that sings of the sweetest gale, for Lucky, it sits still on the horizon, always out of reach, but never sight.

While for others Hope is the tune without words that never stops, to Lucky it is a slippery thing that waits until he reaches out to fly. Hope taunts Lucky from afar while never quite leaving him truly.

He's six when he first learns that hope can fly, and seven when he understands that it can die. What soared in his heart in his youth and dug claws into his dreams in just a year had escaped into nightmares—nothing but a hearse in the streets.

In the streets, like Lucky had to be, from age six and onward. He'd say he's sad to have lost his family, but their memories are gone all the same, and obscured to the back of his mind in exile. A mother, a father, a baby sister he used to hold. In each instance he tries to recall her, her features are only more incomplete.

Lucky is eight when he learns what it means to be a street

kid, when the yelling of shopkeeps and heckling of merchants first tattooed his mind.

Sure, the War Goddess' power could heal, but it couldn't do away with the scarred-over relics of a past a child isn't meant to touch.

Which is all to say, to some, Hope comes as part of the package—life and passion are synonymous. Lucky's sure he's known what it's like to have hope, or to feel love, but that time has long passed.

So Lucky doesn't return to the temple. Without the help of the Siren, he often doesn't manage to come down from his attacks, leaving his irises sparkling silver most of the time—but he can make it. For two weeks, he makes it, hiding the teeth, the eyes, and himself from the rest of polite society—content to go back to his safe places in the alleys and quiet parks. For two weeks, he makes it, until the first snowflakes fall upon his nose. And when for others, Hope is the thing with feathers, for Lucky, it's the pushing, prodding hand of an impending cold winter beckoning him back towards worship.

No matter how little he wishes to see the Siren, winter is upon him. He needs shelter more than peace of mind, and so he opens the door.

The grave is standing in front of the statues, reading the scripture. When he hears Lucky's footsteps, he looks up and smiles.

"Good evening, child," he calls. Lucky wants to bite back a snappy retort, but instead bites his tongue.

"Evening, Margrave." He bows, and when he looks up, the margrave smiles.

"What brings you?" Lucky takes pause for a moment as he sets his things down onto the pew and considers. After an incriminating silence, the grave speaks softly. "Protection from the elements?" Lucky looks back at the grave and nods, stilted and awkward as if he'd been caught in a crime, but certainly morality of the clergy should include keeping him out of the cold, right? The margrave beckons him forward, and Lucky approaches the statues with him, resolutely keeping his gaze away from the Siren. "There was a time, Son, these gods were just like you." Lucky blinks.

"Really?"

"Oh yes. The Book of the Triad details the story in book two. Have you ever read the scripture, Son?" Lucky shakes his head, and casts his eyes down in shame.

"I can't read that well, Margrave." The man nods, and looks back at the marble.

"Well, Son, so it goes; our very own Lady Retribution was once a common child like you. They say she was born on the same day as the Siren came to be." Lucky widens his eyes and looks at the grave.

"They're not twins?" he asks, first on the docket above all the questions swirling in his head.

"They are, they are, Son. In spirit and in mind, but in our mortal definitions? No."

"Why did she get her powers?" Lucky asks. The margrave smiles.

"The Lady is said to have been a mighty warrior, but above that, a diplomat like no other. By the age of fifteen she'd slain the barbarians that once ruled our lands and stolen their treasures for the people. Not to mention," he turns to look at Lucky and smiles snidely, "stolen our Angel's heart." Lucky chuckles. "She was rewarded for her bravery and skill, and our Angel took her under his wing." Lucky can't help but roll his eyes, but laughs nonetheless. "And she was raised alongside the Siren until her coming of age, when she earned her divinity. As the Lady Retribution slept sound in the Heavens above, our earth was beaten by the blood rain for two weeks—the sun shone not behind the clouds, and streets were painted red by the Warrior's wishes. On the day of her awakening, the showers finally ceased, and grew fields of red and white roses in their wake."

Lucky stares up at the marble carving of the Lady Retribution

"I never knew that." Something at the back of Lucky's mind niggles at him to ask the Siren about this, but he pushes it aside. He doesn't intend to see the Siren. Not now, not ever.

"Many don't. It's a true shame how few read the tales for themselves. If they did, you'd have known that our mighty protector, the Bleeding One, was once a poor mortal, too." Lucky smiles. "It is not our choice the position we are born into, Son, but all can make the most of it. She did." Lucky meets the grave's eyes and smiles, bowing his head down in gratitude. "I'll grant you sanctuary here, Son. You may spend the night in the temple, away from the elements." Lucky beams.

"Thank you, Margrave."

"Of course. Do feel free to share the tale—you never know who may need to hear," the grave says. Lucky nods and smiles, and the grave turns away, collecting his things and heading out the door of the temple. He bars it on the inside behind him, granting him some peace and quiet inside.

The marble sculptures taunt him, and he can tell the Siren wants to speak, but he acts as if he's none the wiser and sleeps restfully for the first time in weeks.

There's a storm raging outside, and the thunder rumbles into the thick glass window panes. Alone by the fireplace sits a young boy with tattered clothes, beige and grey, stained and mismatched, with holes on every seam. He stares into the fire so as to avoid looking at the rain, as lightning bolts pierce his periphery, his mind begs him to go outside and relish in the chaos.

He won't, because there's his mother, standing by the door.

"Is it warm?" she asks, with her arms crossed and an easy smile on her face. Her boy nods, but he doesn't speak. He doesn't turn to look at her. "You know what Father said about playing in the rain," she says softly.

The boy nods again, but the pattering on the glass sinks into his mind—gripping his thoughts with talons, sharp and grating. The mother settles down on her knees next to him at the fire, and she hums softly. He hums along. It's his old lullaby from childhood—a faraway song, dissonant in his mind but melodic in the air—the type of tune he could sing but no one could ever play nor write, for each of them will forget it in a dark corner of their perceptions, dusted and dry, once the final notes echo off into silence.

"Where did the song come from, Mother?" The boy's mother stops humming and tilts her head curiously.

"Your father used to sing it. Very long ago."

"And where did he get it?" The woman shakes her head.

"He never did say." The boy nods and resigns to silence—gazing into the flame with his mother at his side, something resembling music filling his ears, but the very corners of his awareness tortured by the flashes of white light from the darkness outside.

"Do you want to hear a story?" the mother says. The boy averts his eyes from the logs for the first time since the storm began, and he asks:

"What kind of story?"

"You never heard how Father's story ended, did you?" she asks. The boy shakes his head.

No, he'd heard his father's legends many a time; listened to him speak in rhymes and sing praises of lands the boy wasn't quite sure he really did see, but such intricate crafting of the tall tales of magic and mystery—no such stories could be made from the depths of a human's mind alone. He had one tale he tended to tell whose final words were lost. His father always seemed to stop himself from finishing right before catharsis.

And so the boy turns to look at his mother, and focuses on her lips. She speaks the beginning words of an epic poem he'd heard before in paraphrasal forms, act one and two he knew by heart. He opens his ears and tunes out the sound of thunder as a portrait of a community is painted before his eyes once more.

"There once was a kingdom on the edge of the wood which war always plagued."

37

LUCKY WAKES INSIDE THE TEMPLE ONCE AGAIN, THE SMELL OF incense wafting through the air, smoky and sweet. He almost has it in him to forget where and what he is, but the grumbling of his stomach rouses him to reality nonetheless, and a sweet voice calls his name.

"Lucas?" He cringes, but he opens his eyes and looks up. He doesn't want to see the Siren, but how could he ignore the gods? "Lucky, you're awake," the Siren muses, and Lucky scoffs.

"Thank you for the information," he says. The Siren smiles, and golden wings of calyx sun rays retract in on themselves, eventually disappearing, as he approaches Lucky's bench.

"You've not been here for a while," the god says, and Lucky rolls his eyes.

"Very good with observations today." The Siren's face darkens, and Lucky almost wants to apologize, but holds his ground. He more than deserves a bit of ridicule. The Siren seems to understand this as well, and softens his eyes again.

"I always have been. What brings you back?" he asks. Lucky nods to the window.

"'S cold." The Siren seems almost saddened looking outside towards the falling snow.

"Right. I should've known." There's silence for a moment as Lucky simply looks at the god. "How did you sleep?"

His old lullaby from childhood, opening notes on the tip of his tongue, but ears filled with silence.

"Fine. Bench is a little hard though." The Siren nods. The bigger questions plaguing their minds are not addressed.

"I could give you another blanket," he says. Lucky looks down, his white fur cover starting to become muddied and stained with blood from nights he bites his lips. He'll have to wash it soon.

"Another?" he asks, and the god nods once again.

"You never wondered where that one came from?" Lucky shakes his head.

"No, I did, I just... I didn't consider it was you."

"Why is that?" he asks, and Lucky doesn't know what to say. *Because I didn't think you cared,* is his first thought, but that doesn't feel right. *Because I didn't truly believe in you,* is the wrong answer as well.

"Because no one's ever cared," is what comes out, and he cringes at his own traitorous tongue. When he opens his mouth to damage control, he somehow makes it worse. "Least of all you." He expects holy hellfire to rain down upon him—maybe he's finally crossed the line. Instead, he gets a shaky, wet voice speaking so quietly that he has to strain to hear.

"I never cared?" the Siren asks, tone bordering on a sadness Lucky's yet to hear from the god. Lucky only shrugs his shoulders and looks down.

"I haven't exactly had the best life. I always blamed it on you guys, back in the day." Back in the day. No, Lucky still does. His sharp teeth and emotionally-controlled eye color. The healing factor that's almost been his doom several times shows itself in the worst possible ways, on the run from townspeople and miraculously regenerating each injury they bestow upon him. It's all the Siren's fault, isn't it? He'd never be here without the god.

"That's... unfortunate," the Siren mutters. Lucky nods, and silence takes the temple once again.

"Have you figured anything out yet?" The Siren takes in a sharp breath, and looks around. It's a simple question, but each of them understands the implications.

"We don't have to talk about—"

"Yes, we do," Lucky interrupts. The Siren stops himself to listen, seemingly caught off-guard. "You've changed my life, I need to know how. This is difficult to deal with, you know? Especially since I have no idea what it means. I don't think you do either." To Lucky's surprise, the Siren shakes his head.

"No... I don't. I messed up, I think." Lucky scoffs.

"You think?" The god simply sighs.

"I've looked into it a little." Lucky resists the urge to sneer at the words "a little". He'd think this would be further up on the god's agenda. "As far as I can tell, my gifts are... normal, so to speak. But giving you the Angel's and Retribution's blessings without their knowledge has made some problems," the god finishes, and Lucky widens his eyes and stares.

"What?" he lets out incredulously. "Are you kidding?"

"What do you mean?" the Siren asks, and Lucky laughs a disingenuous laugh.

"You did this without telling them? That's what the problem is?"

"Well—"

"You mean to tell me this is all because you wanted to go behind Daddy's back?" The Siren's eyes darken and his irises are overtaken with gold. His pupils remain, so far.

"Do not use that tone with me, Lucky. I am not a child," he says, and Lucky scoffs.

"Certainly acting like one! You messed me up because you were too embarrassed to ask the Angel." The pupils disappear, and Lucky can tell he's pushing it, but he doesn't back down. The sharp teeth, the strange dreams, memories of places he's never been—they plague him every minute of every hour, and it's all some divine punishment for the godly equivalent of a child stealing from his parent?

"You don't understand," the Siren says, his voice now dark and commanding, but Lucky doesn't care.

"I think I do. I had a family once, too, you know. Contrary to popular belief, I was normal once. I'm being punished for your petulance now."

"I'm working on it, Lucas! Do not speak to me like that." It's definitely Lucky's last warning, but he's never been the best at heeding those. It's how he survives.

"I'll speak to you however I want! Don't act high and mighty when you're just as clueless as me!"

"Silence." Lucky's tongue feels heavy in his mouth, and he shuts up.

He wants to protest but when he opens his mouth to argue, he chokes on an invisible block in his throat. He coughs, trying to rid himself of the weight, and what comes out is a wave of crimson blood that splatters into a mosaic on the pristine temple floors. Lucky stares at it in shock and metallic tears come to his eyes as the taste settles in his mouth, his throat becoming scratchy and pained. Something crawls up, and he tries to swallow it down, but ends out only coughing up another clot again.

The Siren waves his hand, and the red drops on the floor disappear. Lucky's chest feels tight, and he stares up at the god with fear in his eyes. The god almost looks remorseful, but the look doesn't last more than a moment before he's looking down at his nails calmly, studying himself.

"I gave you many warnings," he says, Lucky tries to apologize, but the taste of iron comes up his throat, and he shuts his mouth. "You're above simple mortals now, but don't forget who gave you that privilege." He turns his attention to Lucky, and stares into his eyes, his smile sharp and off-putting. "I always have the final say." Lucky nods, his breathing becoming shallow. The Siren seems to notice, and snaps his fingers, letting Lucky breathe freely. He smiles, but doesn't look at all happy. "My apologies, I don't know my own strength. Seems I caught your esophagus up with your vocal cords. My mistake." It's not an apology—it's a threat. Lucky may not be the best at social cues, but he can see that clearly. The Siren didn't simply forget his own power, he caught Lucky's air purposefully as a reminder who's on top.

And in Lucky's mind, he can't breathe. His lungs are collapsed and ribs all shattered. He stares at the ground beneath him—concrete under his body, bruises marring each and every inch. This is what happens when he hits the ground. Lucky prefers falling.

The god gives him a once-over with his eyes before talking

again. "*You may speak,*" he says, and the pressure in Lucky's chest recedes instantly. He takes a moment to breathe, swallowing down the blood that threatened his throat moments before.

"I'm sorry," he says, not meeting the Siren's eyes. The Siren hums.

"Sorry for what?" he asks.

"For questioning you. For insulting you. It won't happen again."

"Hm," is his only response. Lucky looks up, and sees the god's pupils return, irises still blindingly metallic. "Do keep this as a reminder, Lucky. Know your place." Lucky nods.

"Right. Of course," he concedes, the taste of his own blood still heavy on his lips. The Siren's expression softens, his eyes melting back into dark brown. He raises his hand and cups Lucky's cheek, smiling at him kindly.

"I do so care for you, Lucky. It hurts me to see you hurt," he says softly. Lucky nods, though events prior challenge the god's assertion. "Don't you forget it, my little moonlight. Hold your head high. My favor is something to be treasured."

"Of course, Siren," Lucky says. The god smiles, and backs away.

"I'll continue to look into your issue, but I want you to remember this." Lucky nods, and the god disappears in a flash of light, leaving him alone in the temple again.

Lucky had begun to hope that the favor and blessing of the gods would mean that his life would be changed for the better, but as he looks up to the eyes of the marble sculpture before him, pastel yellow light shining down on it in rays that once would've been awe-inspiring now only serve as a reminder that Lucky is small—he remembers his place.

Where Hope they say, is the thing with feathers, for Lucky it is the same. But where Hope they say knows how it feels to fly, for Lucky, it is caged.

5

The wind howls, a thunderous symphony of destruction, as the sky tears apart from outside the window, and the cosmos almost screams as it's ripped in two by forces beyond its control. If they're smart, the people run away in a frantic haze of self-preservation, but very few of them make it out alive. The dragons rule the sky, monsters lurk in the night, and the young boy is simply witness to it all—unwilling, unmoving, unable to stop it.

The air is thick, and it's hard to breathe. The ocean once calm and fruitful providing the city with fresh fish now seethes. Waves rock the shores, drowning the kingdom's fishing boats leagues under water never to be seen again.

The ground shakes under foot and any who made the choice to run trip over themselves and each other, few narrowly avoid being trampled to death by the weight of the beautiful oblivion.

And a young boy watches from his window. His mother pulls him away, and shelters him, wrapping her arms around his head and covering his ears to soften the blow—the sound of screams from his community.

"Mom, what's happening?" he asks. With tears streaming down her face, she searches herself for an explanation, but nothing comes to mind.

But stories—stories she's always known. In the tough times it's what got them through life. His father's disappearance, and the death of his *grandmother—she could cover it all up with stories. She knew how to pretend. She can pretend she's okay, she can pretend they're safe, and she can pretend the screams are part of the act.*

"There's a kind dragon, Love, that lives atop that mountain. He's protecting us from the evil ones. We're playing a game with them."

"This game doesn't seem very fun," the boy mutters. The mother nods, and forces out a laugh.

"It gets better, don't you worry."

The fire outside reaches the window, and a young mother pulls her son closer to her chest.

⚬❧⚬

LUCKY AWAKES IN A BLIND PANIC, PATTING HIMSELF DOWN FOR flames he's sure lick his clothing. When he opens his eyes, however, there's nothing but his blanket, and the candles in the temple keeping watch over him.

These dreams don't seem to leave him. The memories of people he's never known and places he's never been, and none of them ever end well. Sometimes there's death, other times starvation, and sometimes, it's so much worse. In his sleep his mind is oft tortured by images of bloodied hands and burning cities, and above it all the chiming of church bells tolling their own death march.

And there's always the boy. The young boy with straight brown hair and his protective mother who stand in the rubble, alone, and a father always spoken of but never seen. Lucky supposes it has to be a side effect of the Siren's blessings, that these days more and more feel like a curse.

Speaking of the Siren—

"Good morning, Lucky." Lucky looks out the window and scowls. The sun barely crested the horizon, let alone risen.

"It's not morning, Siren." The air in the room goes cold.

"What was that?"

"I said good morning, Siren," Lucky amends, and the Siren nods, letting the temperature climb once again.

Lucky looks up to meet the god's eyes, and takes in his appearance. Today he's abandoned the crown, but his robes are still as elegant as before. He's dressed in blue, with the same golden threads connecting each seam. On his shoulder, there's an expertly embroidered lily in white and gold, petiolic windings stitched together with care. There are clear gems with salt-and-pepper flecks of black and grey scattered inside, each of them are held in place with lengths of white cord that stretch across to each shoulder. He looks regal, but to a god, Lucky feels that's an insult. His golden wings are folded neatly behind his back, and today they seem to glow more than normal, emanating a calming, friendly, yellow light.

"Did you sleep well?" he asks. Lucky nods despite himself.

"Yes. It's warm in here," Lucky responds. The Siren nods. He turns away toward the margrave's podium and flips through the book resting on it, back turned to Lucky.

"And... you've noticed any more side effects?" Lucky considers his answer carefully. Should he tell the Siren about the dreams? Would he do anything about it, or would it just make him mad? Lucky's put up with his anger before, he knows the god would never kill him, but nagging at the back of his mind is the torturous semi-reality of what-ifs. What if Lucky finally crosses a line?

He's already crossed so many lines.

"Lately I've been having some strange dreams," Lucky mutters. He almost doesn't think the Siren even hears him.

"Oh." He's quiet after that, as if considering. "What kind of dreams?" He still doesn't turn to look at Lucky.

"Nightmares," Lucky replies. He shifts in his seat, and the god hums.

"Always?"

"Always. Just now it was really strange. The world was just... on fire. And there was this kid and his mom, and they didn't leave. They just sat in the fire, and the mom just told the kid stories and pretended nothing was wrong." The god stills and Lucky looks towards him for a reaction, but finds nothing. His hand rests on the book, and he stares at it, but doesn't turn the page.

"What else?" he asks quietly.

Screams. Agonizing screams, the wet squelching sounds of twisting a dagger, a knife in a wound, flames licking at Lucky's feet. The feeling of an unfamiliar woman's tears soaking into his tunic and blood on the pavement.

"Um, the kid's hair was black. That's something?" Lucky says.

"Fin, get out of there!" someone screams. The world collapses around him as a boy stands in the wreckage watching terrors beyond his under-standing wreak havoc upon his world— the only world he's ever known. Hellfire and ash takes hold of his pant leg and climb up, searing heat spreading over his limbs, and he screams. "Finny, come to Mom!" He can't move. The fire reaches his waistband and he pats at it, but the effort is futile. His hands are charred, and the fire is no less destructive. He stares at the black mess of his burnt hand and tears flow like broken dams.

He hopes, distantly, that his tears could quench the flames, and screams in fear as arms grip him and pull him away. "I've got you," his mother says tearfully, but he only keeps yelling. His mind calls for him to walk back into the fire. He struggles against his mother but she holds tight.

The Siren is unresponsive, staring at the pages blankly. "Do you know his name?"

"No," Lucky replies. He doesn't know why, but something tells him he can't tell the god. The Siren finally turns around to look him in the eyes, and Lucky is held in place by a golden gaze of fire.

"Finny, please, come on, stay with us!"

Fire. Blood, blood, blood, corpses in the street.

"I know when you lie, Lucas," he says. Lucky shakes his head.

"I'm not lying," he says back. The Siren clicks his tongue and steps away from the podium.

"Another one," comes his response, and Lucky can feel the temperature drop. "Why are you lying to me?"

"I'm not," he says, though he can feel the small threads holding onto the god's composure snapping with each word out of his mouth. The ice is thinning. "I don't know his name." The Siren approaches him and kneels in front of his pew, reaching a hand out and cupping Lucky's cheek softly. He smiles with kindness, but his eyes betray his true thoughts.

"Lucky, Lucky, when will you learn?" A sharp pain hits his chest, and his eyes widen. He shakes his head.

"No—wait, please," he mutters.

"Lucky, tell me the truth."

"Finnigan," Lucky says before he has time to process. His mind fights him for power, and his mouth runs without his permission. He can feel the Siren's claws inside his head, and his voice vibrates around his skull like the sounding of a gong— metallic, coarse, and grating. "His name was Finnigan. I don't know his last name. His mother called him Fin."

The Siren seems put off by this answer, and stares at Lucky for a moment, before he can feel his grip on his thoughts release, and he exhales.

"Finnigan," he repeats. It's not a question. He considers, looking down at the floor. "Lucky, did you see how he died?"

Limbs scorched and lungs filled with the sour smelling toxin of the permeating smoke. The boy has a headache that forces him to his knees, and he cries out in pain, catching his mother's attention once more. She needs to run—she needs to get away, but she can't go without him.

"Fin?" she calls out. The voice rings in his head, but he doesn't register its source. Rather, a voice from deeper inside his head calls out to him to finish what he's begun.

He stands.

"Finny?" she yells again, looking at him from across the fissure. Tall flames separate the family on two sides of the burning city. The mother's black hair is singed on the ends, and her dress covered in soot and blood.

Her boy is on the other side of the fire, staring at her blankly, as if he doesn't know who she is.

He walks.

"Fin, stop! What are you doing?" she screams. He doesn't pay her any mind as he walks further into the flame. A rattling voice from inside his mind laughs to him, congratulates him—it sings as the fire licks at him once more, blackened flesh and severed nerves overwhelming his senses. He can scream, but he can't move away.

"How did you know he died?" Lucky asks.

"Nothing to worry about, Lucky. *How did he die?*" The uncomfortable feeling of the total loss of control returns to Lucky, and his chest tightens.

"Fire. He walked into the fire." The Siren releases him again.

"No," is all he says before he stands again and starts pacing the floor nervously. Lucky cocks his head to the side.

"What's wrong?" he asks. The god turns around and pins him with a golden gaze once again, and when he speaks, his voice is no longer sweet and assuring—it's laced with rage in a terrifying symphony of primitive sounds that lacerate Lucky's thoughts.

"What's wrong?" he mocks, drawing nearer to Lucky. "Other than you lying to me? Withholding this information for so long?" Lucky cowers away, and not for the first time, prays to melt into the wood fiber of the bench.

"You didn't ask—" The Siren cuts him off by laughing.

"I didn't ask, did I?" He closes in on Lucky and grips the teen's shoulders. "Do you want your little problem solved?" Lucky nods. "You tell me everything. This isn't a game, child."

"Sorry. Right." The Siren laughs again.

"You think you're all powerful now that you've got a couple little quirks? Why, I should've come for you when you disappeared on me for weeks. I thought maybe you'd learned some respect." Lucky shuts his eyes, and leans away, nodding. The Siren doesn't sound right—his voice is angered and sharp and drips with contempt. It's not at all the Siren Lucky met that day in the temple, with kind eyes and golden wings and a smile that seemed forgiving. How naive he had been.

When Lucky opens his eyes again, the world has gone grey, and he looks to the Siren in fear. He only sneers at him.

"Pathetic. Panicking from hearing what you deserve." His vision darkens. What he knows is warm, inviting gold in the Siren's eyes is now a black abyss of nothingness that stares into Lucky's soul. Inside of it he can see his own reflection, his sharp teeth taunting him with their omnipresence. "You can't get out of everything with the little eye trick." Darker now, and the Siren scowls. "Are you kidding me?"

"I'm sorry," Lucky mutters. "I can't control it." He feels something cold on his face, and cringes when he feels the polar, sub-zero temperatures of his own osmium tears begin to drip down his cheeks and leave almost burning tracks on the way. The Siren reaches up to touch one of the metallic drops, then pulls his hand away immediately upon contact.

"What the—!" he exclaims, letting go of Lucky. Lucky looks at him in confusion. They hurt him? "You little—"

"It's not my fault!" Lucky yells, holding up his hands. The Siren still seems angry.

"Everything is my fault, isn't it?" he says, and Lucky stiffens.

"Well, in this context—"

"*Quiet.*" Lucky shuts his mouth. This time, the Siren had the good sense to let him breathe, so he supposes that's a plus.

Lucky was ready for the blood—he was prepared for the blood to come up his throat.

What he was not prepared for was his saliva freezing inside his mouth, and esophagus going so cold he almost wishes he couldn't breathe.

Lucky gasps and the intake of air shoots pain through his body, being overtaken by chills so intense he can't think straight. He tries to open his mouth to let out the wave of silver, but finds his lips suddenly frozen shut. He shrieks in fear as the liquid simply builds up inside his mouth, and can't help the silver tears that begin to flow once more, immediately boiling once they hit his warm skin, and burning cold tracks down his cheeks. He wipes them away, but they singe the skin of his hands as well.

He collapses onto the floor by the Siren's feet and lets out a cry, begging him without words to stop. The god only stares at him, not a single show of remorse on his face. He drops down onto his knees, and looks at him in a torturous mockery of sadness. He doesn't speak.

Lucky breathes in through his nose, and when he breathes out, cold silver liquid spews out onto the floor in the most unnerving form of a bloody nose possible. The Siren snaps, and it disappears.

"Always so messy..." he mutters. Lucky cringes and looks down at his arms, where red pinpricks have begun to appear on each of his veins, sharp and shiny red points growing with each second. Blood. He can feel it slicing through nerves. He wants to scream. "Yikes," the Siren mutters, "that's enough of that."

The pain recedes and Lucky falls to the ground, warmth immediately overtaking him in such a wave he feels like he's burning up all at once. He covers his mouth with a hand to keep from shrieking as tears continue to slide down his cheeks. He faces the floor, and in the reflection from the pool of mercury he can see there are red tracks down his face from the tears that will certainly scar over.

"You know I don't want to do this to you," the god mutters.

Do I? is Lucky's first thought, but he's had enough for one day.

"I know." Lucky hopes deeply that the Siren can't recognize that lie. He says nothing, and pulls Lucky into a crushing hug, taking care to keep his exposed skin away from Lucky's tears.

"Oh, Little Moonlight. We'll get through this together. You and me, to the end."

"You and me," Lucky echoes. He hopes it isn't true.

THE LIGHT IS DIMMER

"LEARN ANYTHING NEW?" HONORA ASKS. SHE'S SITTING quietly reading a book and sipping a cup of tea. Nikolai takes off his chords and embroidered jacket and is left in just his white tunic, comfortable for the first time today. Beauty is pain, they say.

"Unfortunately," he starts, running his fingers through his hair, obsessively fixing it up, "kid knows about Finnigan." His sister goes quiet and looks up to meet Nikolai's eyes.

"How?" Nikolai shrugs and sits down next to him.

"Says he has dreams. Says he saw him."

"And that's true?" Honora asks. Nikolai nods.

"Far as I can tell." Nora lets out a breath of relief.

"So you didn't look into his mind?" she asks. Nikolai stills momentarily, and it's all the answer his sister needs. "Nicky, that hurts people." Nikolai throws up his arms in defeat.

"Well how is he supposed to learn to stop lying to me! I want to help him, and I can't do that if he's keeping secrets." Honora stares at him with a deadpan expression.

"You messed up," she says.

"How?"

"Your kid's not gonna trust you," she says again, staring at Nikolai intently.

"But he gave me a hug," Nikolai says. There's silence for a moment as Nora considers internally how her brother could possibly be so inane.

"Out of fear, Nikolai. He's scared of you." Nikolai shakes his head.

"No, that can't be true," he says, and Nora nods.

"Your kid thinks you're gonna kill him." Nikolai scowls.

"Don't call him that," he warns. Honora shrugs and looks back to her book.

"It's what you called L—"

"Do not say his name, Honora." Nora only laughs without humor, and her eyes go crimson when she turns again to look at her brother. She throws her book down without marking her page, and stands, towering over her brother.

"It's a *human* thing, you wouldn't understand." She spits the word as if it were venomous on her tongue.

"Excuse me for not being born as you were, Lady Retribution," Nikolai retorts, staring her down.

"As I was?" Retribution parrots. "And is there something wrong with how I was?" Nikolai doesn't respond, and Nora chuckles. "I know last time scared you, Nikolai, but you're making a mistake."

"Last time, what?" The gods turn away from each other, and calm their blazing eyes to meet a blue gaze. They look between each other, and make a silent pact—an unorthodox alliance of doves and crows to save themselves. An alliance that stands on thin ice, ready to crumble under their feet.

"Nothing, Dad."

6

Time unwinds like a tangled cord in Lucky's mind. It trips over knots and bumps on the way, having to slow to a halt to wrangle itself into something fathomable.

He hasn't seen the Siren since the freezing incident, and he thanks his lucky stars. Who in his mind used to be the merciful and loving brotherly figure had suddenly become a twisted image in his head, distorted across broken memories, dilapidated and skewed. Distantly, Lucky can remember the days when he used to speak to the Siren as if he'd known him for years; kneeling before his form enshrined in stone by the hands of prophets. Lucky would speak to him like an old friend, and envision him responding. With kind eyes and a soft smile, he'd imagine the god descending from the heavens to assure him of his future, and tell him everything was okay.

Now, as he stands on the boundary of everything he once was, and everything he wants to be, he thinks of the god only as a Leviathan in disguise. With his bags in hand containing all he's ever owned, Lucky stares back at the village with tears gathering in his eyes, their cold reminding him of a friend's betrayal, and he bids goodbye to the only world he's ever known.

His Creator, who gave his world life, had existed only in Lucky's presence to imbue upon him gifts he'd never wanted. A Creator which should have been a beacon of Hope, who had the responsibility to protect his people. The same Creator who'd given him healing, a shelter, food, and more company than he'd had in his life had also bestowed godly attributes that a mere mortal couldn't handle. And with those gifts, the dreams—looks into a distant past that felt like premonitions—and above all, the Voices.

Gods, Lucky can't stand the Voices anymore. Singing day in and out on the edges of his perception, never in the forefront but always lingering. Opinions and instruction cutting into Lucky's mind like a cold knife blade, as if he needed any more cold. So sharp and scathing that Lucky couldn't feel the fibers being severed until the blood was drawn.

Which is to say, his thoughts or another's, he couldn't anymore tell.

It's wishful thinking, he knows, to believe that leaving the village could throw the Leviathan off his trail, but if the Creature wished to exist pervasively in his brain, then at the very least Lucky could live away from consecrated reminders of his omnipresence. The temple couldn't be a sanctuary to Lucky any more than an aerie to a cod. In his home, he was surrounded by predators.

Squaring his shoulders, he takes one last look at the village, and disappears into the wood.

"The autumn is coming soon," the young boy crouches down in the dewy grass and speaks lowly, softly to a dandelion sprouting from the ground. "You'll come again next year?" he asks. He's learned to take the smallest change in the speeds of the winds as a response, and he smiles. "I thought so. You're much braver than I," he mutters. He sits down in the grass against the trunk of a tall tree and looks up at the sky. He wonders if maybe his father is looking after him now—if even in his absence he takes care of his son.

The wind kisses his cheek and he sighs, looking back down to the flowers. "Thank you. I'm sorry, I was thinking again." The breeze ruffles the flowers' petals, and makes them bob up and down, almost like nodding. Fin giggles.

And the world shifts.

Lucky is in Fin's place, staring down at the weeds as they change before his eyes from bright, cheery yellows into a rotting brown and black textile of death, and he pushes himself away. The wind whips his hair into tangles and his heart stutters as a headache overtakes him.

"You can't run away, Moonlight," a voice calls. Lucky presses his hands over his ears and shuts his eyes, but the voice comes from inside him. "When will you learn?" the voice asks.

"Never," Lucky replies, with metallic tears beginning to stream down his cheeks, "I'll never learn. You're always right, I'm wrong." He can feel the Siren smile, and he can hear it in his voice.

"That's right." There's a pause, before the voice returns. "Oh, dearest little Moonlight, won't you come home?"

Won't you come home?

Come home?

Come home.

Lucky breaks himself out of the daydream and shakes his head violently. From the minute he woke up in the temple two days ago the Siren has been reaching out to him, begging him to return. Lucky can't shake the feeling of the Siren's grip on his mind—his chest feels tight and a headache pounds in the background no matter how he tries to ignore it. He can feel the Siren getting close, reaching to the surface of his perception to pinpoint his location and drag him back, kicking, screaming, and bleeding. Lucky pushes him away each time he gets close, but he can't hold on for long.

"We can talk about this, Moonlight," the Siren whispers to him. "Won't you come home?"

Lucky shakes his head. He doesn't dignify the god's prying with a response. He trudges on.

"You can't ignore me forever," he says. But Lucky will try.

He's back in the fire, his flesh seared. The smell of burning hair and clothing and boiling blood takes over his senses, and he falls to his knees. He can hear his mother calling but it won't register as a command. All he can hear is the laughing from the voice inside his head, yelling at him to pick himself up—screaming to walk forward, encouraging, pleading, egging him on so loudly that he can't hear his own thoughts, if he has any anymore. He stands, and walks closer to the flame.

And the world shifts.

Lucky stands alone in the boy's place. The sound of a woman once screaming for her child replaced only by the voice of the Siren, laughing and plotting and begging him to come home. Lucky tries to ignore it but can feel the fire licking at his feet. The Siren doesn't tell him to walk into it, he only speaks to Lucky in a calm and level voice, faking kindness.

"This doesn't have to happen," he says, "I can fix you, Lucky, if only you'll come home."

Home. Lucky doesn't have one of those. Lucky has a safe temple that's been invaded by the Leviathan, waiting for him eons away in a village he never wants to see again.

He shakes his head and clears his thoughts, and—

he's back again. Standing in the forest all alone. He's lost his sense of direction—he doesn't know where he came from. He looks around in attempt to find the footpath he'd have carved on his way through the brush. He finds nothing but piles of dead leaves, and powdery snow in his wake.

"You're lost," the Siren sings. Lucky grits his teeth. "I can help you find the way out if only you'd let me see."

Lucky can feel crawling in the back of his head, the claws of the Siren invading his senses, and he shuts his eyes tight. Like a tidal wave, his nerves sing, asking him to open up and look around, but he ignores it. His body tries to force him to pull his eyes back open, and he holds his hands over his face, blocking the view. Only when the feeling recedes does he look again.

"You're being a poor sport," the Siren mutters, and Lucky

rolls his eyes. "It won't hurt, only a pinch and then you'll be home. Safe and sound with me." There's nothing safe about that.

Lucky looks through a young boy's eyes as the flames consume him. First, he feels his hair go, then his clothing set alight, then the feeling of his skin melting, blood boiling, and darkness taking hold.

There's laughter, tons of it, so loud and grating that Fin can't help but listen to it and nothing else. It's melodic and kind and captivating, like the last notes of a chamber symphony before a standing ovation. Fin listens. He doesn't think anymore, all he does is listen. He screams as the fire encases his body, but he can't pull himself away.

And when Lucky is put in his place this time, he feels a sense of visceral, unadulterated horror take hold of his whole being, and he seizes up.

"What's wrong? Can't walk away?" something calls in his mind. Lucky recognizes that voice. He knows that person, from a distant future centuries away. He knows this man, but can't put a finger to a name. "Come on, walk out of the fire. It isn't that hard, Sunshine."

Sunshine. The voice spits the word mockingly like venom in a way Lucky can tell there's far more to it than a simple pet name. It's dark and foreboding. It means death. It sounds like the agony of losing control, biting at Lucky's senses. He feels the flames begin to slough off his flesh and grits his teeth painfully, grounding himself, and—

he's in the forest, looking around. That voice taunts him even as the dream fades away, because he knows who it is—distantly in the back of his mind he understands; Lucky knows who killed the boy, but names are fleeting and time unwinds like a tangled cord. There's a village somewhere that went up in flames and a family missing a child. When did he die? A boy who couldn't have been more than ten, name lost to history to become a footnote in Lucky's story that he'll never quite understand. It shoots off a dull pain in his heart when he thinks of dark eyes and straight, floppy brown hair. The wide smiles and laugh like music stain his memory. Lucky's panicking. Lucky's lost. Lucky needs to—

"Come home."

He freezes.

The Siren's voice echoes around his head—the last notes of a chamber symphony before a standing ovation—and Lucky kneels down into the snow. The wet seeps into his pants and his hands are cold.

"Come home, Moonlight." Sunshine. His vision clouds into dark greys far too reminiscent of smoke, and he breathes heavy. "We still have time."

"You killed him," Lucky says. All at once, the forest seems to quiet. "Fin—Finny, you—" Lucky trails off, searching his mind for any explanation that doesn't put the Siren at the scene of the crime, but there is none. "He was ten." There's silence.

"Come home, Lucky," the Siren says. He refuses to acknowledge his words.

"A child, Siren!" Lucky yells into the forest. A bird flies away in fear at the echo of his voice. "It was you!"

Lucky feels a familiar feeling washing over him, the saliva in his mouth going cold and bodily functions slowing as everything dips to sub-zeroes. The Siren is retaliating, Lucky knows. He tries to keep a hold on himself as silver tears begin to flow. He'd looked at his reflection in the water the day after the incident, and he'd seen the long tracks of scars that traveled down his face in the path of his tears, skin freezing and dying, leaving wells in its place. These tears follow the same path.

"Siren, please," he lets out. The pinpricks of red begin to poke out of his skin, and he cringes away, clenching his teeth. His sharpened canines feel ready to shatter.

"When will you learn," the Siren mutters, but it isn't a question this time. His freezing blood spikes out, and he spits out a wave of freezing silver in his mouth.

"I'm sorry!" he yells again. There's warmth, and Lucky collapses to the ground.

The blood spikes thaw and trickle down his arm, painting the snow a sickening crimson. He feels dizzy from blood loss and his head spins with the sound of the Siren's laughing.

THE LIGHT IS DIMMER

"Come home, Lucky," he says, and this time, Lucky knows it's his last warning. He sighs, and takes in a breath like it's his last.

"I'm coming home."

Back in the village, the Siren smiles.

❀

LUCKY WAKES UP WITH A POUNDING HEADACHE, BRUISES AND bandages marring his skin, a sore throat, and aching limbs with no recollection of how he got here.

When he opens his eyes, he sees the Siren God standing above him with a soft smile, looking at him fondly. He smiles back.

"Good morning, little Moonlight," the Siren says. "It sounds like you had a bad dream."

Bad dream?

Lucky recalls small bits of his sleep, but the image is fuzzy and vivid details obscured. It was bad, he knows that, but how bad, he can't tell.

"Yeah," he says lamely in response. The Siren kneels down beside his bench, raising a hand to brush away a stray strand of hair on his forehead. The touch is gentle and warm, and Lucky leans into it. Something about it seems wrong, but Lucky is so, so tired, and the Siren's touch is inviting. Before he knows it, there's something cold on his cheek. The Siren frowns.

"Moonlight, what's wrong?" he asks, and Lucky shakes his head, laughing slightly.

"I don't know," he says. He sits up, and the god wraps him in a hug, resting his chin on Lucky's shoulder and rubbing his back in circles.

"It's okay. Dreams are strange things, but they're not real." Lucky nods, and something in the back of his mind calls out to him to disagree. But Lucky knows dreams are fake, his brain is playing tricks on him. When the Siren pulls away, he smiles at

Lucky, and cups his face in a hand. "Lucky, you'd never try to leave me, would you?" Lucky looks at him strangely. It's a weird question, but Lucky supposes gods have emotions and insecurities, too. Lucky shakes his head.

"Why would I do that?" he asks, and the Siren's smile widens.

"I didn't think you would."

7

The Siren plucks his guitar with practiced precision, stopping intermittently to reach up and turn one of six dials at the head of the guitar at points. He looks for a very specific intonation of each string, sweet notes echoing out around him as he flicks his fingers across each string slowly. He strums out a chord and it buzzes in the air around him, melodic and calm. He smiles to himself, settling the instrument into the crook of his elbow like he has time and time again, in the place where it belongs. He plays quietly, softly, as if wary of prying ears, though he's alone in the great hall. And listening quietly enough, one could even hear him sing along to a tune of his own making, with saccharine lyrics enshrined in his mind, spoken in rhyme, heralding the god's lament. A long-dead ghost lingers near, her skeleton by his side listening soundlessly.

"If I," he sings to her decayed form, "poured my heart out, how would you take it?"

And the world around him fades away, leaving him alone in his own universe of sounds, smells and senses—the sickening choral music of a tragic love song floating around, with the skeletal form of a love lost that never was.

"Wishful thinking, to the warning you might break it."

But who needs an instrument for song when one's voice knows no bounds? The Siren sets down the guitar, but the music still rings through the hall. He closes his mouth and sings no more, but his chorus keeps pace, and he smiles.

He takes his skeleton's hand, and pulls her up for a dance.

"Or if I spoke my mind? Would it grate your ears?"

The song continues in the god's own voice, though he doesn't utter a word. He wraps his arm around the corpse's waist, holding the small of her back, and directing her movements holding her hand. She didn't tend to pull her weight when they danced.

"Or would you listen while the fires wrapped you in? Stay, despite the mess I'd make?"

He sways in time with the music in the air, and he holds her as if she were delicate and breakable, the bony fingers in his hands reminding him of days past. Ah, if only she'd have danced with him before. If only she'd have kissed him before those lips decomposed.

"You know I hate to bargain with fate."

And when the disembodied voice of a Siren God from days past sings the next words, they seethe between his teeth like poison on his lips. Oh, how she loved this song before his vitriol turned the melody sour.

"Talking to a snake."

The song speeds up and slow picking turns immediately to fast, heavy strumming, anger almost palpable. The Siren stops waltzing and begins to throw her around in a dance that's both fast and painfully slow, spinning her under his arms and smiling insincerely as the song turns bitter, morphed into a green-eyed monster the Siren knows so well, rewritten by her betrayal.

"I may be a fool seeking attention, facing flaws of my own invention. Making all the same mistakes. Counting bones, before they just might fucking break."

205, he remembers. A shame. She could've kept that one had she not been so human and so fallible. A knife slipped between

THE LIGHT IS DIMMER

her ribs was all it took for the Siren to be rid of his worst mistake.

Oh, but Lucky. Lucky, Lucky—now he is special. Siren won't let him meet the same fate, if he can help it. Though he tries to run away and talks back to the god, he'll never truly escape. Lucky has no one other than him, and with that, he's pleased.

Serena's piercing green eyes have decayed leaving only white bone in their wake, but Nikolai remembers how she looked at him, like he was the world, and he sighs, spinning her around as the music continues.

"You would have loved him," he says softly, clutching her hands in his own. "Everything our boy was and so much more," he reassures. Her head nods to the side, and Nikolai scowls. "You would have loved him too much," he continues, counting his steps with practiced grace and agility. Serena's dress sways in tune. It's the same one from the day she died, worn and torn with blood staining the breast over her so traitorous heart. Oh yes, she'd have loved him too much. Which is...

"Why I had to do it. But you understand." His steps grow lazy and drawn out, and he tunes out the music, now dancing to a funeral march inside his own head. "You understand it was your own fault. You always were so understanding." She was, back in the day. When the Siren used to disappear for weeks at a time, and leave her to care for the boy, she welcomed him back with open arms and asked no questions, because it was how she loved. She loved depthlessly, endlessly, without question, and she used to reserve that love for Siren.

The memory of the clever boy with red hair and a white streak stains Nikolai's mind, the spill of pitch in the calm waters of his recollection. A boy who used to call him "Dad," and jumped into his arms readily and hugged him tight whenever he saw him—a boy who was a contamination of Nikolai's pure memories since his gift of godhood, and who he would thankfully never see again.

Who asked him once, in another life, why he so often had to

SAMARA KATHARINE

go away. Who was pleased with the answer of "work" and nothing more. Who knew the War Goddess not as the divine Valkyrie choosing who lives and dies, but as his kind aunt who taught him to wield a wooden sword, and gifted him protection for all his short life. The aunt that loved him more than Nikolai, just like Serena did.

Nikolai stops smiling and spins her around again as the music falls back down to a slower tempo more accommodating to his graceful waltzing steps. When she danced when they married, she marveled at his elegance as they flew across the floor—she laughed at his charming words and lilting voice and told him she'd love him forever. Now, eyeless sockets stare at him judgingly and her movements are formless—of course the Siren never expects agility from the dead. It truly is a shame such a beautiful soul couldn't be saved from her own heart.

The song reaches its end, and the Siren drops her into a dip, holding the skeleton just above the floor. Her laughter from their wedding day seems to echo in his mind, just how she laughed when he dipped her the first time, and he frowns.

Mood soured, he lets her hit the floor, before taking his guitar and leaving.

Maybe Lucas would make better conversation.

⚜

LUCKY CAN'T SHAKE THE FEELING THAT SOMETHING IS VERY wrong.

Since that day he woke up from a bad dream in the temple, he can't help but feel on edge. Each time the Siren gets close to him, his mind screams for him to move away as if the god's touch was toxic.

So even when he enters the temple and sees the Siren sitting before his own statue with a guitar in his arms, he shivers. Something feels wrong, and he can't place what.

The Siren looks up at him and smiles, waving him over, sharp teeth on full display. Those have unnerved Lucky much less these days. He needed to learn to get used to his own fangs, and that meant accepting the Siren's as a fact of life.

The god looks ethereal, draped in soft white and yellow fabrics with his cirrus wings spread out behind him, resting on the ground as if stretching themselves. He's gone far more casual than Lucky's ever seen him today—abandoning pristine, ironed suit jackets and lapels for a more simple fluffy-looking yellow cloak with a white shirt underneath. His breast is embroidered with roses and leaves, and for once, he looks at ease. He looks normal.

Human.

He looks so human, Lucky can't help the discomfort climbing through his body at the sight. The Siren isn't meant to be human.

"Lucky, welcome back," he says airily, fingers picking at strings in no particular order, filling the air in the temple with a quiet, formless melody. Lucky nods and smiles, approaching the sculptures to sit down in front of the Siren. He crosses his legs and looks up, and the Siren gazes at him fondly with mirth in his eyes. That's when Lucky realizes, with his legs crossed and tired eyes, looking up to the god, he must look more like a child than ever. When he goes to change his position, the Siren holds out a hand. "No, no," he interrupts as a kind, genuine smile cuts across his face, "it's cute." Lucky can feel heat rise to his cheeks.

"I'm not cute," he mutters in defiance, and the god only laughs.

"Right. Not at all." Deft fingers dance across strings and Lucky watches quietly. Something about the melody is unnerving. "I've missed you, Lucky. What have you been up to this week?" the Siren asks. Lucky thinks for a moment.

"Went up to the capital. Stole some stuff..." he mutters. The Siren frowns.

"Lucky, stealing isn't right." Lucky knows. He's heard it time and time again, and more times than he can count from the god's own mouth.

"It's all I can do." The Siren trips over a few notes and shakes his head in frustration. He's about to speak before Lucky interrupts. "I didn't know you could play guitar," he says, and the Siren smiles.

"Have since before your kingdom was made. Eternity gets boring, you know? Immortality is the loneliest gift you could wish for." Lucky raises a brow.

"Don't you have the Angel? The goddess?" Something dark crosses the Siren's face and he lets out a breath.

"I do, but they find themselves occupied with... other things far too often." Lucky hesitates for a moment on his answer. It feels selfish in a way, to request such a thing, but if they knew him, wouldn't his problem be solved—their blessing granted?

"I'd love to meet them," he says, and the god stops playing. He doesn't look up when he replies.

"What?" Lucky can hear something edging his tone of voice close to anger, and he realizes he might've gone too far. But then again, it would be even worse to not answer him now.

"You know, if they knew me and liked me, all my weird stuff could be solved, right? Their blessing and all that?" He thinks for a second before shaking his head. "I'm sorry, that was a little selfish but—"

"No, no!" the god lets out, and if he didn't sound angry before, he certainly does now. "No, you're right! I'm sure they'd love to meet you, too, wouldn't they? To have another kid to dote over and adore—oh they'd be over the moon!" Lucky opens his mouth to apologize again, but the god is rambling. He doesn't even look at Lucky—doesn't seem to register his existence as his eyes go gold and he stares off into his own world, ignoring Lucky's presence. "What more would I want than to be ignored again in favor of a child!"

"Wait, I didn't mean to make you—"

"No, it's fine, everything is peachy," he says, smiling an obviously fake smile. The temperature in the room rises, and Lucky backs away, shaking his head.

"Wait, stop, I didn't mean anything," he says. His body feels hot, and he closes his eyes, bracing for whatever gruesome punishment the god has in mind this time for his misstep. "Please not again," he murmurs.

And all at once, there's silence, and the temperature drops back down. Lucky opens his eyes slightly to look at the god, avoiding direct eye contact, but the Siren is simply staring him down, unblinking.

"You're afraid of me," the Siren says, and Lucky shakes his head.

"No, I—"

"You're afraid of me," he says again, swirling, sparkly gold melting away back into intelligent dark brown eyes, with something Lucky wants to say looks like sadness; but he's not naive enough of a child anymore to think the god would have remorse for him. "You're scared of me. Lucas, why are you scared of me?" he asks. Lucky opens and closes his mouth a few times searching for a response.

Maybe in his nightmares when he sleeps, he sees visions of the Siren's teeth dripping with blood, or the image of a silver dagger pushed into a woman's chest. Maybe when he sleeps at night he swears he can hear the Siren laugh at him, reliving over and over again the feeling of his blood turning into icicles and slicing his nerves in unbearable pain. Or maybe when Lucky wakes up, he swivels his head wildly trying to search for the Siren—see if he's lurking around the corner or watching him, waiting for him to mess up.

Or maybe in his dreams he sees Finnigan, and he's warned to steer clear of the god.

Is Lucky scared of the Siren? Maybe he is. Maybe more now when he hops along the rooftops, he looks down at the ground below far more often than he used to, staring at it and imagining the sickening crack of bones as he hits the ground. Maybe Lucky feels that at every moment he's with the Siren, he's getting closer and closer to the edge of a cliff, just waiting to be pushed. And Lucky knows what happens when he hits the ground, and every minute of every single day he feels the wind hitting his cheeks on the way down the mountain and his life flashing before his eyes. Has he wasted what little time he has trying to earn affection from gods that see his existence as simply something to be toyed with until it's run out of steam? Do Lucky, and all humans like him, live on borrowed time and stolen lives, waiting, just waiting, to hit the ground?

"I'm not," is all he can say in response to the Siren, shaking his head in feigned confidence. The Siren only frowns, seeming genuinely hurt, but Lucky won't let himself be convinced he means anything to him. He means nothing. Because the Triad is so grand, and Lucky is small—the gods are so great, presiding over his world in peace and standing above it all, where Lucky sits and counts down the minutes on a ticking clock.

And in his head, the clock hits midnight, bells tolling, the sound foreboding a fate so dark and far away—or singing of his demise. No one will mourn the death of the gods' toy.

"You are, I know," the Siren says, and Lucky shakes his head again.

"I'm not, I'm Lucas Barlowe, I fear no one." Siren knows when he lies, he's said it before. The Siren can read his mind and control his actions, and he hears his thoughts loud and clear—and Lucky knows how he sounds to the god. He reeks the stench of a liar because he fears being known.

Because somewhere in a grassy valley that Lucky isn't meant to have seen, there's the corpse of a black-haired child buried *six* feet deep in a *five*-foot casket because at ten years old he's no more than *four* tall, and he wonders why *three* olden gods needed to end the life of the only *two* people he's ever loved, leaving him alone except for *one* face that haunts him even in death.

Lucky knows who killed Fin.

So is he scared of the Siren? Why would he be, when a boy

who reminds him so much of himself is decomposing in the earth, and Lucky never got to say goodbye? Why would he fear the Siren, when he can count down the minutes to a child's death, or recount his mother's last words in perfect clarity?

Why would he fear the Siren, when...

"I've never done anything to you."

... except provide him food and shelter and companionship, and warm arms to lean into on cold nights. When all he's ever done is make Lucky feel safe, make him soft for comforting hugs and kisses on the head, cover him with blankets and protect him from harm.

Why would Lucky fear the Siren to save himself from memories of a past that never happened, and a boy he never met?

Because eternity gets boring, and immortality is the loneliest gift you could wish for. Should it be so surprising that detachment is simply part of the package?

Siren wraps Lucky in his embrace, and places a kiss into his hair, rubbing his back in circles and comforting him in the way Lucky knows so well. He feels a familiar cold sliding down his cheeks, and hopes he doesn't stain the god's cloak silver.

Maybe Lucky is afraid of the Siren. Maybe his melodic laugh haunts his nightmares, and he flashes back to more painful days whenever icicles form on roofs. But maybe, regardless, people also love the wrong people sometimes. Maybe this is just one of those times.

Maybe Lucky is afraid of the Siren and what he can do to him, the same way he fears the dark but welcomes its embrace, and the same way he fears falling but thinks about it too much these days. Maybe Lucky fears the Siren, but can't make his heart stop loving him all the same.

When Lucky pulls out of his embrace, he wipes the tears away, and smiles at the god in silent thanks for his comfort.

"I'd never want for you to be scared of me," he says, searching the teen's eyes. "Please don't be afraid of me." Lucky nods, and feels like a liar, because he knows that can't happen.

He's dragged back into a hug again, and laughs tearily as he squeezes back.

"I'm sorry," he says. The god shakes his head.

"Since the very first day I looked at you, Lucas, all I've ever wanted is to hold you and keep you safe." From his embrace, all Lucky can ever get is bruises.

If he promised not to fear the gods, it would be a lie, but still, he'll never not love the Siren even if he tries.

Because Siren is so great, standing above it all, and if Lucky were on his shoulders, he'd lean down to look at the fall.

8

A gainst Lucky's better judgement, in the following weeks, he lets himself get comfortable around the Siren. It's not good, he knows, and he should push back again before he starts to see him as anything more than he really is. But... all the same, he can't be blamed, because as much as he tries, every time he begins to feel fear and discomfort set in, the Siren does the smallest thing—kisses his head, or holds his hand, or brings him food and talks to him—and suddenly he's pulled right back into his comforting but so entrapping embrace. He's stuck in a divine cage, and the longer he stays, the more he starts to think of it as home.

To top it off, Siren has been very lax with punishments as of late. Lucky hasn't felt his blood freeze or vocal cords shred in weeks, and when he feels the temperature rise, he tenses, and the Siren immediately releases.

His mornings in the temple begin to feel like something that he's never felt before. An oddly domestic, familial atmosphere where he's surrounded by warmth and lo—

No. Maybe not that.

Lucky doesn't want to get comfortable with the standard of living he's become accustomed to with the god. Even when the

Siren doesn't appear that day, he's sure to make his presence known. Every morning when he wakes up, he's met by a loaf of bread or pieces of fruit or vegetables. Hell, he's had butter for the first time in gods know how long, and just the other day with a little bread roll, honey. Real honey. He probably couldn't have even gotten that if he did have a normal life.

He's grown into his figure and can no longer feel his stomach rumble in the day. He can't wrap his fingers around his wrists anymore. It's perfect, and it's everything he could've ever wanted.

But it can't be true.

It can't last, right?

"Ferocious, Lucky. Fur-oh-shes," he hears the Siren direct him, and he turns his attention back to the book in his hands. The god is leaning over his shoulder, looking down at the page and pointing to the word with one finger. Lucky shakes his head as if it could put the thoughts from his mind.

"But that's a 'c.' Wouldn't it say fur-oh-kee-us?" The Siren lets out a quick, breathy laugh and shakes his head. He ruffles Lucky's hair with a hand, and Lucky keeps himself from melting, because this can't last. He means nothing to the god.

"No, it sounds like an 's' and 'h' because it has that ending." Lucky scowls and shakes his head.

"That's dumb."

"True," the Siren agrees.

"I hate this language," he laments, "I bet yours is better." He's heard the Siren speak it before. When he was first "blessed" he heard the Siren talk in a strange staccato rhythm in a language that sounded sharp. Sounded cooler than English, that's for sure.

"It would be very hard for you to learn though," the Siren says with a low laugh. "Maybe your own language first, yeah?" Lucky nods.

"Ferocious pets," he mutters, mostly to himself, getting a feel for the word in his mouth. "An... aff—affinity?" He doesn't quite understand why it was so important to the Siren that he learn to read better, but he'd learned not to make a habit of questioning him. He feels a congratulating pat on his back, and can't help but smile.

"Affinity!" the Siren echoes, voice filled with pride. The way he praises Lucky makes him want to cry every time. It sounded as if they were real friends. Like brothers.

It isn't supposed to feel like that. Lucky is supposed to look at the fall.

"—at that means?" the Siren asks him. Lucky shakes his head.

"No. I don't know that." He could probably guess, but he's lost in thought.

"Well, it just means you really like something, or you have a special relationship or connection with it." Lucky nods. "So you have an affinity for being loud and annoying—"

"Hey!"

"—and I have an affinity for music," the Siren finishes his sentence and looks at Lucky, smiling. "And you, of course." Lucky looks at him for a moment, considering his words. He fights back the tears that prick at his eyes as they do every time the Siren speaks so fondly to him. He wants to say something back, but can't help the voices at the back of his head reminding him he's a pawn. The Siren likes him the same way a child likes a stuffed animal. Instead, he only nods, and sees the Siren's smile drop a little before turning back to the book.

"Ferocious pets, with an affinity for chaos," he finishes the line. The room goes slightly colder as the Siren's hand comes back up to hold his shoulder and pull him closer, but he says nothing. Lucky feels conflicting senses of both validation in his brushing the god off, and a lingering feeling of guilt from the lack of response to an obvious moment of vulnerability.

Does the Siren have vulnerability?

"The sisters loved their cats," he continues, "but they still caused problems. It was clear that Puppet, the black cat, was part... al? Partial. The black cat was partial to Anna, which made her sister jel—jealous." He frowns. "This story is dumb, Siren." The Siren laughs.

"It's a little slow. What, you don't care that they learn to love each other at the end?" he teases. Lucky shakes his head.

"Love is stupid. I'm a strong man with strong man problems." Lucky could feel it in his bones that the Siren wants to disagree, but he's quiet for a moment.

"Even strong men need someone to love. Just to have something to lean on from time to time." And sure, maybe the Siren was right, but shit, he was going to sit here giving Lucky life advice as if he were his father—like he has any idea what Lucky's life was like before he arrived. He scowls.

"Easy for you to say, you and your cool magic family that control everything. I don't have anyone." The god is quiet after Lucky's statement, and his grip on his shoulder loosens.

"You have me, Lucky." It sounds far more like a question than it should, and Lucky recoils on himself. He shakes his head.

"No, Siren. I don't know anything about you." The Siren seems taken aback, and releases Lucky's shoulder entirely, looking at him in confusion. Lucky sighs. "Like, you're cool, but, I don't know—you know everything about everything, and you're the awesome guy everyone prays to. I'm just some kid. I can't lean on you the same way as..." a family. Friends. Humans.

He doesn't get to finish his thought as he's wrapped into the god's arms. "I love you, Lucky."

And Lucky's heart stops.

It stutters in his chest as he flings his eyes open and stares at the wall behind the god, wide-eyed and wild.

"I should've said it before, Moonlight."

"Shhh... I love you. You know that, right?"

"I love you, too, Dad."

A new voice echoes around Lucky's head. A voice that calls the Siren *dad*.

"I hope one day you can love me, too."

"One day you'll realize this was for the best."

A boy with red hair looks up into the Siren's eyes, and nods, wiping tears off his face and smiling sadly.

"I trust you."

He shouldn't. He shouldn't, he shouldn't, he shouldn't, he has to run, run.

Running out of time. Clock ticking, timer counting down, borrowed time, borrowed time, the fall—the fall is coming.

Lucky, you're going to

f

   a

     l

       l

"—ing in love with you since the day I saw you. Whenever you need it, you can lean on me." Can he? Can he, really? When there's so much blood on his hands, and Lucky is complicit in it all by virtue of keeping it secret?

Lucky sometimes swears he feels the blood on him.

"You promise?" The Siren smiles.

"I promise." The little boy is scared. He grips onto his father's sweater hard as he pulls him into one last hug and tries to say everything he never could with one gesture. I love you isn't enough. I'll miss you, and I'll remember you aren't enough. It's a promise in his final moments.

I will love you.

Until I see you again.

"Do it, honey." The Siren's voice echoes inside the boy's mind. He couldn't disobey if he tried.

Tears still flowing, he approaches his mother's body, lifeless on the floor, and pulls out the shiny silver dagger. It's so pretty. It's been on a hook on the wall for so many years. The boy didn't even know it was sharp.

With his hand on the hilt, he holds the cold blade to his neck, and smiles at his father.

And—

"—I'll spend a lifetime convincing you."

When Lucky wakes the Siren isn't there. He's gotten used to being woken with a hand in his hair and sharp white teeth smiling down at him, deceptively fondly.

There is none of that today. Today, he sits up, and spots a woman lounging comfortably in front of the sculptures, twirling a knife in one hand, and looks her over quizzically.

She has long blonde hair that looks silky as if brushed five times a day. Lucky wonders what it would be like to run his hands through it. Resting on it she wears a shiny golden crown, not much different to the Siren's. Sharp and intimidating.

She wears a long red cloak, with white fur around the collar, gold chains and cords draped all over, along with a chiffon dress covering her legs, leaving just enough of her feet exposed for Lucky to see her slick black heels.

Lucky would like to think he's not an idiot anymore, so when the woman smiles at him and bears sharp canine teeth, Lucky doesn't take long to make the connection, looking up to the statue of the goddess.

Had he met her months ago, he likely would've frozen, screamed, thrashed, or maybe bowed down and asked for an autograph (she is the coolest, after all).

Now, Lucky's become strangely accustomed to this kind of thing. The surprise is of course palpable, but comes out not in a terrified shriek like it did the first time he met the Siren. This time, he simply stares blankly, eyes melting into silver.

"Smart kid," the goddess says, and Lucky's brain short-circuits.

"I've seen you before," he says simply, and the woman laughs.

"True. Nikolai apparently is so inept he can't handle a panic attack." Lucky looks at the War Goddess strangely, and tilts his head to the side.

"Nikolai?" Now it's the Lady's turn to be surprised.

"He adores you for so long and doesn't even give you his real name?" she asks, but it's not a real question. "Typical," she finishes, snorting and rolling her eyes. Lucky simply gapes. He shakes his head, and raises a hand to fix his hair idly.

"The Siren has a name?" he asks, and the goddess looks back at him, and smiles. Well—Lucky thinks that's what that is. It looks like a threat more than anything.

"Think I wanna call my brother the damned 'Siren God' at home? Nah. That's Nicky." She seems so... casual. Far more casual than Lucky expected a seasoned combat veteran and Goddess of War to be, but after putting up with the Siren— Nikolai, apparently—for so long? He won't argue.

"Why... why wouldn't he tell me that?" Lucky asks, and he can't help a tone of hurt creeping into his voice. The Lady's eyes soften and she looks at Lucky fondly.

"Ah, kid, I'm sure he didn't mean it like that. He's got a bit of a problem with attachments to mortals, is all." Lucky shifts in his seat. *Oh yeah, he's got a problem with mortals.*

"So, uh, why are you here?" he asks, realizing immediately he could stand to be more polite. "Lady Retribution, the Goddess of War." To Lucky's surprise, the Lady simply rolls her eyes, and tosses her dagger into the air. It disappears before it hits the ground.

"That 'Lady Retribution' business is so pretentious," she says. She disappears, and reappears behind Lucky in a cloud of black, and the teen flinches when she holds out her hand. "Honora. Or Nora, if you prefer. I don't mind," she introduces. Lucky realizes he's expected to shake her hand, not brace to be hit. So he does. The goddess seems to internally question his hesitance, but doesn't comment. "And Nicky was a bit busy today. I figured with how much he gushes about you, I could stand to be in your presence for a moment." Gushes about him? That shouldn't make Lucky feel so warm and fuzzy, but it does. Honora seems to notice, and gives a playful scowl. "Oh come on, you actually like that sap?" Lucky shakes his head and hides his face.

"Shut up."

The goddess laughs, and it sounds so different from Nikolai's.

Where the Siren's shifts so rapidly from fond to menacing, Nora keeps hers cool, even and sweet.

"No shame in liking the guy," she says between laughs, before she sobers herself and leans on the bench behind Lucky and looks into his eyes. Honora's eyes are blue, and bright, and seem somewhat eerily to glow. "But I did wanna check on you," she begins, gaze softening. "I know Nicky can be a bit much. Just wanted to make sure you're doing alright with him." Lucky cocks his head to the side and looks at the goddess with a question written on his face.

"What do you mean?" Nora sighs, disappearing once more, and in a cloud of darkness, appears again sitting on the bench beside Lucky, casually.

"I just know my brother, that's all. He can get overbearing, especially with kids." And there it is. Lucky sees it for one second—an in. He can actually get straight answers without being tortured or mind-controlled or yelled at.

This is Lucky's chance. The Siren is nowhere to be seen, and it seems that this new goddess is at least a little bit on Lucky's side. And even if she doesn't know what Nikolai has truly been doing to him or the harsh punishments he doles out, she has answers Lucky needs.

So when he sees an opening in the conversation for a brief second, he jumps at it. Maybe a little too enthusiastically, but who knows when he'll get this opportunity again.

"Who is Finnigan?" he asks. Honora freezes, and looks him over for a moment. Lucky feels a sense of dread curling up inside him, like maybe he's misread and now the Lady will punish him, too, but instead, she only lets out a breath heavily.

"Right. Nicky said you knew." What? "What do you wanna know about him?" she asks first, then, "What has Nicky told you?" Lucky shakes his head.

"Nothing. Any time I bring it up he just gets all... mad. Looks like he wants to yell at me, freaks out, makes everything cold, does that—" he gestures to his face, "eye thing?" Honora smiles, and the whites of her eyes disappear, instead leaving a pool of dark, shimmering crimson. "Yeah, yeah that thing." Nora laughs for a moment.

"Yeah, he really lets his emotions get the best of him sometimes." She goes quiet, and looks off into space to consider her answer. She doesn't look back to Lucky as she starts talking, lost in her own world. "I suppose it makes sense for him to not want to talk about him. It's hard to lose somebody like that." Lucky stays quiet. That's not the answer he expected. "Well, to cut it short, I guess... Finnigan was our brother." Lucky chokes on air and stares wide-eyed at the goddess.

"What?" Honora chuckles humorlessly.

"Yeah. There's somethin' the scripture won't teach ya."

"...There's another god?" Lucky asks incredulously, mind already racing. The War Goddess shakes her head, and avoids Lucky's eyes.

"Would've been," she corrects. *Oh,* Lucky's mind supplies, *Finnigan is dead.* "Again, it makes sense he wouldn't talk about it. We don't talk about Finny at all these days. The Angel still hasn't quite gotten over it." Lucky is quiet for a second.

"What happened?" he asks, not quite sure what he's really asking for. The goddess sighs, still not looking Lucky in the eyes, staring off into space.

"The Angel was a lot like Nicky back in the day. Before I was born, he got attached to this mortal woman. Krista was her name. Really loved her, assumed a human form and came down and married her," she takes in a sharp breath and lets it out slowly. "I never knew her, but from what little he's said, she would've made a great mom. Kind lady, compassionate, really loved Nikolai and the Angel." She frowns, and shakes her head. "So anyway, got pregnant, had Fin. I was born long after the kid was already gone, but I hear he was a little ray of sunshine. That's what the Angel always calls him. 'Sunshine.' Like he couldn't live without him."

"Come on, walk out of the fire. It isn't that hard, Sunshine."

Nikolai's voice taunts inside Lucky's mind. His father's endearment for a semi-mortal son spat like acid in the Siren's dark and controlling voice. Lucky shivers, and hopes the goddess doesn't notice.

"Nikolai didn't see him much, but I'm told the kid really loved him. Was always on his heels, trying to play with 'Micky.'" She chuckles slightly at the nickname, but Lucky can't bring himself to laugh along. "He and dad's wife would've been immortal sooner or later. Angel would've gifted them..." she takes in a long breath, and closes her eyes. "The kid didn't live past ten. Fire. They think foreign raiders started it, and Krista went the very same night."

And no mention of Nikolai. No mention of a Siren's song entrancing the child. Lucky can feel his heart stop.

"Nicky and the Angel were torn up. Dad gets all sad whenever you bring it up, and Nikolai just gets angry. I can't blame him, I guess. Losing your first brother when he's so young? It must've hit him hard." No.

No, no, no—what? She doesn't know. She doesn't *know*.

"I was adopted a couple centuries later. I didn't see much of the kid, but..." she finally looks at Lucky, and her eyes soften upon seeing the teen's shocked expression. "You two would've been friends, I think."

"Finny! Finny please breathe, come on! You can do it, in and out. Please, baby, please, not like this!" The mother is frantic, she's on her knees before a child with lungs full of soot, matted, burnt hair and torn skin. Tears stream down her face freely and she presses on the child's chest in a steady rhythm that slowly gets more and more off-beat as the reality sets in on her. She cries out. "El! Elric, please, you have to be able to do something."

And there's a new voice in the scene.

"Finny, come back to us, you're so strong." A man. Blond and tall with silken robes of black and white, kind eyes now morphed into something fearful and pleading.

The mother kisses the child's hand, warm and covered in ash. "Please, Fin."

"Stay strong, Sunshine."

He can't hear their pleas.

When Lucky comes to he doesn't know how long he's been crying, or whose arms are wrapped around him. He only knows that his metallic silver tears fall down his face and continue to carve the wells in his cheeks deeper as he's crushed in a colorless embrace.

"Come on kid, I know it's rough, breathe with me, yeah? Just like last time."

"Breathe!" She pounds on his chest harder, leaning close to his face to see if she can hear a breath come out— anything that could indicate he lives, still. "Breathe with me Finnigan! Please, please, pleasepleasepleasepleaseplease." She's pulled away from her child and wrapped into strong arms, and sobs into her husband's chest, pounding on him with a fist as he combs a hand through her ash-filled hair.

Tears aren't meant to be quiet. They're meant to break and bleed and shatter and scream, but from the eyes of the Angel of Dawn, they drip silently into his wife's hair, without preface or preamble.

"Breathe, Finny..." she continues to cry, even in the Angel's arms. "Breathe—"

"—with me, kid. In and out."

Right. In.

Out. His final breath, laying broken on the stones surrounded by smoke.

In.

Out, his life force drains. The beautiful soul of a child too perfect for this wretched world.

In.

"This isn't working. Kid, you still with me?" Lucky nods, but he feels like a liar. He's somewhere else entirely. His name isn't even Lucky, it's—

"Fin. I love you honey." Her controlled breaths turn back into wails. "Why couldn't I save you?"

Her husband shushes her comfortingly, but she doesn't feel a thing.

"Hey, hey, look at me, come on." Lucky opens his eyes. His world is black. "There you go. Keep them open," Lucky nods. He feels a hand on his own, and a calming sort of aura wash over him. The black fades down into grey tones again. "See? You got it. Already lighter. You're getting good at this." Lighter.

"I'm sorry," he lets out, tears clogging his throat begging to push their way up into his eyes.

"No need, no need. It's a lot for anyone to handle. You're okay." How could this woman be so calm and reassuring and level-headed after delivering the worst news on earth?

Brother.

Brother, son—Fin was the Siren's family. Nikolai, how could he? His own brother...

Lucky wants to vomit. Some random kid was enough, but his little brother? His ten-year-old brother.

Lucky chokes back a sob.

He's been spending all his time learning from and loving a man who would kill—murder—his own baby brother, and for what? And Lucky's been hugging him and holding his hand and learning how to read and enjoying it? From the mouth of a liar who convinced his own family their child died because of some foreign brutes and not by his own bloody hands?

And at times, Lucky can feel the blood on his skin.

Here he is, face to face with a goddess missing a little brother, killed by her own brother. Here Lucky is, face to face with a member of a broken and incomplete family, knowing the truth, knowing how her baby brother really died, and saying nothing.

Who is the true monster? The Siren, or the disciple who keeps his secrets?

Lucky cries harder, and Honora hugs him tighter, and Lucky doesn't deserve it. Because where Honora thinks he cries over the loss of a child, he knows what the truth is and that he is just

THE LIGHT IS DIMMER

as much a murderer as Nikolai. The Siren. The Leviathan. He's keeping the secret of the loss of a life far too soon.

"Tulips are lovely, right, Mom?" The mother laughs, and hugs her son closer.

"Sure they are. Looks like you've picked the smallest of the bunch, though." She gestures to the rows of red and white tulips spread out before them in full bloom in the growth of the Spring.

"But this one's young. It won't die immediately." The boy frowns. "I don't want to sit in my room all day watching a flower wilt. This one has time to bloom first," he says. His mother smiles, and kisses his cheek.

"I guess you're right."

"I'm sorry," Lucky cries again, and Nora hushes him. He doesn't know when he got it, but now there's a red cape draped over his shoulders, white fur tickling his jaw.

"It's alright, you're okay." He shakes his head.

"I'm sorry." *That you never met him. That I can see him. That he's dead. That I know why. That I won't tell you.*

He burrows further into the goddess's chest, and thinks, not for the first time, of falling.

If he could stop on the rooftops on his way to the temple, and sit for a moment to consider. As if everyone who's ever lived hadn't looked off the edge of a steep drop and considered. Because if even only a little, everyone wants to know what it feels like to fall. It would only take a little jump.

But not yet. Not just yet.

He thinks distantly of Nikolai, off somewhere living his immortal life, singing his songs or strumming a guitar, or simply observing, and wonders how he became a monster like him. Maybe, just maybe, Nikolai always knew he'd keep the secret.

Maybe Lucky has the heart of a monster and only the Siren ever knew.

He lets out more tears, and in the back of his mind, a grandfather clock strikes twelve.

9

Nikolai should've known that sooner or later the end would finally come. Thousands of years of weaving webs of lies and tapestries of tall tales thrown together on the coldest backdrop he could find. The moniker of the Just and Pure they had to him ascribed, only to spend a life in lies. A silver tongue stained in blood and wilted flowers left behind.

Who, he often wondered, was the true God of Blood? Though war in its many forms plagued his sister since her birth, no more blood has been spilt down the family tree than rests in the palms of the Siren. Blood pooling in his hands and dripping between cracks in his fingers—drops that he should've known would one day hit the ground.

And when Lucky enters the temple that day, his face tells Nikolai it's finally over. Nights he'd spent holding fires in his hands to keep the child warm all in vain, as they always have been, for he's never meant to have a happy ending.

When Lucky enters the temple that day, Nikolai sees the sorrows of children hundreds of thousands of years before him painted in grey scales in his eyes, and Nikolai waits to hear the news. That he'd found someone new to love that's better than the Siren ever could be, for there's never any outcome that doesn't end with the god alone once again.

Maybe Lucky almost had loved him, but when he enters the temple that day, his expressionless face that speaks of agony beyond his years tells the Siren that he's once again stepped over the edge. For each day of his life, balancing precariously on the precipice of alienation and acceptance, and always waiting to be pushed. He wishes he didn't know what it's like to fall.

When the Siren meets Lucky in the temple, his eyes are dark and framed with sorrow, and not for the first time, Nikolai considers that maybe his many deceptions have caught up to him. For what else, if not the villain of everyone's story, could a whispering god possibly be?

For what else is the Siren possibly meant for than to bleed secrets like ink spilling off a page, or the water off a duck's back that means so little to natural life, only to cause the flurry of ripples, tears, and waves in the water from whence he came? For when the Siren's only in his life meant to do good, he always ends out here—leading those he loves to the cellar to wait for them to fight.

> *Deep with deception, secrets I bleed,*
> *to be lost in the cellars in darkness,*
> *does he, my warnings, finally heed,*
> *or to my tauntings reply?*

And so, if only for the possibility that the conversation wouldn't be had, the Siren smiles wide and approaches his ward with open arms. The boy with a smile like sunshine and eyes of painted valleys avoids his gaze and ducks under his grasp. He hopes distantly that maybe he's for so long taught his arms what it feels like to be full that the absence won't be missed too dearly when he can never hold Lucky again.

But Hope, he knows, is the thing with feathers, and won't hesitate to fly away.

"Lucky," he says with a tilted head, his smile faltering. Though he knows the end of his charade has finally come, the facade won't fall until the final bell tolls.

"Nikolai," he greets back, and the Siren takes pause. The child strafes his perception toward the sculptures, and the god finally lowers his arms. Have they been trained what it feels like once again to embrace, or is the emptiness his only fate?

"Where did you hear that name?" Though he speaks with venom and his eyes melt gold, he can't help his tone in his mind at least from wavering, caught off guard by the use of a moniker so long forgotten by humanity. The name is his own, he cannot deny, but would he have willingly chosen to be referred to as something so sickly, sweetly mortal? Because while Lucky is a pure and perfect beacon of Hope the same way the Siren once would've been, the crushing weight of an immortal life and the world upon one's shoulders has made him blind to the beauties of humankind. A god is only meant to be bitter—with a name so sweet on the lips and human in the heart, could ever he have become what he is today?

"Your sister," Lucky replies, and the Siren scowls, turning to approach him at his place by the statues. He looks up with narrowed and saddened eyes to the marble sculpted form of the Siren before shifting his gaze to Honora; and if Nikolai sneers upon seeing his expression soften at the look of the War Goddess, none shall know. Another, he thinks, choosing his sister over him?

Once again, humans fall victim to the most traitorous, tell-tale heart. Would Lucky one day hear the pitter-patter of lives so selfishly taken without regard, only for Nikolai's own satisfaction? For what is the god if not a silver blade, sharpened to a razor edge ready to strike out at the first inconvenience? If ever he has not been a weapon, let forces greater than himself give a sign.

For this misdeed, should I wish to leave in the past

to my vaults I'll lead in search of a Cask?
My friend, you are weak
it is not revenge I seek,
but you will forgive my greed.

He places a hand on the child's shoulder and pretends not to notice how he shivers and shifts; his touch once comforting and warming like the heat of a summer's sun now chilled as if it were the boy's own tears—cursed to carve wells into his youthful cheeks as a punishment for, what? Is this as it is meant to be? His touch not meant to comfort and hold close memories of nights spent awake, his hand in golden blond hair singing as he sleeps; but rather his hand was always meant to draw blood, and poison the water from whence it was drawn.

"I promise, I meant to tell you," the Siren lets out with a throat closed and windpipes twisted and braided into obscurity. Should he have been cut open, so mortal veins and gears and wires exposed, only then would his inhumanity be revealed.

"Which part of it, Nikolai?" Lucky asks, and the Siren takes in a breath.

"Do not use that name," he warns, but Lucky bristles. Does he already know? Have the Siren's attempts at burying a past, too dark and bleeding for a child, doomed him to the footnotes of history? God of what should have been speech and soliloquy drowned into that which humans truly use his gifts for? For if his literature is only the voice of madness then what a crazed lunatic he was always destined to be.

"It's yours, isn't it?" Lucky speaks, memories of nightmares and daydreams and Voices screaming in his head, directing his anger to his own Creator. "Just like how Finnigan was your brother's?"

"How do you know about Fin?" the Siren asks, biting tone and intentions laid bare on a cold backdrop of silver and gold.

"Your sister. You let her live." Emotions flooding against a strong dam could once have been let out in waves of tears and apologies, but life has poisoned his once immune immature mind, and all his soul has known for centuries is the seething of anger behind marbled walls.

"*Silence.*" He couldn't disagree if he tried, and the teen's jaw goes slack. "You don't know when to stop," he says.

Red liquid begins to bubble out of the child's mouth, but unlike the many times before, his tears won't fall. Something in the Siren wishes that the liquid moonbeam drops would fall down his cheeks and carve their paths like a stream unhindered through the river basins of the wood. If only to know that Lucky listens when he speaks, or takes his words to heart—or to prove that unlike him, Lucky was still pure and innocent enough to cry freely. But tears as visual evidence can only so often fall.

Should they, in your nightmares, so concede
to have fallen victim to such
a disagreeable deed,

"You forget so often, Lucky, that though you are better than before, stronger than you once were, you are nothing without me." Lucky nods, tears still refusing to fall. How far could the Siren push until the silvery pools of emotion the boy called eyes began to overflow with the metallic confirmation of his breaking point? "Baby," the Siren coos, taking his face in his hands, "Baby, Moonlight, you have to understand, what are you if not a comet pulled from orbit? Like the moonlight reliant upon the sun, my dear, you would cease to exist if it weren't for me." Lucky nods, and stays silent as the Siren's power demands. "Dearest Lucky, little Moonlight, you are just as I say—without me would your shine be taken away? And yet still, you wish to question my will? As if without me you'd still have somewhere to orbit—no, no, Dear, though you're more than you once were, it is a virtue to learn when appropriate to *bow.*"

At the word, Lucky drops to his knees before the Siren, and he smiles.

"You may speak, Moonlight."

"Your brother," Lucky spits immediately, with blood spilling from his mouth, teeth painted red. Something about the way Lucky says the word sends sharp pain shooting into Nikolai's chest that he doesn't recognize. Brother. When was the last time he'd thought of someone as that? "Your son, Nikolai! Your wife, your mother, all of them!"

"She was not my mother. Krista was not my mother." And if sometimes Nikolai wished that maybe she had been? No one needed to know.

"How long did you expect to get away with this?" Lucky asks, and the Siren can hear choked back sobs in his voice, but he doesn't falter.

"For just as long as they got away with what they did to me, Lucky! Under the same weight of the torture they'd so justly inflicted upon me, would I expect your knees not to buckle? You'd have done the same!" Lucky spits plasma from his mouth, some painting his pants in drops of crimson, the rest pooling on the ground.

"For what torture? Do you hear yourself? For the sin of living, I'd have done the same? They were innocent!" The Siren scoffs and waves his hand in the air, and Lucky doubles over with a headache slashing his skull in two.

> *for what actions should they seek to repay*
> *for the torture, pain they set into my veins?*
> *Dear friend, it is not a game to be played,*
> *rather misdeeds to a misdressèd stage.*

"She made a promise, Lucky. She was meant to love me and only me! *Til death do us part,* or whatever other lies she spit. You wouldn't understand it. You wouldn't understand how it feels to have that promise broken for a stupid child." Lucky stares at the god for a moment, dumbfounded with an expression which you'd give to the dirt under your feet. *Disgusted,* the Siren realizes, *Lucky is disgusted.*

"You were jealous of your child?" he asks incredulously, and the Siren sneers. "That's why they're dead? Because you couldn't stand not being the best?"

"Jealousy is for the weak," he retorts, instead of acknowledging the rest of the teen's accusation. Lucky spits back immediately with just as much venom.

"Then maybe you're not all you think. Maybe you're just as weak as the rest of us." The Siren stares at the teen with anger in his eyes, pupils falling away to a swirling abyss of gold. Once comforting, now is reminiscent only of lava, copper wire, hard and grating metal staring into Lucky's soul. He's fiery. He's angry, and Lucky doesn't back down. What do the humans do when this feeling of tightness in their chest where their heart is supposed to be overtakes them? What should a god do when the same feeling bites into his brain and tears off pieces of his consciousness without remorse. What does a god do when his child, the silvery moonbeam which he's protected so long with all his heart, decides he's no longer worth it? When he finally allows his heart to love again, and bleeding memories of his past corrupt his present?

Well, he does what anyone else would do.

He laughs. A sadistic smile cutting across his face showing off sharp teeth, perfectly pearly white and pristine—a pure vision of excellence that must be intimidating, he hopes, to an orphaned street child like Lucky.

"I'm not all I think?" he lets out, laughing darkly. "Lucky, look at you! You think yourself strong enough to stand up to a god? It's almost cute."

"And you think yourself strong enough to take on the world. To take on death and fate itself against all odds. You think yourself perfect and just and pure, and one day it will all catch up to you," Lucky spits, and the Siren seethes.

Should they in your nightmares, scream
that your savior is not all that he seems,
that his countenance brings kingdoms to knees,
or his favor upon your soul a disease?

"I need not be confident I can take on Fate, Lucky, only you. Only the people who wrong me."

"And the cost to your family? Your friends?" Lucky posits, and the god only laughs—closer and closer to a manic cackling than humorous laughter Lucky once knew.

"Cost? Lucky! Look me in the eyes and tell me I care about the cost!" Lucky shrinks away as the Siren yells louder and louder. "Look around you! Do you think everyone else shares in this delusion of yours, Lucky? Cares of cost? Your worldview relies on the hope that someone would give up everything for a kid they've never met, and you've gotten too big for your boots with these small powers I've *so kindly* given you," his speech becomes more heated with every passing second, and his arms and hands feel so empty. Robbed, once again, of something to hold by the love of another. Oh, it's always the same. The world comes crashing down on poor old Nikolai for having the good grace to give away his heart to a piteous creature who comes to fall for his family all the more. What a shame.

The Siren grabs onto Lucky's shirt and pulls him up to meet his eyes. He smiles, and between one blink and another, they stand together on the highest balcony of the capitol's palace, a cool zephyr ruffling Lucky's hair. Because above all else, whether Lucky has immortality the same as Nikolai would never matter, because unlike the gods, Lucky has no wings.

Nikolai had pondered from time to time how perfect Lucky would look with a spiraling flow of silver behind his back, lighting up everything around him like sparkling mercury. Lucky would look so good with wings. He'd be so perfect with a silver circlet resting on his golden hair—each tip of his crown embedded with rubies and diamonds, cut as sharp as his wit and brilliant as his spirit.

The Siren says none of this.

"You think your little dreams entitle you to knowledge you're not meant to have. You think the words of my stupid brother buried six feet underground give you the right to question me?"

Should the buried ones
not meant to speak, speak
of me as the villain of late-Greek,
or thoughtlessly spin their lies.

"You knew, Lucky. You knew since the very beginning this could only end badly. I know you thought of it. I know you thought of this, Lucky." He gestures wildly to the open sky around them, for he knows that since they'd met, all Lucky could think about was the edges of roofs.

"I didn't know anything! I thought maybe I could trust you! Look where that went!" The Siren's cirrus wings spread behind him in a shining golden feathered cape, and the palace behind him seems to light up in yellow and orange, reminding them painfully of better days past when bright candles burned in the temple and fate smiled upon the two of them.

"You can trust me, Lucky, if you'd just let yourself! But you can't. Just like everyone else." He laughs another dark laugh with poisonous edges, dripping the blood of women and children all on his hands. "Do you think I wanted this, Lucky?" He pulls Lucky close to his chest and gives him a hug, something he knows has to be goodbye, because this was never meant to end any other way. Lucky tries to squirm away, but Nikolai knows the effect he has on him. He'll be melting into his warm embrace in 3, 2, 1. "My baby, my child, my little moonlight. This wasn't how it was meant to be. But you understand, of course, it's your own fault. You always were so understanding." He tries to hold Lucky in a hug for as long as he can, because as sure as he is that this has to be the end, he just can't let go.

Had he played along, responded to the Siren's taunting; maybe he wouldn't have put in the last brick, and maybe Lucky's story could've ended happier.

"You understand, of course, this is your own fault," the Siren whispers again. He buries his face into locks of golden hair and takes in for the last time what could have been—the perfect child who would've stayed with him forever. The perfect child who one day he'd have gifted immortality to live with him for the rest of his never-ending days; a child who would've hugged him and sang with him and learned how to read—who he'd have taught to play guitar and speak in rhyme and taunt Honora until the end of time.

Should they, dear friend,
speak of a Cask,
in a cellar with sins long ago passed—
Let it be said, I speak of no Amontillado,
nor do I spend days
Framing Fortunato.

What's a god to do, he wonders, when the promising vision of a future finally his own comes crashing down on him all over again? What's he to do when he'd let his heart love the wrong people far too many times, the people who could never love him back?

And at times, the Siren can still feel the blood on his hands, and the silver ring on his finger. Though through decades and centuries of atonement for which he'll never be recognized. He's not taken the life of another since Serena, there is only one truth in this world—that no matter what he does, he'll always be the monster the world wants him to be. Because he's the villain—he knows it's true, and life has decided to turn a man to a fuse. So he best give them what they ask.

✦

"You understand, of course, this is your own fault," the Siren says into Lucky's hair, and he bristles, trying to pull out of the god's grasp and run while he still can.

Because you're so grand,
and I'm so small.

Lucky pulls himself from Nikolai's arms and stares the god in the eyes—a reflective pool of golden light still carrying a sense of something almost apologetic. But Lucky has long since abandoned hope of any sort of humanity inside this creature—whatever he may be.

If I were a fraction of what you claim to be...

He leans down to look at the fall. Off the balcony, down to the city center below. Concrete and rocks and cobbled stone paths marking the drop a death sentence.

"It didn't have to be this way," the Siren says, almost sadly, pulling Lucky back into his arms as if attempting to distract from the realization he's just made. Lucky fights his grip, but the Siren holds his embrace tightly. "It didn't have to be this way," he mumbles into his hair, voice breaking on every letter, and his downwards inflections so characteristic of the god Lucky loves now soured and saddened.

"Do it, Honey," a Siren from centuries before sings into Lucky's mind. "Come on, walk out of the fire. It isn't that hard, Sunshine."

"I do so love you, Lucky. I hate to see you hurt." Lucky feels the cold sensation inside him take over, gripping each and every fluid in his body and dragging them down into sub-zeroes in mere fractions of seconds, but he won't let tears fall.

✦

Nikolai forgot how hard it was to do this. Saying goodbye. No matter how much he wanted or needed to, it could never be a quiet affair, and golden tears begin to stream down his face, burning his cheeks as they go, the heat of a thousand suns condensed into a teardrop. Apt, that his moonlight should be killed in such a way. Silver and gold, both too brilliant to exist together in this terrible world.

☙❧

"I LOVE YOU, LUCKY."

Lucky can smell the stench of a liar in every word the Siren speaks, but can't tell if it's because it's true, or he doesn't want to believe it. Because Lucky loves a murderer, and that murderer loves him back.

"I never wanted this, my dear. I love you, Moonlight, so much, but I'm afraid..."

...of heights...

"... it was never meant to be," he finishes, smiling a sad smile at Lucky with a voice that sounds choked with tears. And Lucky's throat is on fire, and his eyes can't lie anymore, spilling out silver.

☙❧

IN THE CENTURIES THE SIREN HAD SPILLED NO BLOOD, HE forgot how it felt to see someone he loves be taken from him. Something pulls Nikolai to think that it's better this way, but for once, he can't bring himself to believe it.

In the centuries since he'd killed someone, he forgot how it felt when their hand finally left his.

No one could ever teach an old dog new tricks, and Nikolai could never not be the monster he was always meant to be.

☙❧

AND OFF THE BALCONY DOWN TO THE STONES BELOW, LUCKY learns, not for the first time, what it feels like to hit the ground.

The bells in the temple clocktower signal the time as twelve, and they toll in time calmly as his bones crack onto the stones. People scream, and disperse away from the body in the street, and he can hear a crunch as sickening as he'd always imagined it would be.

⚜

AND NIKOLAI CAN'T TRAIN HIS ARMS TO REMEMBER WHAT IT'S like to be full, nor could he teach his heart to love the way he was supposed to.

⚜

"NIKOLAI! NIKOLAI, WHAT HAVE YOU DONE?" LUCKY HEARS one last voice before the world fades away. The only world he's ever known is thrown into darkness, and he wishes that maybe he could watch it all one last time between shades of grey.

☙ 10 ❧

"To my worst nightmare,

I know you'll never see this. Sometimes, though, I feel as though it's simpler to speak my mind when there are no witnesses. I know I'll never get the nerve to say it out loud, after all.

Though even if my existence rests in saving this world, I never could in all my years save myself. Even still, I've taken notice of you—as you match my energy exactly and speak to me as if I were an equal. You know that not to be true. It was as if you were born to be my Heel.

Though I know that's selfish. You weren't made for me, nor I for you. A part of me is still trying to grapple with that fact—that I can't have you even if I tried. For you, the pure and kind and perfect woman, could never in a million years dream to spend your days with me, whose history, though I deny and try to clear it from my mind, is drenched in blood and death. For though they call me the Angel, it's never clearer to me than when I look into your eyes that the truth is so far from. Why, I often ask, could I possibly have found my divine epithet when on this earth has existed, you?

I'd be so inclined to believe that you'd fallen from Heaven if that wasn't my job.

And though I am the one they pray to in any of my forms, I believe

99

wholeheartedly that you must be a punishment from something Greater than I could ever be, because I know how it is to feel so in love with all you can be, but never can truly have. No, love, though I know that I am the One above all else, the truth is, I have never been a saint. I've never been a faithful subject. So if a Heaven I know not of one day returns to take you back, who am I to object?

I find myself thinking often, that if circumstances had been different, I could've fallen in love with you the right way, for whatever the right way may be, I have done only the opposite. In another time, maybe, I could've loved you properly.

Sometimes I'm not fully convinced I really do love you, because you torment my mind. I do everything I can every waking moment to try to forget you exist, to put you from my thoughts. And pray tell, Love, would a man in love try that hard to escape it? I don't know, but I do know that I often try to hate you. Sometimes I stay awake thinking over every possible character flaw I can—searching for a single reason to convince myself you're not worth all the time you spend in my thoughts. Sometimes I stay awake thinking to myself that I need you to tell me you hate me, that we could never work. Sometimes I feel I need to hear you say you don't love me so that I can move on.

You have a steel trap around my heart. I would say it was fated that my heart would become yours, but truthfully, I don't think it's ever been anyone else's. It couldn't have been, even in my hundreds of thousands of years of which I've lost count, mortals come and go, but you are perva-sive. There is a strange sort of... omnipresence of you.

I know you'll never read this, and I know I'll never say it. So let me say it now: I love you. I love you more than anyone should love another person. I love you the way that the stories always said but I thought was exaggeration. I can't feel anything but warm and safe with you, and I hate it so much. Because truly, do I really know you? Even after all this time, I try to tell myself over and over that this version of you I know cannot be real. This version is just too perfect.

I shouldn't even be thinking like this, but I can't stop. I've tried, time and time again, because though I am everlasting and have eternity laid out before me to discover myself and whatever secrets of the universe could possibly exist outside my perception, you, my dear, are mortal. I could save you, I've considered, but would you wish to be saved from Death in the way that I have? For omnipotence and my eternal existence in my beginning years I'd grown to think of more as a fallibility—we, the divinity, are cursed. And I, even more than any other, as I have to watch you live and die through mortal means within your control, should I not seek to destroy all potential harm. Would you accept me if I walk into your life for my own selfish purposes?

Here's my confession to you, my love, to my innumerable sins which outnumber your own, and to my greatest sin of falling in love with a fantasy; for only should you exist as a reflection in the water. And with my crimes immortalized in ink, it is only in this life that I should venture to an admission of guilt, which will stand the test of time, even as the stains of yellowed weathering grace these pages, or very well my own tears so unjustly fall without my permit.

Let it be said, my dear, through my words and your memory I can only be assured, someone will remember us, my love, in another time. Even if they may tell my stories wrong, and speak of me in praises that I never myself would've wished to have earned, someone will remember us, in another time.

Though my mind wishes not to acknowledge that presently there is and may never be an Us in the way that I would've wished, my firmest hopes of prosperity rest on the prospect of you, in my protection, so much as you should need, for as long as is necessary.

Even I should never have expected to be immune to the human's heart; as I'm sure anyone who may ever lay an eye upon my overwrought pronouncement may understand, love has made me a fool.

With my love and kindest regards, from one Angel to his Archangel, and in more ways than I could care to admit, from one human to another. As sincerely as I may be, to my love.

-Elric"

"ELRIC, YOU KNOW WE DON'T NEED THAT!" KRISTA LAUGHS, and the god nudges her playfully. She nearly drops her basket of fruits, and shoots her husband a glare, though with no real heat.

"We need it, I promise." He plucks the expensive bottle of wine off the merchant's stand, and without fanfare hands him a fistful of gold, far more than what he ever would've asked. He affords him no explanation before smiling at Krista and walking away.

"You know, one day people are going to begin to wonder where you get so much gold," she says, and he shakes his head, waving a hand.

"Ah, love, it's old money. Some—" he gestures to nothing in particular, thinking. "Some very rich and very dead uncle," he finishes, and his wife laughs.

"Oh, and what's this uncle's name?" she asks. He smiles.

"Mr. Man Person, of course. Why, you met him before he sadly died in a very human fashion. Don't you remember?" Krista shakes her head and laughs.

"Ah, how could I forget our dearest Man Person?" Elric snickers and presses his back to the door of their small cottage, pushing it open. Immediately, something collides at top speeds with his leg, and he rolls his eyes playfully at Krista. She shrugs.

"Afternoon, Finnigan," he says. He sets the wine bottle down on the table and picks his son up, holding the child at his hip.

"Dad!" he shrieks. Elric cringes as Krista laughs, beginning to put away their shopping. He should teach the child to manage his volume, he thinks, though that may be too much to ask of a four-year-old boy. His energy simply can't be contained. Elric shakes his head and boops the kid on the nose, making him laugh.

"Where's big brother Nikolai, Fin?" he asks. Not a second later the young god appears before him, covered in scrapes and scratches with leaves in his hair, smiling innocently. Elric sighs. "Again, Nicky?"

"They weren't even close to catching me this time," Nikolai brags, and Elric laughs.

"Almost like you have deific abilities." Nikolai shakes his head, and moves around the table to reach where Krista stands, plucking an apple out of her basket.

"Nah, this is pure skill."

"Mhm. How many of them this time, Nikolai?" Krista asks, and Nikolai's face lights up.

"Twenty-six of them, three with horses, too." He smirks. "They still couldn't get me." Nikolai had a habit recently of going out to terrorize local police forces to see how far he could push. Elric certainly didn't want to encourage the behavior, but it wasn't as if there was any true, tangible risk to it, so he let it slide.

"Good job, Nicky. Pass me that knife?"

"Oh, Krista, don't feed his ego," Elric jokes, and Nikolai turns around, feigning offence.

"I have nothing of the sort! Oh, dear Father, how I am wounded." He pretends to faint backwards, and Krista turns around at just the right moment to catch him in her arms. Elric laughs and repositions Fin on his hip.

"You won't feed your brother's ego, right?" he asks backhand-edly. Fin giggles and bounces.

"Nicky is the coolest!" he exclaims, and Nikolai puts on an impish grin.

"Even the kid knows it," he says, and Elric simply sighs. With a smile on his face, he leaves to put the child down for a nap.

"*Finny,*

Happy fifth birthday, my sunshine! Why, it feels not a moment has passed since I first saw your face, and yet, another year of your life has already been completed. And you still have so far to go.

You've grown so immeasurably in your little time. From waking your mother and I five times a night to learning your alphabet, and beginning to go to school! How is it that you've grown up in just the blink of an eye? Is it simply that from the lens of my immortality all you do seems so small?

No. Everything you do means the absolute world to me. To have you in my arms day after day and hear your laughter— and even though your older brother is sometimes hostile, you speak to him with such joy that my heart melts. You know how 'teenagers' can be, yes? It's far worse when that so-called teen is a couple decades old and magic. He'll get over it eventually. I'm sure he does so love you.

Sometimes I think of the day you're finally of age and I can reveal all to you, give you my letters, and tell you stories of days long before your arrival when the world was far different than it is presently. But I will have to wait—so very impatiently, and in bated breath, of course—for you to grow. Don't tell your mother, Sunshine, but when you've matured, I wish to bring you both back to my home for what could be eternity, if you so wish. I decided this year. How so darling you two will look with wings like Nikolai's! Yours, I think, will be yellow—so bright and cheerful as your innocent soul. Your mother will match me, I'm sure of it. She'll have my black feathered crow's wings and rule with me as the Goddess of Death, and what a picture-perfect family we'll make.

Oh, Sunshine, what would I do without you? You, your mother, and your brother are my whole life, and I wish only peace and prosperity for you all. You have a god's blood in your veins—never forget. Your life is sacred, not only to me, but this universe.

When I first held you I could see the future in your eyes. You'll forgive me for being a sap, just this once, I hope, for upon lifetimes and lifetimes within an unfeeling universe, it is such a rarity to me to feel so sincerely for anything or anyone. Looking upon your countenance, an emotion so very foreign in my thousands of years makes itself apparent. I'm unsure how I've ever lived without it.

Oh, dear, I'm so sorry this letter could not be as long as your fourth birthday's—I've been quite busy. I look forward to many more years with you, sunshine. I will accept nothing less than the best.

I love you, Finny. Never forget.

-Dad"

"Dad!" The door slams shut and Fin jumps onto Elric's lap as he sits on the couch, and Krista laughs from her place in the kitchen, bent over a bowl of dough making cookies.

"Hey Finny, how was school?" It felt as though between one blink and another the child had grown from infancy to the blooming, bright young boy he'd become. In only eight years of age it was already clear to his parents the mark he'd one day make on this world. Why, if he didn't become the most renowned of engineers and scientists this universe had ever seen, then Elric would've been made a true fool out of.

"It was good!" he says. He drapes himself dramatically across his dad's legs, and rests his feet on Nikolai. The young god backs away with disgust shriveling up his face, and Elric frowns at him, though Finnigan doesn't seem to notice. "I started this weird religion class, and my teacher says magic is real." Elric laughs lightly.

"True, though not so much magic as divinity." Fin scowls.

"I don't know what that word means, Dad," he says. Nikolai's mouth tips up in anger, and Elric makes a mental note to talk to him about it sometime very soon. He can't be acting like this in front of his brother.

"You'll know one day soon. How's your friend? Arthur?" he asks, and Fin rolls his eyes.

"Archer, dad. And he's fine. Did you know we're gonna get married?" Krista perks up at the sound of this and looks to the child while Elric laughs.

"Is that right?"

"Yeah! That's what you do when you're like really, really, best friends. You have to get married. We're gonna get married," the kid says. Krista smiles, looking back to her cookies, rolling out the dough onto a tray.

"You don't marry your friends, Fin," Nikolai says, and Elric can hear a note of frustration in his voice.

"Yes, you do! That's what mom and dad did!"

"Dad and Krista didn't just get married because they're friends," he scoffs, directing his attention back to the book in his hands, not sparing a glance to his brother.

"You wouldn't get it," Fin says, shaking his head, "you don't have friends." Nikolai looks up from his book and sends a death glare to the child, and Elric can see calyxes of shiny gold climbing up into his irises. He resists the urge to laugh as he attempts to diffuse the situation.

"Now, now, Fin, that's rude."

"But—"

"No buts, Finnigan. Apologize to your brother." With a huff, Fin sits up and crosses his arms indignantly, but still does as he's told.

"Sorry, Nick. That was mean. I still love you, even if I'm your only friend." Nikolai's glare darkens, and now Elric really has to try hard not to laugh.

"Finnigan."

"Sorry. That was mean too." He stops himself there, and Nikolai rolls his eyes, leaning back against the couch with his book in hand.

"Thanks," he says simply, before adding; "It's Nicky." Elric hides his disappointment. Elric would prefer it sooner rather than later if Nicky could get out of his strange jealousy phase.

Though Elric's told him many times that he can love both him and Finny equally, Nikolai seems to have gotten it in his head that the new addition to the family is his replacement. Elric can understand why, of course—though Fin was born out of his love for Krista, Nikolai simply came into existence the same as Elric did those eons ago. Elric can still remember his son's words, rattling in his brain like a torturous echo, from nights before, filled with tears.

"*Because he's something you chose, and I'm something that happened to you,*" Nikolai had said.

"*That's not true. I love you both to the ends of the earth, no matter how I got you,*" came Elric's reply. At times he feels he can still hear Nikolai's sobbing from that night as he lay in bed, clutching his blankets close to his chest as if it could be a protective barrier against his too-human emotions. "*And,*" Elric had continued, pressing a kiss to the god's forehead, "*I'll spend a lifetime convincing you.*"

❧

"*My dearest Finny,*

Even now I still feel I can hear your and your mother's laughter dancing around the halls of this house. From the very day you were born I had expected you and Nikolai to grow up together. We could all exist in harmony until the end of time.

Even in death, sometimes I still believe in the possibility, though I know it can't be true.

Heavens, where do I begin? Not a year has come and gone since your passing and yet it feels like thousands of immortal lifetimes wrapped together in a tapestry of sorrow, hung above my windows to block the sun. So very appropriate, it feels, that after the death of my Sunshine, I should be tormented by the lack of light. I run blind in darkness through this terrible world with my heart aching to see you again.

And though I've been, in my past, so eloquent in my writing of my thoughts to you, since your death, the most expressive words can't come to mind.

My dear, since your time, I've lost the poet in me.
As I insert
needless
line breaks,
that feel significant but
hold
no bearing.

Where once lay potential, in pretentious purple prose, now can be found but nothing than peppered plot holes.

Because what can I say? I've lost the poet in me since that day I saw you die, and I don't read literature anymore because it looks me in the eye. Author's descriptions of a feeling that has left me as you and your mother did stare into my soul and ask, in no uncertain terms, if I am to keel over and be struck down by such humanly affections. The answer each time is yes.

In your absence I've taken to sleeping as if rest were the reticence of death. For if I close my eyes a second longer, the world I know may slip away from me—and without this earth, the only remnants of your existence that I may convince myself I've not gone mad would disappear. Even the gods may grow weary from time to time, and without your mother by my side and your laughter through my walls, there is nothing to lull me to sleep but silence. I cannot stand silence anymore.

Your dear brother, bless him, convinces me to sleep. Oh, dearest Nikolai from time to time comes to my side and weeps at the loss of his baby brother and his mother, and whether it be comfort he seeks or simply someone to cry alongside him, we are in our grief together. It is so very true that I never could have made it through this without him. He wakes me from my sleep and talks me into eating, and he sits me down to talk when I go silent, lost in thought.

I visit the cemetery each week, and replace the wilted flowers by your graves. Never shall I leave the symbols of death such as the decay of nature for you to look at—oh, how you did love flowers.

Each time I see a child lean down to pick a dandelion out of the earth, I see in their eyes the joy and youth that once did inhabit your soul and I can't help but feel a sense of attachment to them. Each and every one I bless with protection from such nightmares as control my own sleep. They may rest peacefully, just as you do, now.

I shall leave this letter at your grave just as I always do, and I will replace your flowers and speak to your mother, and never will I stop wishing it was me instead of you.

I love you, Finny, now and forever, and in eternal rest your soul shines as bright as it always has.

Happy eleventh birthday,
-Dad"

NIKOLAI FIDGETS WITH HIS SUIT NERVOUSLY, AND GLANCES AT Elric every few seconds for a reassuring glance. His expertly tailored white suit will be sufficiently wrinkled by the end of the night if he's to continue with such anxiety as he has. Golden embeds in the breast and shining cufflinks glisten in the sunlight, the leaves and flowers in the arches above the altar wave in a cool breeze. If there ever was a more perfect ceremony, in Elric's omnipotence, never did he witness.

"I do," Serena says with a bright smile, and Nikolai's face lights up. Elric hadn't seen his son so happy in decades, and the sight of his joy brings a grin onto his own face. He holds his own hands in his lap to keep from clapping and hollering.

He couldn't have asked for a better daughter-in-law. Serena was intelligent and kind, and spoke to his son with such affection it was almost sickening to be in the room with them. Her long dress matches his boy's eyes—bright gold head to toe with a chapel veil spread out behind her in a wave of sparkling sunlight, and her red hair is done up in a regal braid coiled around her head. And from the way she smiles, Elric has no reason to ever distrust her love for Nikolai. They really are a picture-perfect couple.

"And do you, Nikolai Wood, take Serena to be your lawful wedded wife, joined in heart and spirit in the eyes of the gods, to love and treasure 'til death do you part?" Nikolai nods so enthusiastically Elric worries he may give himself whiplash, and has to hold himself back from laughing.

"I do. Yes. Yeah," he says, and Serena laughs at him fondly. Elric follows.

"Then by the power vested in me, so granted by our Two gods above, I pronounce you Mr. and Mrs. Wood." Nikolai pulls

Serena close and kisses her, still with an endearingly stupid smile on his face. Elric laughs, finally unclasping his hands to clap and cheer for his son. When they pull out of the kiss, Nicky doesn't spare a single glance to anyone in the audience. He simply stares at his wife lovingly as she laughs at the expression on his face— so annoyingly affectionate.

Ah, young love.

It's clear when Nikolai speaks he means for no one to hear, but Elric can just barely pick it up.

"How do you feel, Wife?" he asks, and Serena smiles.

"Better than ever, Husband. Extraordinary. Excellent, even." Nikolai chuckles and grasps her hands.

When he says, "Now you're stuck with me forever," Elric can tell he truly does mean forever. She shakes her head, and tilts her head up to look into his eyes.

"Longer," she says, pulling him back in for another kiss.

Elric can't help but smile brighter.

৩৯৯

"MY CHILD,

I wouldn't have believed it had I not lived it! Why, am I truly so old that I now have a grandson?

Just yesterday, it feels, Nikolai had come into existence, and now, he has a wife and a child! Oh, he's so very stressed as of now, but such are the trials of new parenthood! You truly are a lot to deal with, little Leonato. A ball of pure contained energy, you are! Not to mention one of joy, and a beacon of positivity to all who've ever seen you! I have to spend much time teaching Nicky the ways of being a good father. He's picked up so fast. Not that I'm surprised.

Will you have your father's quick wit and razor-sharp intelligence, Leo? I have to believe so. Even if not, I've already witnessed you take after him for so much. In you I see his bright smile, emboldening ambition, and craving for understanding of the world. You're a curious young boy, just as he once was and still is. And you take from your mother as *well, I've seen! It should be considered a gift, truly, that you take Serena's kindness and humility rather than Nikolai's ego. Don't ever let him read this letter, Son, he'll not take that so humorous as the two of us do! Our little secret, here, eh?*

In the little time you've been in this world, you've already made such an impact. It will be many years before you'll learn of your uncle Fin, but by the stars, you remind me so much of him. Maybe it's the way you cling to Nikolai's side as if he were a lifeline, or maybe it's the way you speak to me as though I were a wizened elder ready to teach you all of the secrets of this curious world. (Please Leo, I am not so old. Have mercy upon me. Of all things to take from your dad, why the senile jokes?)

There's so much for you to learn and see, and though your father laughs at my attachment to you and readiness to accept you as my own, I am so very ready to show you it all. The universe has given Nikolai you so generously as it did give him to me. The joys and wonders of having a son of his own, I can already see, are beginning to soften him to this world. It is because of you that I believed existence has managed to endear itself to him. You'll never quite understand how entirely you and your father and mother own my heart, and maybe I never will either, but believe me when I say it: you are going to go far, and I will not rest until I've seen to it you get only the best out of this life.

With much love to you my dearest grandson,
-Grandpa Elric"

"Nikolai, I know this is a lot to take in, but——"

"No, Dad! You know nothing! Why—why couldn't you have told me first? Fuck, I knew you liked her but... we're a family, we make these decisions together, Dad. Why would..." Nikolai sits down and runs a hand through his hair in frustration. Elric thanks his lucky stars that Honora needs so much sleep to get used to her newfound godhood. Heavens forbid she'd have to hear Nikolai's anger.

"Nicky, it's going to be fine. Take a deep breath, right,

Honey?" Nikolai tries for a moment to do as he's told but can't keep his breathing steady for more than ten seconds before breaking down again. For the first time in years, Elric watches his son begin to cry, and can feel a sense of overwhelming guilt climbing up his throat. He leans down to pull Nikolai into a hug, but he's pushed away as angry tears stream down the god's face. He looks up to him with a face of pure dejection, and Elric suddenly feels so small.

"Was I not enough for you?" he asks, and Elric takes in a heavy breath. Nikolai's golden tears land on the floor, hot and sizzling, carving paths into the hard wood. "Was I not enough for you, Dad? Serena, Leo?" He pauses for a moment and breathes. "Fin? When is it enough, Dad?" There's a sharp pain in Elric's heart at the mention of his late son's name.

"Nikolai, of course you're enough, you're all enough."

"Then why, Dad?" Elric considers for a moment, his son's teary eyes making him question himself despite everything.

"You know how big my heart is, Nicky. There's space enough for all of you. Special spaces for you all that I just keep making, not room being taken up." Nikolai just stares at him for a moment, lips pressed together into a thin line, clearly keeping cries at bay. No matter how much Nikolai wished he were above the wiles of his human heart, he felt just as deeply as the rest of them. "I promise. You'll never be replaced, Nikolai. I love you just as much as I always have." Nikolai nods slowly, but Elric can see doubt in his eyes nonetheless. This time, when Elric reaches to hug him, he doesn't move away. "I love you so much. Just as I always have, and always will."

"I know. I love you, too, Dad." Elric breathes out heavily, and hugs Nikolai tighter.

"I love you, Nicky. And," he continues, echoing words from lifetimes ago—from memories pressed together like puzzle pieces that though recovered will never quite be the same, "I'll spend a lifetime convincing you."

"LEONATO,

How quickly and entirely you've welcomed your new aunt into your life, it's almost astounding. You, like me, have a heart too big for your own good. To watch you run into her arms the moment you see her with shouts of 'Onny!' just warms my whole being. I knew from the start that you had as traitorous a love as I. Your capacity for affection surprises even me, and why, how high a bar that is.

Your father asks me from time to time if I believe you like Honora more than him. Parenthood is fickle like that, isn't it? Often I'd considered maybe Nikolai loved Krista more than I, back in the day, so I can't say I don't understand. You just have too much love inside your soul to be able to afford it to so few people.

How time has flown since your birth. You've just begun school, and Nora is teaching you the ways of combat. Well, I'd of course prefer she'd not teach a seven-year-old to wield a sword, but you find it so very entertaining. What a strange bonding activity it truly is, but I suppose I can't judge. I used to take Nicky soul-reaping when he'd first come into being.

Nikolai has told me that I need not write you so many letters the same way I did Fin, but old habits die hard. I still have eleven years until your coming of age, so I'll use it to my advantage as much as possible!

That being said, of course, by Nikolai's insistence I have decided I could stand to make my letters shorter, so this must, regrettably, be where I leave off for the day, though I could say so much more. Happy birthday, Leo.

As always, with much love,
-Grandpa"

ELRIC FINDS HIS EYES BETWEEN EACH WORD DRIFTING BACK TO his son sitting beside him. While he's shed far too many tears in the few hours he's been here, Nikolai is stoic and calm, and stone-faced with not a hint of sadness.

Everyone grieves in their own ways, but Elric takes notice of his son's strange method.

He would think, of course, that at the funeral of his wife and son, murdered so brutally in the witching hours of the night, that Nikolai might stand to let his more human vulnerabilities come to light, but his face is straight and controlled, even as the margrave calls him up to give his eulogy.

Nikolai looks to the small casket containing his eight-year-old boy, and for a moment, all is silent. Elric doesn't think that anyone in the chapel even dares to breathe in the seconds that Nikolai's face twists into a strange, pained expression at the sight of the coffin, draped elegantly in white muslin with young white gladiolus, lilies, and pastel purple lavenders in floral arrangements across the top.

Even though all in the cathedral understand that inside that coffin lays a young boy gone too soon, too bright and innocent for this world, it's the stark contrast between the long casket of Serena, and the less than two-meter one of Leo that truly creates the cognitive dissonance of the day, bringing tears to onlookers' eyes.

Nikolai sheds none as he stands before the lectern.

"As parents," he starts, projecting his voice through the grand hall, "we never even begin to imagine the possibility that one day, our child may pass before we do." He takes in a heavy breath, and Elric thinks he sees him blink away a tear. "I certainly never wondered what I'd say on the day of my son's funeral. I never thought I'd live to see the day it came. The same as I never considered what I might say standing before the deathbed of my wife. The woman who I'd promised to protect and cherish 'til death do we part. Well, is it so untrue to say I've failed?"

Elric remembers the very moment his son told him the news that day.

"*A murder,*" Nikolai had said. "*Someone broke in. Both of them. Gone.*" And Nikolai had lamented into the early hours of the

THE LIGHT IS DIMMER

morning how he should've been there for them—how it was his fault they were dead. Elric mourned with him for so long his voice grew hoarse and pained until neither could cry anymore and had to fall into uneasy sleep.

The tears from that night are gone, leaving only a detached Nikolai standing at the podium with a straight face, projecting a facade of acceptance Elric knows is a ruse. Inside, he must be in turmoil.

"To my love, Rena, fly high. Never doubt even in death that I've loved you forever. You were kind and reassuring, and held my hand through many a difficult night. You were understanding and accepted me despite my flaws, and you pushed me to be a better me every single day. I've thought too many times since that night that I wouldn't be able to continue without you, but please sleep assured that I know you would've wanted me to go on. You had so much left to offer us all, and we must leave it here, until one day I see you again," Elric's already cried too much today, but he can feel his emotions boiling over yet again. He sniffles, and Honora pulls him into a hug, rubbing his back in comforting circles.

"It's alright," she says, though her voice cracks at every syllable. "You'll be okay." Elric nods, but can't find it in him to believe it.

"And to Leonato," Nikolai continues on, his voice now shaky. "Leo. How do I even begin to explain how entirely all of our lives have been altered in your absence? Never in my years did I believe that one day I'd have to speak of you in the past tense, but here I am." He smiles sadly and raises his hands in concession. Elric knows that Nikolai deals with grief through jokes. "I told you once, long ago, the second you were born that I would protect and cherish you to the day I died, and—" he wipes his now watery eyes with the back of his hand, "—and I never knew that would turn out to be a lie. In so few days since your death, I've already found myself looking out the windows and seeing you playing in the grass with Honora, or hearing your long-winded, misconstructed speeches in the night taunting me while I try to sleep. It's been far harder to sleep peacefully without your mother's warmth by my side, or the knowledge that just a room over, you're having sweet dreams."

No one mentions how many of them know that Leo was tormented by night terrors so often in his sleep. It's more comforting to imagine that his days were spent in happiness. Elric will try to push the sound of his grandson's screams at night from his mind.

"And you'll forgive me for all the tears I've forgotten to shed in your absence, because though I know it to be true, my mind wishes to convince me that you're not gone, and that soon enough you'll come into my room and beg me to teach you the piano once again while I try to work. You'll forgive me for the fact that in my denial, I've forgotten to grieve the way I should, because it's not yet sunk in that I'll never again hear your laughter, or watch you bake with Serena, or send you off to school, or hold you in my arms and give you all the hugs that you deserve—that you'll never have again." He looks back at the caskets and addresses them directly, as if the rest of the people in the chapel didn't truly exist, and once again, he was face to face with his wife and child, simply speaking to them as he always has. "I hope with all my being that Death is kind to you both the way this world never could be. I hope so deeply with everything I am that the rest of your days in what lay beyond life are in comfort and peace spent, and that you have for the rest of eternity in death what life could never give you." He takes a breath. "And some day, I hope I'll see you again, and that we'll once again be a complete family like we always wanted. Until then, sleep peacefully, my loves. I'll love you, from today until the death of the universe, just as I always have. Until I see you again, sleep sound, angels."

He steps away from the lectern, and keeps his eyes to the floor as he returns to sit by his family. Elric and Nora give him hugs, and whisper kind words to him.

He doesn't speak.

❦

"THERE WAS NO SOUND THIS MORNING. OR AT LEAST, I DON'T *think. Nature was silent, and the birds spared no calls or caws, and the wind spoke no words. Mist fell over the horizon in thick layers as the cold began to freeze up the cool humidity from the day prior, coating all the land in a cool blanket of grey. Something pulls me toward it, strangely, begging me to open the doors and welcome the unknown into my life, but I resist.*

It's been tolling all night. The church bell—loud and commanding—sinking into my mind, taking over every single thought. I find it rather distracting.

No one else seems to hear it, but I don't believe they need to. Something tells me it's only for me to hear.

Strange, truly. Though I look over the horizon, I can't find a single church poking out above the skyline, so it truly is an enigma to me where the sound even could be coming from. But that's fine, maybe it is simply inside my mind. It seems as though it's only for me to hear—as though maybe today, life will change.

But I am not so superstitious to believe that my own inner machinations can truly mean anything. I should go back to sleep, I think, it's far too early in the morning for such waxing philosophical about the meaning of mundane things. I've tried to sleep, truly, but all I can hear are the bells. It's—"

Elric turns his head away from his desk as the door opens and immediately slams shut, and he's met with the sight of Nikolai being thrown onto the wood floor by Honora, whose eyes are bloody red to the very core and alight with fire—angry, and foreboding of something terrible. Nikolai looks up into Elric's eyes, and he registers that Nikolai is afraid.

"Nora?" Elric asks uneasily. Honora huffs and kicks her brother's form at her feet, and Nikolai groans in pain.

"Tell him what you've done!" she bellows, and for a moment

even Elric is intimidated by the sound of the unfiltered, seething contempt in his adopted daughter's voice.

"What's going on?" Elric asks, standing from his desk to approach his son. As he nears closer to Nikolai, Nora yells.

"Don't touch him!" and Elric does as he's told, backing away. In the back of his mind, a timer ticks down loudly, signaling to Elric that an era of secrets he didn't know of has come to an end, and he's about to witness the undoing.

Tick.

Tick.

Tick, it goes, as time unravels like a tangled cord before his eyes.

"Dad, Honora just doesn't underst—"

"I don't understand?" she cuts her brother off loudly, dark red eyes alight with fire. She's lost her temper. Honora always has such a tight grip on her emotions, always able to keep visual evidence of her anger at bay, but now, Elric sees the bleeding red of her eyes almost glowing in the dim light of his office. "I think I understand perfectly, Nikolai! Tell your dad what you did!"

Tick,

tick,

tick, the timer counts down, unwinding in the back of Elric's mind, tripping over knots along the way, sounding the tolling of a church bell.

"Nicky, what is Nora talking about?"

"Nonsense, truly," Nikolai lets out uneasily, laughing a sound of clear discomfort. No one else laughs. "She's seeing things. Don't believe a word she says."

"Cut the bullshit, Nikolai! Elric, your son has been lying to you. I saw it with my own eyes. Tell him how you killed your child." Elric takes pause and glances to Nikolai, still laying on the floor, but now sitting a bit straighter. He can see tendrils of golden light reaching up into his irises, which signal to him that not only is Nora speaking truth, but Nikolai is scared of it.

"Child? What is happening, Nikolai?"

"All your son's excursions to the human world haven't been simple observation, Elric. And not only now is there blood on his hands, but he had to make the kid's last moments torture— pretending he actually cared about him. Tell your father how long you spent playing with your food!" Nikolai's eyes are fully gold now, and his face is fearful. He glances around the room wildly, seemingly searching for an escape. Elric kneels to look him in the eyes.

"Nikolai, what did you do?" After a moment of hesitation from the god, Nora kicks him again.

"Say it!"

"Fine!" he yells. He sits up and stares into Elric's eyes with purpose. "I killed him. I killed them, all of them! I fucking did it! Is that what you want? I pushed the kid off the balcony, I watched him die, I'm a fucking murderer, is that what you need to hear? Because no matter what I do, no one can ever choose me! It's always you, it's always Honora, or whoever else they've decided is more worth it." Elric stares at him with wide eyes and glances between him and Nora, who suddenly seems just as shocked.

"Nicky, what are you saying?" Nikolai smiles a sadistic smile, his sharp teeth drawing golden blood from his own lips.

"I killed Lucky, Dad. And I'd do it again."

There's something about death that Elric never quite understood.

Sure, he was the progenitor. The practitioner of what all in humanity considered immoral. His sole purpose in life was to bring to the people what they'd write as being met by the most irreparable evil, the counting down of minutes on a ticking clock, and that so quiet *tshh* as the sand timer falls.

And truly it should be known, of course, that life is but a blip in that radar; an eddy in a current of entropy. What means so much to them means so little to him. Just a brief chemical reaction that lights up in darkness, a flame that burns bright in adversity, high and mighty and eye-catching beyond all else, but its fuel spent, eventually, dissipates.

All who live know this—that such accidents of life can't be contained and all motion slows, but should the soul conceive its own nonexistence what would be the use of self-preservation? So they lie, and deny, and pretend the facts can't hurt them. The wish to defy nature is short lived, and that evil must be consolidated with the fragile concept of fairness in the human brain.

And knowing all this, still, there's something about Death that Elric never quite understood.

There is no preamble to the end.

One would think the story itself would qualify enough as preface, but in the end, it never does make sense how the light goes out without a grand declaration. Final words are spoken and sometimes they mean something—sometimes you hear everything you needed, or you wish you had—but others are mundane. In the blink of an eye, the life inside can vanish.

Does Death care if you end your story at the climax? If your character arc has no foreseeable finish when the cord is finally cut, or the last domino, finally

dropped

onto the ground?

No.

Death wouldn't care even if your final thoughts are cut off, forever fading out into silence. Whether your chapter is ended when it's meant to, mid-sentence, or maybe mid wor—

So Elric stares at his son unblinkingly, and from the silence in the room, one could hear a pin drop. Because what else is he meant to do? The first he's heard of a Lucky, and he's already gone? And from the way Nikolai tries to maintain a snide smile, but his eyes well up with wetness, Elric can see that maybe there was supposed to be a prologue to this death, or that he'd meant more than any of the thousands of lives taken each day that Nikolai wouldn't have batted an eye at. And still, with such a weight bearing down on his son's shoulders, Death has no preamble, or final declaration. It comes when it does, and none are the wiser.

Of course, the Angel of Dawn is not the most articulate man to ever have lived, and despite eons of knowledge that humanity could never imagine, when hit with the news that someone important is gone before ever having been, words fail.

"What?" he asks.

"All of them, Dad. Everyone—Fin, Serena—I thought it would help. I thought maybe for once in your life you'd think I was enough," Nikolai says, and Elric simply continues to stare.

Nikolai has always been enough. When, when was he not enough?

"Stop, stop. What is Nora talking about?" he asks, though his heart stutters at the silence in the room, and the air of anger and fear. The tension crawls up his chest and closes his throat, and though he wants answers, his brain can't seem to comprehend how much he fears them. Though the answer climbs to the forefront of his mind, each moment the quiet stretches, he pushes it back, because surely, surely not.

"Tell him!" Honora barks.

"Nikolai, you didn't kill someone," Elric says, but there's no reason for him to have found himself in this situation had it not been true. Though he tries to state it calmly, his voice wavers as the upwards inflection betrays his lack of confidence.

"I did," Nikolai says. And Elric's world breaks. How long had his boy spent cultivating his image as the just and pure? Who'd help mere mortals in their plights for eternity if ever he needed to? It couldn't be true, surely. Nikolai didn't have a bad bone in his body. He was hotheaded and quick to anger and irresponsible with his mind control, but to end someone's life before their time was up? Not even Elric, as the Angel of Dawn and the god of this irreparable evil, would think to do such a thing.

And admitting it so calmly? Why, was it not enough to be approached by Death so unceremoniously, but his own son, who he'd raised with a wise mind, sharp tongue, and—at least he hoped—clean morals, could say something so earth-shattering as if it were the complexity of a drop of water?

"Nikolai..." he tries to speak, but his son raises his hand. Elric counts the sizzling hot golden tears that fall down his face one by one until he composes himself and set his lips in a line—cold and unforgiving, the same way he was each time the truly awful of humanity had to be punished.

The same way as when he served justice as it was meant to be.

But in his heart, Elric can feel the aching sensation threatening to pull him down to the gates of the inferno. Something eats away at his consciousness—not only is his son not what he'd claimed to be, but that no justice was about to be upheld.

"It's true, Dad. All of it."

"No, you're lying—was it a criminal?" he asks, and Nikolai shakes his head, face straight and eyes set. He's acting calm, but from the current of his gilded eyes and the rage emanating off his sister, there's no escaping this. He's guilty of something.

"No, it wasn't." And bile rises in Elric's throat, not only from the admission of the death of an innocent, but the mere fact that though clearly his son understands what he'd done, there's a sense of underlying disconnect from the situation in his speech. Where Nikolai was known to give impassioned speeches and soliloquy to the very ground he walks upon day to day, his tone contains no promise of prose or poetry to explain his wrongdoings.

No, he refers to his deed as not an extension of himself and his sins, not something he is actively a part of, but something that has happened—as if he were an outsider staring in on himself from a distance.

Whoever had left this world without Elric's knowledge—without the time of day so much to give them an exit monologue or celebration of life—whoever they were, to Nikolai, they were an "it."

"Nikolai, what have you do—" he's cut off abruptly by his son sitting bolt upright and staring into his eyes with a fiery passion that he'd never seen before. Should he think of Nikolai as being passionate about his music or his literature, or the greatest poets of the world that he'd trained in eloquence, none of that passion was matched by the emotions curled behind his eyes now.

Though it looked like passion, there was something laying under. A creeping sense of dejection and fear that made the blade in Elric's heart twist deeper.

"I did what I had to!" he yells, and the dam of composure

he'd attempted to build breaks with the force of a tsunami. "Can't you see, Dad? Everyone, everyone you ever meet, every little mortal you ever speak to has to take precedence over me! Over us! Since day one!"

"What are you talking about?" Elric asks, and Nikolai lets out angry and nervous laughter.

"What am I talking about? Finnigan, Dad! Krista, and Leo, and Serena, and—" Nikolai doesn't speak for a moment, the concentrated look on his face betraying the fact he's considering his words heavily before letting them out, and Elric wishes he'd kept it to himself. "—and Honora." Nora stills at Nikolai's side and casts a look to Elric before dropping her gaze back down to her brother. "Your little mortal pet projects. All of them. Every single one; I asked you, Dad, why I was never enough. And you kept taking it further."

"Nicky—" Honora pipes up, but Nikolai turns around swiftly to face him, and shoots him a forced, cruel smile.

"Don't you dare take this from me like everything else. Don't start this with me, Honora. You weren't the first offender, and you certainly weren't the last. My dad's stupid bleeding heart just let you in! Don't start with me, Honora! You'll never understand, no matter how much you try. If I could, I'd have gotten you, too. I wish you'd drop fucking dead."

And there's silence in the room again.

Elric takes in a breath.

Honora stares.

And Elric can't say he's seen this expression on his daughter's face before. Nora's eyes reflect a sort of dejection and sadness Elric hasn't seen in all his time, and when her voice finally comes out, Elric doesn't think he's ever heard it so strained or shaky.

"W—what?" she asks, it's a question Elric fears the answer to more than anything else.

This is the point at which the Angel of Dawn backtracks on the conversation, finally putting the pieces together.

I'd have gotten you, too.

You weren't the first offender... my dad's stupid bleeding heart.

I wish you'd drop dead.

In retrospect Elric should've understood sooner, but his brain forced all the evidence to the back of the charter for his own sake, because he couldn't consolidate the ideas in his mind.

He couldn't think of Nikolai—sweet, innocent Nikolai, in his basket as a child, eyes glowing brightly, and tiny fingers holding on to Elric's hand, gurgling and laughing and clapping his hands. He couldn't think of his sweet Nikolai as what he knows the only explanation is.

He couldn't, for the life of him, consolidate the idea of his baby boy, whose leg his mortal son clung onto, being the same one to take his final breath. The image of the young Nikolai crying in his bed at night fearing being replaced by Krista, and the image of her final ragged breaths echoing through the empty house all those years ago.

He couldn't imagine the same Nikolai from his wedding day, smiling and jittery and anxious in the dressing room, being the same one to drive that silver knife through his wife's chest, and even less could he imagine his Nikolai buzzing with new parenthood energy taking that same knife to his son's throat.

I'd have gotten you, too.

But that was the only thing that could possibly make sense.

Elric didn't notice the emerald tears beginning to drip down his cheeks as Nikolai opened his mouth again.

"Yeah, that's right, Dad. I was just never enough, was I? Even when I tried to carve my own damned path, everyone flocks to you. My own son loved my sister more than me! Do you know how that feels? Everyone, every time. Serena, and my friends, and my—" he takes a breath, "my Lucky. My little moonlight." Elric stares at him through teary eyes.

"I'd never let anything hurt you, Sunshine."

Fin smiles.

"I almost had faith again, Dad. I almost had faith that maybe

I deserve anything—that maybe just once I could have some-body who wouldn't use me or abandon me. I almost had faith that he could love me, Dad. And you," he turns to Honora, "took everything. Again." He laughs, but it's hollow and hiding some-thing deeper. "I don't know what I expected. I don't know what I expected." Nikolai suddenly presses his lips together and curls in on himself, head in his hands and knees pressed to his chest.

"I don't know what I expected, Dad. I don't know what I expected." He repeats it like a mantra as Elric's green tears fall to the marble floor, flowers and grasses bloom up from the impact. His own golden drops sizzle at contact with the cold stone, carving molten holes below him. Honora is silent. "Everything. He was everything. Every single—he was the light of my life, Dad. I had it under control. I had it under control. I don't know what I expected." He takes a breath. "He was afraid of me, Dad. I knew it, I knew he was, I just couldn't accept it. He was every-thing, and he was scared of me, and what was I supposed to do? My years have made me blind to what humans need and I panicked each time, Dad. Then he met Honora, and I couldn't take it anymore. Dad, I had it under control, I swear I did."

Elric is barely listening, mulling over the implications of his son's words torturously. The voice of his long dead wife in the back of his mind reassures him from years ago that Nikolai would get used to it.

She was always right. She was right about everything she ever said, and the only times it mattered, she couldn't predict it. The only times it mattered. When she said Nikolai would be okay. When she said Fin would live.

There are a few things a person can do upon learning their son has killed their family. There are a few things a person can do upon understanding, finally, that Fate hadn't simply chosen for their life to go terribly wrong—for all that they love to be stripped from them.

Elric? He cries.

Hard, and long, with aching sobs that rip through his gut and let the ground around him bloom out into a forest of its own right, saplings of oak trees sprouting up by his feet, and dandelions tickling his clothes. His emerald tears drip down onto the floor, bring up new life in their wake. He can't help but hear an ode to death in the sound of the petals opening and plants reaching up, breaking cracks in the floor. Within moments, the flowers at his feet wither away and die, wilting brown and curling in on themselves in a pitiful display of their non-negotiable mortality.

He hears the bells tolling once again. It's rather distracting. He was right, he realizes in that moment—he was right about the bells. This morning when he'd awoken at the break of dawn and pink sunlight filtered through the vines climbing his walls, he'd heard the bells of a nearby church that didn't exist. Though he looked over the horizon through the fog in search of the source, not a spire came above the skyline, nor a clocktower reaching up to the heavens. Elric was right, he understood, that the bells were meant only for him.

Because somewhere underground, his son's body has long since decayed and let itself return to the earth from whence it came. Somewhere in a valley deep his child was never meant to see, there's the corpse of a black-haired child buried six feet deep in a five-foot casket because he's no more than four tall, and he wonders why three olden gods needed to end the life of the only two people he's ever loved, leaving him alone except for one face that haunts him even in death.

Because somewhere underground, or hell, even above it, another child has fallen victim to his own bleeding heart and watching eye. Maybe if he'd have had the sense to hide the telltale heart beneath the floorboards to fester and beat and infest his thoughts, then his son wouldn't be dead, or his grandson dead, or whoever Lucky was, dead.

The bells of the clocktower tolling the death march of a love lost that never was chime to the rhythm of the beating of a heart, and Elric can hear it clear as day—as if his sins so innumerable have manifested themselves in the music of his betrayal. He can hear their hearts beat. The hearts of everyone he's caused the deaths of, and when he looks upon the garden grown from the tears of his crimes, he can't help but feel enraged.

For he cries because the weight of his own misdeeds upon his shoulders all but crush him, and the tears of his evil infect the ground and spring the beauty of nature in its wake, taunting him with its glory and perfect innocence and purity. Inescapable evil blooms because of his tears and sits at his feet, asking for its charge and waiting for how they may be of service.

Elric deserves none of it.

If he's sentenced to damnation, he'd go with one sin or a thousand. What's one more?

So Elric does what he's never had the spine to in his thousands of years salting the earth and playing games with life he now knows to be more precious than silver or gold.

He touches his son with the hand of Death, and he puts him to sleep.

"Elric!" Honora screams, and the Angel raises a finger to his mouth.

"Not gone. Comatose. For as long as it takes," he says, and Nora nods.

"And you'll forgive me for all the tears I've forgotten to shed in your absence, because though I know it to be true, my mind wishes to convince me that you're not gone, and that soon enough you'll come into my room and beg me to teach you the piano once again while I try to work."

The words of a liar echo in the Angel's head. A liar that he calls his son. A liar that he raised into this. A son driven to madness by rejection. It should be easy to articulate in the same manner of eloquence as Elric always has—his droves of information of languages dead, alive, and in between; it should be easy to speak in rhyme and give his brain a bite of literary intelligence just like he always has. But it is not. Because for a long time, Elric has lost the poet in him. With the rest of his family, he died. Since the final sparks of life in that brief reaction they call existence dropped away and the flame went out in their eyes, Elric's been a walking corpse for quite some time.

It should be easy to, in the same manner of eloquence, speak in a way that can be understood so that generations of poets could look back on the moment and understand what he'd gone through. But what use is poetry without the black tongue painted in silver that had driven his family to their deaths?

There are a few things a person can do upon the realization that their life is a lie.

The Angel doesn't know the other methods, so all he does is cry.

I've lost the poet in me.
I promise you I didn't try.
After all I didn't mean to,
he didn't even say goodbye.

Why should I think myself
a poet, when all my work is dry?
As I insert
needless
line breaks
for space
to occupy?

I've lost the poet in me,
but believe me, I didn't try.
He left one day without warning,
wouldn't look me in the eye.

He said he didn't intend
to die that day,
but he had no alibi.

He walked alone
on the shores of death
while life passed
him by.

And I wonder just from
time to time
if Death has been kind.
Or maybe it's better, in some
way, than being
trapped inside in my mind.

But I know he writes
soliloquies when he has the time,
he just doesn't give them to me,
and I'll pretend that's fine.

I've lost the poet in me,
and sometimes I walk the shoreline
cursing his name into the wind—
I know he's waited for a sign.

Inspiration, the wingèd devil
drops down into my rhymes,
but he pulls it away
back up to Death
with his noose of twine.

So I've lost the poet in me,
he doesn't want me anymore
Because I've waited far too long
to settle any of his scores.

And I know that night,
he died on those shores,

but I go back out of spite.
For when another tortured artist
steps through his doors,
he'll already be
planning his flight.

✦ 12 ✦

Nikolai sits silently on the carved marble floor, tracing the patterns in the calico stone, watching minutes tick by at a snail's pace. Elric and Honora haven't visited since he woke up. He's not even sure they know he's conscious again. He's not sure how many days or weeks it's been since his father put him to sleep, but he doesn't want to guess. Every passing hour is another that his family has forgotten about him. Abandoned him. He doesn't want to think about it.

So he sings. Quietly, trapped in by his father's magic, making sure he can't escape, he composes little symphonies in his head and puts lyrics to them in post. He can never quite remember the words once he's moved on to the next verse, so he alters them as he goes. When the chorus comes around he changes the lines and puts it to a different beat, and when he's come out the other side it's almost a new song entirely. But each time he tries to start a new melody, his voice shakes and his mind reels. Each time he tries to begin a new song, his thoughts travel back to golden hair and sharp teeth—silver eyes, and the slow, steady breathing of a sleeping child.

Most of his music is about Lucky.

He's sure, somewhere deep inside of him, that if the teen

were here with him he'd light up the room with his blinding smile, and Nikolai would see him suck back his lips to avoid his sharp canines just like he'd taught him. He'd lean onto Nikolai's shoulder and watch his fingers with interest as he plucked out a formless tune on a decades old guitar, and he'd hum along to the melody, and he'd look at him with those bright, painted green eyes and Nikolai would envision a future together. Away from his father, he'd grant the boy parts of his powers to stay with him forever, and raise him like a son, and speak to him like a brother.

So it's safe to say maybe now that the smoke has cleared and he's been forced to reflect, he feels a little bit bad for killing Lucky. Maybe he wishes he'd done it differently, or maybe he wishes he'd given the boy a better death. Something more becoming of his otherworldly perfection.

It's... unfamiliar. Guilt is a strange emotion. It makes his chest tight and stomach twist into a knot, and he can't avoid it. He can lay down and roll over, and drink water and breathe deeply, but the feeling of guilt remains, heavy in his heart and omnipresent. He tries not to think about it, but it keeps coming back. It comes and goes in waves and hits him at the most inconvenient of times, and as he tries to sleep, it controls his thoughts and won't let him rest.

He doesn't understand it. All of the others, he'd never once considered that if he could go back he'd do it any differently, but now? Now the fear in the boy's bright emerald eyes as he stared up to the god on that balcony haunts his dreams.

So the Siren has taken to sleeping as if rest were Death being shy. He closes his eyes for a moment, seeing blond hair and green eyes at the corners of his vision, and hears the dull crack of a skull on concrete. He can't keep them closed any longer.

He wonders where Lucky is now. He'd been dragged out by Honora within moments of Lucky's death and didn't see the aftermath. There were screams from the people below as they backed away from the child on the stones, and a sickening sound as his bones gave in, but Nikolai didn't see the rest of it.

Would his boy receive a proper funeral? Would he be buried in the community cemetery, or simply thrown to the outskirts of town to decompose?

Maybe that's what's causing the Siren to feel guilt the most. He'd never tried to imagine Lucky's death, but if he had to picture it in the time he'd known him, he would have thought that he'd wrap the boy in satin and twist flowers into his hair, and make crowns of poppies and lay him down on a bed of yellow roses, and imagine that he was asleep peacefully, and not gone forever. Heavens know he's earned a long sleep, and with the Siren's watch, he'd not be disturbed in his eternal rest by the lack of eulogy at his grave, for Nikolai would always be there in spirit.

Maybe that's what hurt the most—that his moonlight had no one in this world but him. No one would care for him as much as Nikolai did to give him a real sendoff.

The god tries to pretend he can't feel hot golden tears drip down his face.

He pretends he doesn't miss his moonlight's sweet voice or irritating laugh, or the way he looked up to his eyes as if he were the whole world. The god pretends he doesn't wish he knew where his baby was now.

He pretends he doesn't wonder where his sanity's gone.

"But–"

"No, Honora. That's the end of it." The Angel of Dawn crosses his arms and leans back against the wall, avoiding eye contact with his daughter. He knows by now Nikolai must have awoken and must be awaiting judgement, but it's taken far longer than he'd expected to decide what he must do.

The truth is he knows the answer, but he won't let himself understand it. He won't admit that he knows how to end their suffering. But who can blame him?

"Elric, he's dangerous," the War Goddess says again. It's been the same argument, around and around in circles since they first put him to sleep, and they've made no progress.

"You think I don't know that?" Elric asks indignantly, finally meeting Nora's blue eyes.

"You sure are acting like you don't," his daughter shoots back, with narrowed eyes and a defensive tone.

"I can't just do that."

"Yes, you can. You know you can, you're just hiding from it," Honora snaps, pointing a finger in her father's face. "You're trying to delay the inevitable. If it's not today, then it will be tomorrow, or the next, or years later, but it'll happen, Elric. This world doesn't have a place for people like him." Elric slaps his daughter's hand away with anger in his eyes and raises his voice.

"I can't, Honora! He's my son."

"And my brother!" Honora shouts back. Elric goes quiet. "You think I want this?" she asks, and Elric doesn't respond. "My brother is a murderer, too, not just your son. Do you think I've been awake all these nights pacing tracks into the floors because I want him dead? Because I don't care what happens to him? I've had to come to terms with this, too! Not just you!" she yells at him with wetness clouding her eyes. "I went to Leo's funeral, Elric. I was there. I remember feeling heartbroken and on the verge of tears for days on end. Do you think I'm unaffected by this?"

"Nora—" Elric tries, but Honora raises a hand and stares him down with a gaze of fire, and Elric backs off.

"I feel betrayed, too. This is my family, too. I don't push you because I don't care, I can't let anyone else be hurt by him, Elric." There's silence in the room that echoes off the marbled stone. Gold, ruby, and emerald engravings on the walls taunt Elric from afar as he stares up into the tendrils of pure gold, wondering why it had to end like this. There's a way Nikolai's story could've ended that didn't involve this conversation, but the Angel would never know how it goes.

"What if we can change him," Elric mutters, but he knows he doesn't truly think it possible. If his son was capable of changing his ways, he would've done it before any blood was ever spilled. The world changes around him, and Nikolai changes by not changing at all. Honora simply stares at her father, and lets out a heavy breath.

"You're scared," she says simply, and Elric nods. "Elric, I get it." A pause, then, "I'm scared, too." Elric's never heard his daughter say that before. "I don't want him to go. I don't think..." Honora looks away from Elric, hiding her face. "It won't be the same without him. Nothing will." Elric can swear he sees a drop of a blood-red tear fall before Nora wipes it away with a fiery anger.

"Then we don't have to kill him," Elric says, back to bargaining now that his daughter is showing doubt. "We can find another way, he doesn't have to go."

"Elric," Nora says with a forced laugh, "what other way? You know there's nothing we can do."

"Well..." Elric starts, and Honora turns to look at him.

"Well, what?"

"I could just—"

"No."

"Nora, hear me out."

"No, I know what you're going to say, and the answer is no."

"But it could work! He'd still be alive. He wouldn't be himself, but that's what we want, isn't it? We could still have him, just without the..."

"Madness?" Elric nods.

"Without the madness." Nora sighs and runs a hand through her blonde hair.

"It could work, but we have no one else to give it to. We'd need a new vessel that we can actually trust."

Elric considers this for a moment. He could make amends. He could right his son's wrongs and fix everything. Maybe then he'd be absolved of his own sins of allowing Nikolai to go so far.

With how much Nikolai loved the kid, it must not be such a leap in logic to assume that maybe he'd be strong enough. After all, he already had all of the Siren's own gifts before his death. Elric looks at Honora, and immediately the goddess's expression hardens.

"We can't do that," she says.

"Why not?"

"You can't choose the kid's fate for him," Nora says, and Elric straightens his posture, pushing himself off the wall.

"But we can fix them. Both of them."

"But then you'd be just like Nicky!" Nora shouts, and Elric draws back, offended.

"I am not like him."

"You want to make decisions for Lucky. You think you know what's best for him—so did he. You can't choose for him." Nora looks around for a second, trying to collect her thoughts. "What if he's better now?"

"What?"

"What if he's okay? What if now that he's away from Nikolai, everything is fine? What if Death is treating him better than we ever could?" And Nora may be right. Maybe life for the child was nothing but suffering. Maybe he's better now that he's been released. Maybe Lucky would rather stay dead than be forced to do it all again, but he's their only option. Otherwise they'd have to kill Nikolai for good.

"But if we can't use Lucas," Elric says. He doesn't finish his sentence.

"You're being selfish."

"Well allow me to be selfish this one time! You know you don't want Nikolai dead, we all know it! To hell with being self-ish, I want my son! If we can't use Lucas, we can't have Nikolai at all." Honora sneers.

"Would Lucky even want Nikolai to be saved? This isn't about us! If Mr. Just and Pure can't live up to his name, then we have to, and where's the justice in using a dead man's name to justify the salvation of his tormentor? We don't need another vengeful god ready to rain holy hellfire on our people. You're being insane." Elric flinches away at his daughter's outburst. He'd never once say that he's afraid of his children, but at this moment, he just may be close.

But still, even in the worst of times, sometimes people love the wrong people. This is one of those times. Elric can't find it in himself to think of a world where he's without his son—mad and murderous as he may be, he's Elric's. The Angel can't imagine a world where Nikolai isn't there, in whatever form it is. Whether he be divine or mortal, Elric's made the mistake of making him feel unwanted once.

He can't do it again.

"That's my decision," he says with a tone of finality. Honora gawks at him before scoffing.

"You're an idiot," she says simply, and Elric nods.

"Love makes you a fool."

"Love makes fools more foolish than before, but can't corrupt the minds of the wise," Honora returns, and Elric smiles.

"You can go ahead and think yourself the only wiseman here, but you'll thank me later," he says, "Nikolai lives."

⚘

THE SIREN SINGS, ALONE IN HIS GILDED CAGE. HE CUTS himself off upon hearing the quiet patter of footsteps outside, and perks up as the door swings open, and his father and sister step in. "Dad?" he says.

"Hey, Nikolai." His father locks the door behind him once again, and the Siren is forced to understand the fact that he's not being released just yet. "Good to see you up." Nikolai can't bring himself to smile.

"It's been a few days. I started to think you'd never come." Elric smiles sadly, and Honora continues to be silent and stoic. Good. Nikolai doesn't want to hear from her anyway.

"I know. We just... had a lot to talk about." Nikolai scowls. What should be so difficult to discuss about the fact that you've driven your son insane? An apology would be nice.

"And you decided...?" he posits. Elric and Honora share a glance between each other, and Nikolai can feel his heart climb up his throat. Whatever the news is, it isn't good. Elric kneels down to his eye level and takes his cold hand. Nikolai can feel the rejection incoming, just like it always has.

"Nikolai... you know I love you," Elric says. The Siren raises a brow.

"Do I?" Elric pauses and presses his lips into a line. He doesn't let go of Nikolai's hand.

"I hope you do," he says, "but if not, let me say it again; I love you Nikolai, and I want you to know it." Nikolai stays silent, watching tears form in the corners of Elric's eyes. "Which is why I can't let you keep doing this. To yourself or anyone else." He takes in a deep breath, and Nikolai's eyes follow the movement of his chest. Up. Down. "Which is why I have to let you go."

And the earth shatters.

And there aren't enough words in the thousands of languages living and dead that could possibly explain the pain that shoots through Nikolai's whole being at that statement. His emotions climb up his throat, and he swallows down the tears before they can meet his eyes.

Nikolai should've known that sooner or later the end would finally come. Thousands of years of weaving webs of lies and tapestries of tall tales thrown together on the coldest backdrop he could find. For which the moniker of the Just and Pure they had to him ascribed, only to spend a life in lies. A silver tongue stained in blood and wilted flowers left behind.

Only this time he has nothing to latch onto. There is no immediate escape. He can no longer bargain with fate. Even if he had a dagger or a balcony or a wildfire fueled by anger, none of it would be able to touch his father, even if he wanted it to. In his years since he killed Leo, he'd forgotten what it was like to say goodbye for the last time, and with Lucky, he understood once again. But now? Now he sits across from his father facing rejection for the final time, and he understands what it's like to be on the receiving end.

He grips his father's hand tightly, as if he could train his arms how it feels to be full. As if he could teach his fingers to forget the warmth of a family. He squeezes his other hand into a fist tightly, as if he could make his nerves forget the feeling of a ring on his hand, because after all this time, despite everything he knows, sometimes he thinks he can still feel a diamond ring on his finger, and his wife's delicate touch sliding it on.

Maybe, if he holds on tightly enough, when he's finally let go, the absence won't be so missed that he'll crumble in on himself again—the pressure of a thousand lifetimes of suffering weighing down on his shoulders, because it's all he deserves. If he holds on tight enough, he can pretend he's wanted.

"I didn't want to have to do this," his father says tearily. "But you've forced my hand..." Elric looks down at the stone floor. "I just—I suppose the only thing I have left to ask... where did I go wrong?"

"What?" Nikolai mutters, and Elric laughs shakily.

"Where did I go wrong, Nicky? When did I convince you that you could only get my attention if no one else had it? When did I fail, Nicky?"

"Elric—" Honora tries to speak.

"No, Nora. I want to know. Nikolai, where did I go wrong?"

It shouldn't be as hard as it is to pinpoint the first moment where Nikolai decided nothing was worth it anymore. When he decided he'd sink into oblivion, and take everyone else down with him. It shouldn't be hard, because he knows in his mind he's spent eons blaming Elric for everything he's done—every bruise on his body, every drop of golden blood, and every death on his filthy hands. It shouldn't be hard, but it is. He can't think of where Elric went wrong. He knows there has to have been a time, but he can't pick it out among the waves of anger and fear hitting at his skull in the moment.

He stays quiet.

"Right," Elric says, nodding slowly. "Right, I get it." Nikolai doesn't know what he thinks he understands, but he doesn't ask. He doesn't need to. "Nikolai, I hope you know I love you. I've always loved you, from the moment you came to me. I was blessed with your existence, and I don't know what I did to deserve you. I just... I hope you know that. Please, know I love you." Nikolai nods.

"I love you, too, Dad," he says, but something in him doesn't quite believe it. Elric smiles.

"Good. Good, yes, I love you too. Just, remember that, okay? If you never remember anything else, Nikolai, just remember I loved you, and I always will. Okay? Can you do that for me? Even if you can't remember my name or my face, just, please, know that," he lets out breathlessly, with viridian tears falling down his cheeks. Flowers spring up out of the stone when the drops hit the floor, but no one spares them a glance. Nikolai stares at him with questioning eyes, and nods slowly, squeezing his father's hand tighter.

"What are you saying?" Elric shakes his head and grabs Nikolai's other hand. When his emerald teardrops land on the backs of Nikolai's hands, intricate patterns of white chrysanthemums and tulips climb up his skin and arms, tattooing him in his father's memory. He stills. Elric never let his tears touch anyone. He knew it was permanent.

"Please, Nicky. Please just promise me you'll remember that." Nikolai feels fear grow inside him at his father's tone of urgency, and he agrees frantically.

"Yes, yes, I'll remember. I'll remember, I promise. Why would I forget?" he says, words coming out like the flood of water from a broken dam.

"Good. Thank you, Nikolai. I love you," he says. "Just remember that." Nikolai wants to open his mouth to question

Elric again, but before he can, a sharp pain rips up his spine. He yells, looking down to see Elric's hands glowing a dark green. He closes his eyes and screams in pain, and when he opens them again, all he sees is gold. But slowly, the color drains, and Nikolai watches his own father's normally sky-blue eyes shift into their emerald state, then, into gold. He finally realizes what's happening.

"Dad, wait!" he yells, but Elric doesn't let go. Verdant teardrops stream down his cheeks, tattooing Nikolai with a beautiful forest of flowers. Honora steps in when Nikolai starts thrashing, trying to wiggle out of Elric's grip. She holds onto her brother's shoulders and grounds him tightly, keeping him still as he feels his divinity being drained from his very soul. "Wait, stop!"

"Nikolai, this is for the best," Honora says, and the water built up behind the god's eyes spills. To his horror, the drops don't burn on the way down. His tears don't paint his face sparkling gold. They only drop down his cheeks, and pool at the corners of his mouth, tasting of salinity.

Mortality.

His body feels heavy, like he can't hold up his own weight. There's a tightness in the skin on his back as he feels his calyx wings be torn out of him and into the light pooling in Elric's hands. His whole being feels ripped apart piece by piece, skin torn and twisted, and his very existence ripped away by a claw, dragging along his ribs and making him bleed on the way out. When he opens his mouth next to scream, a current of golden blood worms its way out of him, and he gags.

"Wait—wait, please," he bargains, but no one listens. His voice is hoarse and quiet, and talking takes all the energy he has left.

A whole life of misdeeds flashes before his eyes as everything he once was is shredded. When he falls over onto the stone floor, and heaves out a final breath, he feels a kiss on his cheek.

"Remember that, Nikolai. Please."

And it all fades to black.

❧

THAT NIGHT, AN ADDENDUM IS MADE IN PERMANENT GOLDEN ink in each and every existing Book of the Triad. When the margraviate wake up the next morning to the new verses, frantic preparations are made within the hour to modify each temple in the kingdom; to commission new statues and rewrite sermons and prayers.

That night, two new lives arrive with matching white streaks in their hair. A young god made of moonlight, and a man in the kingdom with amnesia, forgotten who he is.

That night, as a golden-haired child sleeps on in the Heavens, the moon shines bright in the sky. For the next morning, the next night, and each morning and night after, a full moon captivates the common people; midnight at dusk, midnight at dawn.

That night, the Angel of Dawn rewrites the Book of the Triad, with one minor correction.

The pious attend the service and look between the statues of the Triad.

The Angel of Dawn—the creature of the shadows. The grim reaper that guides the kingdom's dead to what lays after death, if there is anything.

To the Angel's right, Lady Retribution, the War Goddess, depicted in a long red cloak and a crown.

To the Angel's left, the kind eyes, curly hair, and bright smile of Innocence—the young God of Spring; the young god of rebirth, revival, forgiveness, and kindness. The next chosen mortal child of the Angel, gifted his godhood to please the Angel's bleeding heart. A beacon of hope to the scared children of the kingdom's streets.

And in the back of each temple, the statue of the exiled Siren God. The former god of literature and music, and speech and communication. The God of the Silver Tongued, whose words were drenched in blood from the very moment of his birth. The exiled and excommunicated god of all things artistic, and all Just and Pure.

But maybe more accurately, as the graves preached, and the songs sang, the Leviathan—dead God of Madness.

13

Lucky is stuck behind a closed door when he comes to. Through his time in between life and death, he's learned well enough that trying to snap himself out of it won't fix anything.

So he sits up.

He waits.

The next thing he notices besides the closed door and darkness outside his window is the comforting warmth wrapped around him. He's got... a bed. A big one at that, with three soft pillows at his back, and stacks of blankets weighing down on him.

Well, that's unusual, he thinks. Normally limbo's favorite places are the dark alleys where he used to live, or the sounds of Fin's death in his mind over and over again. He's not normally given a breather in his deceased mind's machinations, but he'll take a little reprieve where he can get it. He stretches out his arms to his sides, and groans when his neck painfully cracks, releasing tension. He looks over his body. No bruises, no cuts. Okay, so he wasn't going to start off already hurt this time. He can work with that.

He cracks his knuckles and looks around, being made aware of a strangely elegant room surrounding him. Paintings and wreaths and laurels of flowers adorn the walls, and vines climb up the windows. Not overgrown, but rather kept cleanly and precisely, with wildflowers growing off each of the petioles. Not so much a mark of abandonment or forgotten ruins, but rather nature's touch politely asking to reclaim the room, and the people within letting her. It's oddly calming.

There's a desk on the opposite wall from the bed, with pots of ink and pens and parchments covering it. A notebook is left open on top, but Lucky can't be bothered to strain to see what limbo's written in it for him, so he keeps looking around.

There's a door that probably opens to a bathroom or a closet, and a dresser with a mirror on top just enough out of Lucky's way that he can't see himself in it. He sighs, and falls back over onto the mattress, preparing to close his eyes before a sharp pain hits his back, and he bolts back up. He rubs down his spine, but hits nothing.

Stupid phantom pains.

He plants his feet on the ground off to the side and stands. He wobbles a bit trying to get his footing, which is also something that's never happened in limbo. His joints feel sore and out of use. He considers for a moment just climbing back in bed and waiting for a new afterlife to come around, but decides against it. It's been the best start to a morning he's had in a long time.

The floorboards creak slightly as he sets his full weight on the wood, and he hears a sound. He stills, and grounds his feet, not daring to breathe.

There's shuffling outside the door, and he strains to hear, but finds a dull headache clouding his senses.

"—ora?" he hears a vague voice, and freezes. Looking around, he can only plot out so many escape routes. The thick vines cover his access to the windows, and he doubts the door to his right would do him any good. For all intents and purposes, he's trapped.

"—wake?" He catches another half a word from outside, from a voice he can swear he recognizes. It doesn't sound like the Siren—heaven knows Lucky's seen enough of him in limbo to last another lifetime—but it's something familiar.

There's a knock at the door.

Lucky holds his breath.

"Lucas? Are you awake?" a voice asks quietly, softly, as if any louder would break Lucky. He doesn't respond. The person knocks again. "Hello?" Lucky takes in a breath.

"What do you want," he says, less a question, and more a demand. There's hostility in his voice, but why should he even try to be kind when there's no way this scenario ends well? Just like all the others.

"Can we come in?" Why ask permission?

"Sure."

The doorknob twists, and the hinges creak as it opens slowly.

And Lucky stares into the eyes of the goddess—Honora—and who he can only assume is the Angel of Dawn, with blond hair and bright blue eyes, and a long cloak of green, white, and black—massive feathered wings stretched out behind him, spanning wall-to-wall. Which begs the question:

Where is the Siren?

"Hey, kid," the Angel says with a light smile on his face. Nora remains stoic as always.

Lucky doesn't open his mouth. He simply stares at them. "Um... how are you feeling?" the Angel asks. Lucky once again refuses to respond.

After a moment of awkward silence, the Angel glances to Nora with a pleading face.

"I told you to give him time," she says without taking her eyes off the younger. Lucky finally cracks.

"What is it this time?" he asks. "Come on, spit it out, we don't have to play this game." The two look at each other, even Nora seeming a little bit confused.

"What are you talking about?" the Angel asks, and Lucky scoffs.

"Let's go, painful death or whatever. I'm ready. This is the weirdest one you've tried so far, though." Lucky's face won't betray the fact that for the first time since he was shoved between life and afterlife the vignette actually feels real. He won't let his mind have the satisfaction of knowing it's tricked him.

"Lucky, are you alright?" Honora addresses Lucky directly. He rolls his eyes.

"Get on with it, please," he says.

"We're not going to kill you," the Angel says. Lucky raises his brow.

"Nice try." The two stare at each other for a moment, and there's silence for a moment.

Except... it's silence.

Real silence.

Not the fake silence of limbo. There's no sound of high-pitched ringing in his ears invading his hearing. No, there's... only quiet.

There isn't the sound that always follows him in limbo of the Siren's laughter, or of Finny's screaming. It's only the quiet of the room and the steady breathing of its three inhabitants, which is even more strange, because Nora and the Angel never would have appeared in his nightmares in limbo.

Lucky bites down on his tongue and shrieks as metallic silvery blood starts dripping from his lips. The two gods gawk at him, and his mind reels.

"What is this?" he yells.

If it can bleed, it can die, the Siren had once told him.

He hasn't bled since he first awoke in limbo. He was already dead.

If it can bleed, it can die, but Lucky's been dead for ages. Lucky's not been alive since he last saw Nikolai's dark eyes. Lucky hasn't understood the weight of a heavy breath leaving his chest since he heard the crack of bones on stone and felt reality drop like a guillotine onto his skull. Since the darkness closed in on him and he followed light down to Hades, only to be dragged back up by the Siren's claws into whatever exists between his earth and his fate.

Somewhere back on the streets of the capital, Lucky's broken and twisted limbs should be presently devoured by vultures as townspeople stand by, his flesh torn and drenched in sweat and blood. That was the last time he was supposed to bleed.

But if it can bleed, it can die.

Which means Lucky can die.

Again.

"I'm alive," he says under his breath. The Angel nods. "I'm alive."

"Yes, you are."

"Why am I alive?" He means to ask calmly, but understanding stabs into his gut with force, and it comes out as a shrill yell, begging for explanation.

"We brought you—"

"You brought me back!" he screams. "You brought me back! For—for what? For more torture? Where's Nikolai? Let him kill me now, please, I can't do this again!"

"Lucky, calm down, we're not going to let you die again. We brought you back because—"

"You're sick!" he interrupts, vision melting into shades of grey. "You're insane. You're all insane, you're all just like him. Where's the Siren? Please, just let me go." There's a familiar cold sensation on his cheek, and he reaches up to wipe the tear away, but only ends up nearly punching himself, dragging his hand down his face aggressively as if he could peel away his own skin and escape from whatever cage they have in store for him now. He can't do this. No matter how much the Siren's melodic laugh echoes in his mind, and his embrace calls to him even from the grave, he can't do it again—let himself believe that he'd found a family and let it be ripped away, again, and again. He won't allow them to convince him to love again.

"Lucky!" Retribution yells. She grabs onto Lucky's shoulders, but Lucky thrashes and throws her off. He bares his teeth as if somehow he, the mortal child Lucky Barlowe, could intimidate the gods. It's not like they've never seen sharp teeth and ill intentions before—they have them all themselves.

"Let go!" he exclaims, backing up until his thighs are hit by a sturdy nightstand. He reaches down and braces himself on it, clutching the ebony wood like it's his only connection to the earth, clinging onto existence as if it'll be torn apart before his eyes again. His vision darkens.

"Lucky, you're panicking again, deep breaths."

"Fuck you!" he shouts. "It won't work," he lets out breathlessly.

"Let us explain, it'll be okay. Just calm down for a second." Nora approaches him with her hands outstretched like she were placating a wild animal—and Lucky may as well be one; caged and enraged, baring his teeth and waiting for an outlet to strike.

He's never attacked the gods. Maybe that will be enough to get them to let him die.

Nora touches his arm, and he rips it away with a strength he didn't know he had in him. "Don't touch me," he says through gritted teeth. The ferrous taste of his own blood still lingers in his mouth, proving to him with every passing second that he's back. He's alive.

He's a puppet. *No one* mourned the death of the gods' toy, and they never will.

"Lucas, calm dow—"

"*Shut up!*" he screams, and all at once, everything breaks. The formerly dim room lights up, casting bright white rays over the walls, and Lucky's back screams in pain as he feels something being torn out of him. A silvery aura surrounds him, sparkling and blinding, engulfing his entire being in a protective shield. The Angel and Lady Retribution fall deathly silent, as does the nature outside. Moonbeams stream in through the window and the temperature drops. The two gods stare at him.

His peripheral vision catches sight of a tendril of brilliant light at his side, and he turns around to find the culprit.

Giant silver seraph wings.

Lucky's giant silver seraph wings.

He looks around. The moonbeams, the wings, the glowing, the silence, everyone following his command.

Everything clicks into place.

Lucky opens the dam, and tears fall from his eyes like torrential rain. He falls to his knees and sobs into his hands, feeling his skin sing from the cold bite of his cries. The light in the room dissipates as his energy depletes rapidly, and his wings are called back into his body. His hands begin to turn blue and black, freezing inside out, but he can't be bothered to care.

He thought he'd have run out of tears to cry by now. He thought he'd have run out of emotions to feel, but no—if there's no joy, if there's no love, no anger, and no hatred, there is always one constant. There is always grief. It's the only emotion that's followed Lucky his whole life. It's his most loyal companion. There are things he can leave behind, but sadness is not one. The pure, complete dejection he's always felt could never be abandoned; Lucky doesn't know if he truly still is himself if he's not hurt.

Life keeps giving him gifts. Life gave him Nikolai, and Nikolai's blessings, and food on the proverbial table, and a safe, warm place to sleep, and a second chance at living.

It's like life keeps handing Lucky lemons, but his tongue tastes sour. The world is yellow, and Nikolai's gifts were yellow. All Lucky knows is lemon cake and lemonade and the acidic air of citrus surrounding his every move, and all Lucky can think about is lemons. Because life keeps handing Lucky lemons, and all he wants to do is throw them back in its face.

It just won't *stop.*

And Lucky bites his tongue again, just to prove to himself it's true—as if he could wake up and prove to himself this was all just a nightmare, because he's certainly not had enough of those.

But the metallic fluid fills his mouth and starts to drip down onto his hands and into his lap, because Lucky can bleed. Because Lucky is alive.

His hands feel cold and painful, and they're blue and black all over. Lucky feels the chill down to his bones, but he can't be bothered to care.

After all, it will heal.

Because Lucky is a god.

The thought hurts him down to his core. He'd thought originally when he'd first met the Siren that he was blessed above all else to have contact with even one of the gods, but to meet all of them? To be one?

He looks up, and the two gods continue to look at him silently with concern written over their features that makes Lucky want to scream. Why would they be scared for him when all they've ever done is hurt him? How is this any different? Honora's presence once would've been comforting, like when he met her in the temple, when she calmed his anxiety, taught him how to control his temper, however futile the efforts may have been. But now those sky-blue eyes that hold fear for Lucky's well-being are mocking him, just like the Siren. What reason has Lucky ever had to trust a god?

Though the weight of his words fall on his tongue like an anvil the second he opens his mouth, he can't be blamed for abusing his power in the little time he has it, for the smallest mercy they refuse to grant him for all the suffering they've inflicted upon him.

For eternity, goes unsaid.

"*Get out,*" he commands, though his voice shakes on each syllable. They exit the room immediately and leave Lucky to his own devices. Without missing a beat, he simply screams into his hands.

Eventually he'll have to stand, soak his digits in warm water to ward off the frostbite, and come to terms with his circumstances, but that moment will not be now. For now, he sits on the cold, hardwood floor and sobs into his hands, letting the emotions built up during his time in limbo flood over and out, and onto his flesh. Because in the time between his death and apparent rebirth, all he's known is misery over and over again.

It's not even so much that the pain and torture inflicted upon him was the worst of it—the worst always came when he was happy. There would be times he'd come to a new limbo inside the temple hugged into Nikolai's side, and he'd stay there. There would be no pain, and no screams echoing in his head—it would only be him and the god, quiet, peaceful. Happy.

And then it would be ripped away.

Sometimes the Siren would play music and sing to him and let him lean on his shoulder, and then the second Lucky felt at home for the first time in a long time, it would be gone.

Home.

That's something else that changed. Lucky doesn't quite know when he began to think of being with the god as going home, but it's a feeling that didn't leave him, even in death. And maybe it's simple naivety, or maybe selfishness, trying to convince him that the god had ever held anything other than disdain and malevolence inside his heart. But Lucky thinks he knows what the problem truly was—he'd gotten too attached to a person he began to think of as family that could never love him the same, no matter what he felt to be true.

When his hands go numb, he doesn't care to look. When the two gods break out of the power of his charm and begin to bang on his door and ask him to come out, he doesn't acknowledge them. They don't deserve it.

They've done nothing to earn his forgiveness, and they never will.

He ignores them until the pounding becomes too much to bear, and finally brings himself to utter words he'd been avoiding since he first made his discovery. The word feels poisonous in his mouth, and brings back memories from a lifetime before that he wishes he could leave behind. But even still, as he loses all feeling in his fingers, he decides it's worth it for something similar to peace of mind.

"*Silence.*"

✣ 14 ✣

Nick wakes up.

Or at least, he thinks that's his name.

When he looks around, his surroundings are unfamiliar, and he can't seem to remember where he is, or how he got there.

It's empty and dark, and he can see the moon through tall windows. Other than that, there's no light. He stands up from what could be considered a bed, in definition only, and his feet touch the floor. He's barefoot and his clothes are wrinkled, but in pretty good shape. He has a nice cotton shirt and soft pants, and, to his surprise, gloves. Thin, off-white muslin, not nearly enough to protect anyone from the elements. It's not too cold in the room, but out the window, he can see the dredges of melted winter snow flowing down the stone streets, so for the time being, he doesn't take the gloves off.

The room is, nicely put, minimalist. There's a little, dusty mirror on the wall, and he approaches it cautiously, wiping off some grime to see his reflection. He traces the outline of his face, from his dark eyes to his jawline, up to his brown hair. He reaches up and tugs at the white streak in his fluffy hair above his right eye, and raises a brow.

He racks his brain for some memory of where he's come from, and can't find anything. He does, however, have a feeling that that didn't used to be there.

In the corner he spots a familiar spot of leather—a guitar case leaning against the wall. He approaches it, and pulls at the latches to reveal a polished cedar body and pristine tuning pegs. There's an 'N' carved into the headstock and painted in gold. His eyes rake over it, and he furrows his brow in confusion. It's a familiar instrument. When he settles it in his arms and picks out a melody he can't quite remember the origin of, he feels without question that it's his, but he doesn't know why.

He sits back down on the bed, and strums a few chords, but gets quickly irritated with his gloves. He pulls them off, and patterning of green reaches down his fingers. His eyes catch on the ink, and he pulls up his sleeve to reveal a full arm of floral markings, from his elbow down to the tips of the pads of his fingers. He frowns.

Studying the wild tattoos, he finds a certain sense of nostalgia overtaking his thoughts, but can't pinpoint from where.

It's still dark outside, and he can't bring himself to light a candle to get a closer look at anything—as if he'd be able to find a match anyway.

He resigns to wander.

He drops the guitar back into the case and locks each of the golden latches. Pulling on a brown jacket he found on the floor of the room, he trudges out the door with the instrument in hand. The kitchen and living room of the house are small and not necessarily notable. He figures he'll take to exploring that part of his predicament later.

The air is chill. Not overwhelmingly cold, but enough for the last bits of winter's snow to hang onto the stone streets for as long as they can. Nick figures when the sun rises higher, the straggling patches will say their final goodbyes. It's almost saddening, though he doesn't quite know why. The warm weather doesn't feel... right. As if Nick was meant to live in the cold of the dying days of late autumn, sparing his time for doomed petals blooming in the cracks of the stones. It's nice to be out in the chill, but he can't shake the feeling that when the spring lilies begin to bloom, he'll be hiding himself away.

There's no one outside at this time of night, and birds returning from the south fly high over his head. The only noise is the sound of his thoughts, and the soft crunching of pebbles beneath his feet.

He exhales, and a cloud of steam materializes in the air. He smiles.

He wonders if he has anything to smoke on him. He doesn't really know if he actually smokes—he can't remember smoking before, or much of anything for that matter—but it feels right. He'll have to leave it be, though, because a swift search of his pockets reveals nothing. He's not sure he'd be able to light it, in any case.

A crow lands atop a stone wall beside him, at his shoulder level, and he reaches out with a finger to pet its head, but it squawks and flies away. He frowns and traces the bird's path into the distance until it disappears along the skyline, where he can see flecks of orange peeking up above the treetops. There's something unfamiliar in the strange sense of unease he feels in the dark, cold and alone, with not a soul awake to speak to. He should welcome the rising sun with open arms, but can't recall if he has anyone to look forward to seeing in the morning.

Maybe he used to. Maybe someone would come looking for him and help him remember what he's doing.

Who he is.

His mind doesn't rest for too long on that thought. It feels unlikely.

He continues walking, taking in shops and houses with inexperienced eyes, and understands with a feeling of déjà vu that the streets of this village have seen his presence before, but can't place why. Coming upon a fountain, with water frozen down to the stone and drips of melting ice falling onto the ground, he sits down and looks around. A town square of some sort, with stalls and businesses crowded around trying to find the prime real estate and most foot traffic.

He runs his hand along the sharp edges of the ice, and nicks himself slightly on a corner. He looks down at the small bead of red running down his finger, and squeezes the cut closed. His eyes linger on the blood as it drips slowly down, off his hand, and onto the ground, seeping in between the cracks in the cobbled path. It seems wrong. Not for him to bleed, but...

Well, he doesn't know what. Something in his stomach just turns at the sight of the red liquid. It's not the blood itself, but something else entirely. He lets out a breath and tries to ignore it.

He opens up the case once more, and fiddles with the tuning for a moment, the first string dipping down two notes lower than normal, and the second, one note. He doesn't quite know why that feels right to him, but the tuning sets him at ease.

"*You've got crowns and competencies beyond what you'd need,*" he whispers, not quite sure what the lyrics mean, "*in a normal fucking life.*" His hands flick over the strings in no particular order that he can distinguish, but it still comes out as a coherent melody. His fingers seem to move more with muscle memory than anything else.

How strange that the mind can forget, but the flesh never falters.

His fingers know the shape of the tune, drifting out into the air. The more he thinks about it, the less he understands where the music comes from, so he closes his eyes, and his notes ring. Quiet, so as not to be a disturbance. Only enough for him to hear his own voice.

"*And I'm sorry,*" he mutters, "*I'll never be what you expected of me.*" He laughs ever so slightly. "*I guess I can't be cured.*"

A small bird watches him from the roof of a small metallurgist's shop. He can feel its eyes prying into him, and it shouldn't be so uncomfortable to be watched by a creature without the capacity for judgement, but it makes his skin crawl all the same.

"I guess there's a reason, and maybe it's justice, you should back away when I'm seen."

He stops singing and cringes, shaking his head. He shouldn't be out in the early hours of the morning bemoaning his life's problems, negligible in the grand scheme of it all. Especially when he can't be sure what those problems are.

So instead he picks at the strings one by one, letting out a flowing piece. A song that sounds like forgetting, staccato notes dragging him through the melody. At times he slows and tries to recall whatever it is that he should be playing, moving his fingers along the strings and feeling the ribs of the cold steel. There's something obscene about it all. As the metal digs into his fingers, he can't shake the feeling that these strings aren't even right—maybe he should be playing with a rounder body, and softer strings. Quiet. Classical.

He stares down at his fingers from time to time as the metal bites him, and feels moisture pricking at the corners of his eyes. Something tells him that it shouldn't hurt as much as it does, and when he releases the strings to examine himself, he finds red marks pressed into his flesh. The tears gather at his lashes and he blinks them away. He's not even sure what's so sad about it all. Does he need to build calluses? That shouldn't be so absurd of an idea for a musician, and yet, it sits so uncomfortably in his chest, pulling at his heart. It feels as if his veins twist and knot on top of each other—like if he were to be cut apart all he'd see would be braids and ropes yanking each other around, the mortal instruments of his life fighting against his very existence.

For some reason, it feels right.

He lets a tear drip off his cheek, and his mind whispers to him that this is correct. Karmic retribution for a past that never happened, or a life he never lived. Something too long ago to feel guilt for—a history that everyone but he can remember.

A tear drips down onto his guitar, and he flinches, pulling

away, as if he expects some harm to come to him. Logically, nothing happens. He wonders what he thought would happen.

The sun crests the horizon, and he stares, before shaking his head and packing the guitar away again. He wanders aimlessly down darkened streets watching alleyways for lurkers, but the rest of the city sleeps, as he should as well.

He comes upon an ornate building with columns in front, stained glass windows peering into the dim hall, with dead plants lining the outside. It must be beautiful in the summer when all has bloomed.

He pushes the door and it opens with a metallic creak of protest from the hinges. He mutters an apology under his breath. To a door.

Inside, the walls are hung with intricate paintings and murals, the glass windows each with their own symbol. A green leaf on the tallest, a red crown to its right, and a yellow music note on the last. In the front on a platform are three stone sculptures staring at him, and behind them all stands a tall man with curly hair and a sharp smile. His gaze lingers on this sculpture. Why is he cast to the back? Who is he?

Why does he look like Nick?

Nick reaches up to the white strands of his hair and tugs on them absentmindedly, twisting them around his fingers as he glances around the building. His eyes land on the podium before the dais, and he walks up to it, taking a small leather-bound book off of it, and flipping through the pages in no particular order.

From what he gathers, it's a religion. "The Book of the Triad."

Yeah—yeah, that seems right. Nick remembers a religion. Albeit, not the contents or scriptures, but he knows it exists. It's the smallest, most insignificant piece of the puzzle, he thinks, but he welcomes anything closer to figuring out where or who he is.

He turns his head back to the statues, and stares at their faces. The person on the left, the tallest, has curly hair like him, and a bright smile. He's dressed in long flowing robes, and is, overall, the least imposing of all of them. The rest look angry. The statue on the right has a scowl on his face, and a sword gripped tightly between his fingers, a crown on his head. The one in the center seems to reach out to pull the other two in with giant feathered wings, cocooning them at his side. Protective, he decides, more than angry, but it still isn't a welcoming expression.

And then there's the guy in the back; he looks kind enough, but his smile is dark, and his eyes feel misleading. He holds out his hand before him and clutches a book. Nick strains to look over to see if anything is carved into the stone pages, but there is nothing. He supposes he can't expect such excruciating detail.

His robes are sculpted such that they almost look like real draping fabric. Nick almost feels that if he reaches out, he'd be able to fix the positioning of his long sleeve, but he doesn't dare touch the statue.

He looks around the chapel—maybe a church, or temple— and sees small rays of sun reaching up to the sky. No one in the village will wake for at least a few hours.

He puts his guitar case down on a bench, and takes off his gloves, placing them at the feet of the nicest looking statue. He looks young and small—though Nick has to assume that gods age unlike mortals, this one looks like a child, and his smile is so innocent and pure. Nick wonders what his story is. Maybe he'd have to find a scripture of his own to read.

Nonetheless, he bows his head and looks to the floor, kneeling in front of the sculpture. He isn't certain how exactly to refer to these people, or what he may be speaking to them for, so he closes his eyes and lets the words flow naturally.

"Hey," he starts lamely, and laughs at himself. "Uh, I'll be honest, I'm not quite sure who you guys are or why I'm here. Or where I am for that matter. Who I am. And I don't suppose you'd care to give me a hint." There's silence around him. A crow calls in the distance. "But, uh—well, I woke up in a strange house. I hope it's mine, otherwise that would cause some issues. I think my name is Nick. Nicholas? I don't know, but the name feels right, so I think I'll keep it."

It's quiet still, and for the first time since he woke, Nick begins to wish that maybe someone would respond to him. He's felt perfectly comfortable in the silence, wandering in the cold, but inside the warmth of the chapel, he feels caged.

"I probably shouldn't be trying to talk to you. I don't even know your names. If you're real." He doesn't know if he expects some divine power to strike him down for questioning their existence, but that would have been better than being ignored. "I've felt strange all morning—or I suppose, not morning, the sun's barely risen. Forgive my distorted sense of time, I'm not in the best state of mind. I tried to play guitar. It seems like I have a gift for music, granted, from where, I don't know, but it's a start. It's all a bit of a puzzle right now. I keep collecting little pieces— I'm sure I'll figure it out eventually, but if I could get any clues from you... or maybe even why you've decided to wipe my brain, in a sense, that could be worth something?"

"..."

"Right. Right, yeah. It's a weird thing to ask. Um," he pauses and takes a look around, trying to put together a coherent thought. "I have these strange tattoos."

He pulls up his long sleeve to reveal the wild decorations from his shoulder down to his fingers, and not for the first time, studies them intently. So much that he loses track of time, and a few minutes pass in absolute silence before he finds it in him to break away and speak again.

"They're odd. I feel like they're new, but I don't know why. They're not scarred but they're not bleeding and fresh, so I'm not quite sure how long I've had them." He laughs and shakes his head. "Sorry, you don't care. Forgive me, I haven't had many people to talk to this morning, for obvious reasons. But I suppose if I begin to ramble you could simply strike me down. Or however that works." He thinks for a moment, then sighs quietly. "Ha, if I had to spend all day listening to prayers like you guys, I'd probably give up my power anyway. How do you not get tired of it?"

Nick looks around, and stands up to approach the podium again. He flips through the beginning pages for some clues, and presses his finger onto the ink on the twelfth page, looking back to the statues.

"Let's see," he mutters, reading a description. The Progenitor from which the other gods originated is written as a kind older man with black feathered wings. He smiles. "You're the... Angel? Angel of Dawn." He scans the page to the bottom before flipping over, and finding nothing. He flips through the book more, and lands on a passage about the second one, the Lady Retribution. "Now that one I believe," he mutters, laughing airily. "You look like you could throw me across the sea without breaking a sweat."

He doesn't find anything about the younger-looking one, but after a few moments, lands on an excerpt discussing someone called the Siren. Though the passage is hastily crossed over in dark ink, and beside it reads a note. *"See revision."*

He looks around, spotting a smaller journal on a small shelf under the podium with browned pages torn at the edges. He picks it up.

"The tale of the Mad Leviathan," reads the first line. "The falling of a god from his very own Grace, overcome by grief and jealousy, seeking to repay sins never committed. The Angel's only biological son, dead."

Nick's eyes turn to the shadowy figure on the dais behind the three main sculptures. The one that looks a bit too much like himself for comfort.

"Mad Leviathan?" he asks. "What does one do to earn such a title?" If it's true that this god is exiled, he won't be getting a response very soon without his own research. So he continues to flip through the journal, before the narrative shifts in the middle pages, detailing the ascension of the youngest god, and he laughs quietly. "Innocence? That's apt."

Staring up at the eyes of Innocence, he feels a certain sense of familiarity, and steps away from the podium, still clutching the book in his hands. He has a face that reminds him of something —a memory far away and dusty in the back of his mind. He can almost picture the face moving, the smile laughing, and the eyes closing and wrinkling up in joy. He smiles. It's a sad smile that makes him feel more alone than the empty temple and sleeping city ever could have on its own, but he smiles all the same.

Nick doesn't voice it, but he can feel he remembers those eyes. Bright green and full of life. He's not sure how.

He shakes his head, and turns away from the young Innocence, holding the journal, and pulling on his coat once more. He grabs the Book of the Triad off the pedestal, before turning back to look at the four sculptures one final time.

"I'm sure you won't mind if I take this. It seems I have some studying to do." He takes a breath. "I apologize for disturbing you. I hope at our next meeting, I can offer a bit more of interest to you." Feeling a bit awkward, Nick flips around in the Book, landing on a page of prayers. He furrows his brows. "Um, goodbye, and, blessed be the pious?"

He picks up his guitar, and shoots the statues a dorky salute before leaving out the doors he came.

If crows pile onto tree branches and rooftops and watch him return home, he doesn't notice; but if he feels eyes on his back as he exits the temple, that's none of the business of the sleeping village.

15

"Like the show, kid?" The teen seems snapped out of a daze, and looks up into Nick's eyes, before an unfamiliar emotion flashes across his face, and he looks away. Nick raises a brow.

"Yeah. You're good. At music, I mean." Nick lets out a breathy laugh and smiles, setting his guitar down in its case and putting away his notes in the pockets.

"Thanks. I'd hope so, considering you've been here for an hour." The kid's face heats up, and Nikolai watches with concerned amusement. The teen studies him when he looks back, from his eyes to his shoes, with a strange look on his face. "Is something wrong?" he asks, and the boy shakes his head slowly, still looking him over.

"No, it's nothing. You just... remind me of someone I knew, I guess." Nick smiles, but can't help but feel a little bit uneasy.

"Another devilishly handsome minstrel around these parts? I've yet to see him, but he must be a charming young man," he jokes, and the kid's laugh is strained. Something about the teen is just... wrong. Obviously, living in this agrarian economy kingdom full of hermits tending to their gardens, Nick had seen his fair share of strange people, but the teen seemed off in a way he couldn't describe. Maybe it was how his eyes were a bit too bright green, but that didn't seem like it.

His eyes are drawn to the streak in the child's blond hair, matching his own.

"Yeah. Cool guy," the teen responds, and Nick feels an awkward air set in. He's unsure what else to do.

Even though Nick's only barely gotten his footing in this strange village since he came to three weeks ago with no recollection of who or where he was, he still can't pinpoint the kid's face. Making a living playing in the square from time to time, Nick's seen quite a lot of the townspeople, so to not be at least slightly acquainted with this kid caught him off-guard. He'd expect to have remembered someone with such an obvious, notable characteristic like the white streak.

"I'll—uh. I'll leave you to it. Thanks. Yeah." The boy stands up, and fishes through his pockets for something. He approaches Nick with his hand outstretched, and Nick reaches as the kid drops a heavy weight into his clutches. He looks down to see five gold coins resting in his palms, and looks up to the teen with confusion.

"Are you sure?" he asks, and the boy nods hastily, shoving his hand back in his pocket. He hasn't taken his right hand out of his pocket the entire time he's been here, Nick notes. "Really? That's a lot of money, kid." The boy scowls.

"I'm not a kid, and yes, I'm sure," he says with a sour expression, and Nick nods slowly, a bit suspicious. He hopes to the gods that this kid didn't just steal from his parents.

"Well, thanks. That's really kind of you." The kid smiles but it doesn't quite reach his eyes, and Nick puzzles over his expression. "What's a child like you doing to have the means to throw around gold?" The kid's face heats up again, and Nick grins, certainly unsure of who the teen is, but enjoying his company all the same. The people milling around the square part for them like the sea and give them their own space, which Nick is grateful for.

"Not a child! I've got a good job, alright?" he stammers, and Nick laughs. "What's that for?"

"Nothing, I'm sure you have a great job," he parrots, and the teen crosses his arms indignantly, which is when Nick spots the sun reflecting off one of his limbs strangely. He looks down to the kid's hand, and the color drains from his face. He studies the prosthetic hand closely. The polished metal covered in thin silver windings like vines. Nick feels sick as his gaze travels upwards to where the vines of steel wrap around his forearm and dig into his skin to hold the prosthetic in place. If it weren't so grotesque a sight it might have been slightly poetic, as if his hand were collateral damage to nature reclaiming her children. As it stands, the bruises around where the metal digs in only make Nick's stomach churn.

It looks expensive. Nick would definitely not be able to afford such a complex instrument, so he wonders how this kid possibly found the means, even with his "real good" job. It's emblazoned in the center of his "palm" with the smallest indication of a crown engraving. Did he work for the emperor? Even still, why would the emperor care to provide such an interesting replacement for a servant?

When the kid notices his staring and hides his hand back in his pocket, Nick sees the muscles in his forearm flex, and the blond cringes visibly. Nick can't imagine the type of pain that comes with feeling your tendons stretch under vines of metal pressed into your flesh.

"Stop staring," the teen mutters, and Nick breaks out of his daze, looking back up at his face where he picks out dejection and inner turmoil. He shrinks in on himself and smiles sheepishly in apology, feeling guilty for his obvious shock at seeing what must be a traumatic memory for someone so young.

"My apologies. I didn't mean to." The kid scoffs.

"Yeah, you did," he says, with a bit more grit and determination in his voice than before. "You never think you mean to," he finishes, and Nick sighs.

"Yeah. I'm sorry. You just don't see too many people with such an expensive-looking prosthetic around here. Forgive me." The child sighs, and, to Nick's surprise, takes a seat next to him.

"Well, ask away I guess," he says. Nick doesn't want to bother him any more than he has, but he does have questions, and an open invitation for them to be answered. It certainly wouldn't hurt...

"What happened?" his mouth runs before his mind has time to catch up, and of course he asks the worst question possible. The kid stills, and Nick blanches, opening his mouth to take it back, but the teen beats him to it.

"Frostbite," he says simply, and somehow, Nick thinks that might be the worst answer he could've gotten.

"Winters are harsh around here, I'm told," he replies lamely.

"Something like that."

"Only big question I have, I guess, is what's the point of the —you know," he gestures vaguely to his own forearm, and the child nods.

"From what I understand it's a bit of a pulley system." He pulls his hand out and pokes at the windings of silver gingerly. "These are hollow, and there are cords inside 'em. They're digging into my nerves, so when I flex my muscles, the cords are pulled, and they move my fingers." Demonstrating, he points to a place on his arm and Nick watches as he flexes the tendon slowly, and just like he said, his index finger curls in towards his palm. Nick can't help but be a bit amazed. The kid smiles. "Modern engineering is a miracle. Doesn't mean it doesn't hurt like hell though." Despite himself, Nick laughs, and after an awkward moment, the teen joins.

Nick reaches out slowly, and holds his hand up in the air between them. "The name's Nick" he says. A strange look crosses the blond's face, but he disregards it.

"Lucky," he says. He doesn't shake Nick's hand, only eyeing it strangely as if it could jump out and hurt him, and after a second,

Nick takes it as his cue to withdraw. Another strange thing that he'll choose to ignore.

"Pleasure meeting you, Lucky," he says, smiling. Lucky's smile is strained, and Nick can tell he doesn't truly mean it when he says,

"You, too." Then, "Nick," almost as an afterthought. The air is awkward between them. Sensing that he's overstayed a welcome he never got, Nick stands and takes his guitar case in his hand, tipping his head to the kid.

"I'm here most weekends, if you ever wanted to come around." He doesn't stick around for Lucky's reaction.

🥀

MONTHS PASS BEFORE NICK SEES THE BOY AGAIN, AND FOR A while, he forgets that he ever was waiting for someone. After all, time waits for no one, and it continues to pass by as Nick finds his footing in this strange new world. He picks up odd jobs performing, and goes to the square each weekend when he can, but since Lucky's disappearance, it feels empty.

It feels familiar, in a way, for Lucky to disappear for weeks on end.

When Lucky finally shows his face again, he's changed. His hair is a bit longer, and his face is more sullen. Nick notes that he no longer moves his hand with such noticeable agony as the first time they met, which sets him at ease. Nick sits on a bench in the temple. He'd just been talking to the statues once more after spending longer than he'd like to admit studying them and the kingdom's history. He reported back his findings, but of course it's nothing they wouldn't already know themselves. When the door creaks open and the boy steps into the warmth of the temple as spring begins to grow across the land, Nick is annoyed at the interruption, but happy to see him.

When he spots the teen's face, he waves him over with a smile, and Lucky approaches him cautiously.

"Long time no see!" he says, and Lucky gives him a fake smile. He sits on a bench across the aisle from Nick and trains his gaze on the older man. "Where have you been?" he asks. The kid shrugs.

"Things, you know?" he says. Nick's about to speak again when Lucky says, "Didn't know you were a devout." Nick chuckles and shakes his head, letting his arm rest across the back of their bench comfortably. He can't help but feel eyes on him. Eyes that aren't Lucky's.

"Not really. Just wanted some quiet," he says instead of the truth. Lucky nods, and levels his gaze at the statues. Nick does the same, and studies the face of Innocence for a moment, before saying out of the blue, "He kinda looks like you." Lucky seems to take pause, examining Nick's face.

"You don't say," he lets out between his teeth.

"Yeah. Same hair at least." It's at this point a smile forms on his face and he reaches up to his own tufts of white. "Hey look," he says, "we match." Lucky's smile is strained, but Nick has learned to expect that.

"That we do," he says. Nick laughs.

"Strange. I don't think I had this before. Maybe I was simply meant to meet you." Lucky tilts his head.

"What do you mean, 'you don't think'?" Nick shrugs and lets his gaze wander the grand hall.

"Strange situation, but I'm not quite sure who I am."

"Depressing," Lucky says, and Nick laughs.

"No, no—for real. I woke up a couple months ago and was just here. Amnesia or something." Something flashes behind Lucky's eyes, and he stares at Nick intently for a moment, before speaking with a quiet and soft voice.

"You... don't know anything?" he asks, and Nick shakes his head.

"I mean, I know how to breathe, but about nothing else." Lucky looks at him blankly with a dark expression on his face, until Nick gets uncomfortable with his laser-focus and begins to look around aimlessly again. Lucky mumbles something under his breath, and Nick looks back at him. "What was that?"

"Nothing. Nothing at all." The feeling of being watched intensifies, even as Lucky turns away from him and closes his eyes.

When he looks up to the eyes of the statues of the gods, they simply feel eerie, almost as if the sculptor had carved their eyelids deeper and twisted the visage so that the statues look right at Nick—into his soul. They must have always been like that and he never noticed. There's no need to try to find deeper meaning in the mundane of daily life. Gods know Nick doesn't have a great memory anyway.

TIME WAITS FOR NO ONE. AS WEEKS PASS, NICK FINDS HIS WAY in this strange new world. He picks up a job at a bakery and learns to cook, and grows closer to the strange timid boy with the white in his hair. He can't help but feel an instinct to protect the kid, as if he were his own family, so when he meets him in the temple or Lucky finds him in the town square playing a tune on his off days, he makes an effort to get him to talk as much as he can. He doesn't quite know why it's so hard for the boy to open up, but he doesn't push when Lucky gets uncomfortable.

He's noted several uncomfortable subjects to steer clear of.

First: Lucky's childhood. Lucky doesn't seem more than sixteen or seventeen, or maybe a very mature-looking fifteen-year-old, but even still, talking about his upbringing immediately grinds any conversation to a halt. This extends so far as to Nick asking about Lucky's exact age. He can tell from the boy's face and stature that he's clearly younger than Nick by a wide margin, but he'll never know for sure, because the question of his age is met each time with "What's it to you?" Nick relies on his intuition and thinks of Lucky as in his late teens. Nick first noticed this as a problem when he asked Lucky where he went to school.

From Lucky's silence, he had extrapolated that maybe he's a drop-out, or skips school every day, but as the conversation continued, he realized more and more that anything relating to how he grew up, his favorite activities, his childhood memories —everything made him squirm. So Nick dropped it.

Lucky's family. If Nick were a lesser man, he'd consider the possibility that maybe Lucky is homeless or doesn't have a family from the way he blanches each time he's asked about it. But each time they meet, Lucky arrives with outfits embroidered with intricate silver threads and warm fur around his neck, even as the weather begins to pick up into the early months of Spring. He clearly has someone looking out for him, but by his insistence, Nick will never know who that person is. The first time this was made apparent to him was when Lucky showed his face a bit later than they normally met.

"Dad want you to finish your carrots or something?" he had jokingly asked. Immediately at the word 'dad' the color drained from Lucky's face, and he cast his glance away from Nick towards the cobbled street.

"I had things to do," was all Lucky said, and Nick couldn't help the suspicion climbing up his chest. He made a mental note that 'dad' was not something he should say, for whatever reason.

Next, Lucky hates fire. The only time Nick managed to convince Lucky to come home with him and have some tea, Lucky nearly had a breakdown at the sight of Nick lighting a candle in the dining room. He tried to keep the evident distress out of his voice, but the sheer terror painting his face alerted Nick to this next sore subject. When Lucky spoke, his voice shook slightly.

"You can put it out. I don't mind the dark. Really," he'd said, smiling tersely and shifting his weight from side to side. Nick wanted to ask what was wrong, but at this point, he knew better. He blew out the candle, and made a special effort to stand in front of the kettle as he turned on the burner so Lucky wouldn't see the flame. They drank their tea in relative silence, and Nick was the one to carry the conversation for the most part until Lucky seemed to calm down, and returned to negging him like usual. He left late that night, and his smile seemed more genuine than normal, but still stressed. When he was gone, Nick relit the candle and stared at it as if the flame had the secrets of the universe.

It was much colder in the house without Lucky.

Finally, Nick knew that Lucky didn't seem okay.

Every time he saw him, he'd keep his gaze pinned to the ground, and when Nick would reach out to ruffle his hair, he'd flinch away from the contact. Nick didn't want to bring it up, but it became far too much to simply pretend he didn't notice— something was wrong. It hurt his heart, because each time he'd see the child, he'd feel so strongly that he needed to reach out and hug him goodbye—protect him and show him he cares, but Lucky doesn't seem to want to be anywhere near him.

And that's okay. It's okay, but Nick can tell there's something else to it.

So when he finally settles down at the kitchen table across from Lucky with a cup of green tea in his hand, he looks at the boy fondly, and tries to find a way to phrase his question. He's buttered the kid up all night with homemade muffins and honey candy that he bought for far too much money from a beekeeper, but the main event is coming now.

"Lucky?" he asks quietly, and the teen looks up over the rim of his cup with a brow raised, meeting Nick's eyes. "Can I ask you a question?"

"You just did," Lucky shoots back immediately with a smirk on his face, and Nick rolls his eyes. "Fine, go for it." Nick takes in a breath, and tries to think of a way to back out even now that he's come this far, but time waits for no one, and it won't wait for him to gather his courage.

"Lucky, is everything alright at home?" There's an uncomfortable silence in the room for a moment, and Lucky's eyes seem to widen, his pupils growing just slightly bigger as he looks around

Nick's kitchen wildly. He looks like a caged animal searching for an escape. "You don't have to tell me everything, but I worry about you, Kid."

"Not a kid," he mutters, instead of answering the question. The denial doesn't come with the usual fire it normally has, which worries Nick even more.

"Lucky, I'm serious," he says without thinking, and Lucky looks up to meet his eyes swiftly with a strange mixture of joy, anger, and shock painting his face all at once. Nick can tell he's struck a nerve, but he can't back down. He needs to know the kid is safe. He takes in a breath as Lucky stares him down. "Really," he lets out, "if anyone's hurting you..."

"No one's hurting me!" Lucky exclaims suddenly. He flinches and a drop of tea falls down the side of his cup and onto his hand. He keeps eye contact with Nick trying to look confident, but Nick can see a tendril of fear creeping up into his eyes. Nick sighs.

"You promise?" he asks, and Lucky nods aggressively.

"Yes. Yes, I promise. No one—no one's hurting me." He takes in a breath, then, quietly; "Anymore." And Nick's heart shatters, a sharp pain shooting into his chest, and he lowers his brows, feeling a tear coming. He swallows down the sour taste in his throat before it can reach his eyes. He reaches across the table to take Lucky's hand, and the kid stills, but doesn't pull away.

Gods above, Nick is going to find whoever hurt him and make them regret ever being born.

Anymore.

"Lucky," he starts softly, and Lucky shakes his head.

"I don't need your pity. I'm fine." He pulls his hand away, as if Nick's heart didn't already hurt enough.

"Lucky, I hope you're telling the truth." There's an echo in Nick's head. *I know when you lie.* He shakes it away.

"I am!" he nearly yells, and Nick fights hard to keep his cool under the pure sense of bloodlust washing over him, keeping himself from murdering whoever caused Lucky this much pain so that he can't even accept a hug from him.

"And this person can't hurt you anymore?" he asks, not sure if he's trying to pacify Lucky or himself. Lucky nods slowly.

"He's gone," he says, a hint of shakiness dropping into his voice. Just as Nick starts to see the light begin to hit his eyes weird again, he closes them and looks away. "He's—my brother's gone," he finishes.

"*I'll be your brother,*" Nick's instincts scream, "*He didn't deserve you.*"

Instead, Nick simply nods, and looks around, before asking, "Lucky, can I give you a hug?"

Lucky doesn't look at him as he considers his answer, but silently, shakily, he nods, and Nick rounds the table to kneel in front of him, pulling him into his arms.

Lucky lets out a muffled sob, and Nick feels something cold on his shirt. He doesn't have the emotional energy to question it. It seems the room's dropped a few degrees anyway.

He shushes the child quietly and rubs his back, and for the first time, Lucky melts when he hugs him harder. In another situation, Nick might be happy that he finally got Lucky to open up and let him in. In this situation, he fights back tears.

"I'm so glad you're okay," he says, and Lucky nods quietly without responding. "I'm sorry that happened to you," he continues, and Lucky shakes slightly. "I care about you, Lucky. So much." Lucky nods, but Nick isn't quite sure he truly understands.

But that's okay, he figures.

Something tells him, in any case, he'll spend a lifetime convincing him.

16

Lucky sits across from Honora, watching her hands dart across the board with suspicious eyes. They'd been at the game for about half an hour, and had made no headway. Lucky had more pieces than Nora, sure, but each one that made up the difference was just another pawn. No matter what Lucky did, Honora always had a way to combat it. It took her no time at all to figure out that Lucky had a reckless playstyle, chasing pawns and moving out into no-man's-land ambitiously, and Lucky had never played against someone so good at defense. Something told him he'd be in this chair for a long while.

"You're quite good at this," Nora breaks the silence, and Lucky looks up.

"I know," he says simply. Honora finally makes her move, dropping her bishop down on a diagonal from Lucky's king.

"Check," she says. Lucky moves his king one to the left. "How did you learn the game?" Lucky shrugs.

"Sometimes people would play with me. Mostly pity, I guess." Nora snorts and brings out a knight.

"Bet they stopped pitying the second they saw what you could do." Lucky scowls and captures the knight with ease.

"People never stop pitying those they think are lesser than them," he says, leaning back in his chair and huffing. "No matter what, it would always be the same."

"Hm," is Nora's only response as she moves out a pawn two spaces forward, and Lucky smiles. He captures it, and Honora stares at him. "You can't do that," she says.

"En passant, Miss Wood," he taunts. "You'd think Lady Retribution herself would be better at strategizing." At the goddess's continued look of confusion, Lucky huffs, and sits up straighter to explain. "If the enemy passes right by you on their pawn's first move, you can take it on the diagonal. You wouldn't let a soldier walk past you on the battlefield, would you?"

"If it puts my men in danger," Nora says, picking up a rook, "I would keep to myself." To punctuate, she takes Lucky's attacking pawn. Lucky scowls. He moves on Honora's rook to make a point, though he knows it puts his bishop in harm's way.

"Check," he says snidely. "What was that about putting men in danger?" Honora simply laughs lightly, and Lucky scowls. That's the thing about Nora—no matter what Lucky did, he never seemed to get on her nerves.

Lucky was consistently toeing the line as close to the breaking point as he could, and yet nothing would make these people—creatures—crack. Lucky waited each day for them to finally realize he's too much work and throw him back out on the streets. He abused his divine powers at every possible point; he curled light around himself to become invisible and spy on them, he broke their things with the sheer sound of his voice, he ordered them around and used the Siren's power to keep them away. They never did anything.

It can't last, he knows, but for some reason, it has.

They had no right to continue to be so kind and tolerant after they ruined his life for the second time. When would they stop pretending this was permanent?

So when Nora laughs, Lucky's blood boils.

"I guess you got me on that one," she responds, moving her king away. Lucky chases.

"Check," he says again. Nora moves once more, Lucky follows. "Check."

"Kid, do you really want a stalemate after half an hour?" the goddess asks, and Lucky bares his teeth.

"I want to win," he says, and Nora shrugs. She pushes her rook into Lucky's path, and Lucky takes it. "Check." Honora shakes her head, capturing Lucky's bishop.

"How's Nick doing?" she asks, and Lucky freezes.

"You can't distract me," he replies with venom in his voice, retreating a knight, and Nora shrugs.

"Not trying to, just curious." Lucky levels her with as dark a glare as he can muster, and for a moment, spots of his vision turn grey. He blinks them away. "Don't act like you've been so secretive. We know you're visiting him." She moves a pawn, Lucky sneers.

"What's it to you?"

"I'd like to know. I won't interfere—per Elric's orders, I can't —but I want to hear how he's faring. It's only fair that you should tell me, sneaking away so often to see my brother."

"He's my brother, too," Lucky shoots back, and Nora looks up. She studies Lucky's face intently, and for a moment, the room is so silent one could hear a pin drop.

"Oh?" she replies. Lucky moves his queen. He says nothing. The only person he's ever admitted his affections for Nikolai to is, well, *Nick* apparently. He can't even be bothered to remember his own name.

Each time Lucky sees him, he wishes that he's finally regained his memories and figured out who Lucky is and what he's taken from him. Would he be mad when he found out? Would he see Lucky's taken his place and hold it against him? Logically, Lucky knows that Nikolai can't hurt him anymore, at least not physically, but the very concept of Nick remembering who he is and betraying him again causes him more pain than the Siren's orders ever could have. When Nick hugs him good-bye, bakes him bread, and makes tea, or when he pulls out his guitar and sings Lucky a song—even without the possibility that he could ruin his life over and over again, it makes Lucky's heart hurt. Because Nikolai sings to him all the same, but without the chorus of bells underneath his voice that once entranced him. His words are human.

"Yeah," is the only thing he can think to say. Nora moves a pawn. Lucky moves his rook. "Why don't I start badgering you about any dark past you may be hiding, huh? Is that fair?" he taunts. The goddess gives a simple shrug and moves another piece.

"Ask away," she says, "but don't expect much."

Lucky drops his queen down across from Nora's king, and the goddess dances away, followed by Lucky poising a knight for attack once again. "Check." Honora scowls and Lucky fights a snide smile off his lips as she moves away once more, and he chases her down with a bishop. "Check," he says defiantly, because above all else if he can't have higher ground over the gods physically, or with his power, he can play games of the mind. That's the problem with giving him the strengths and weaknesses of a master manipulator—Lucky knows when he can and can't win.

"Where's your tragic missing family?" he asks. Honora smiles.

"Parents? Dead. My little brother? Died hundreds of years ago. Other than that, nowhere. I never got married like Nick," she says. Lucky raises a brow and looks up to meet her bright eyes.

"So there were no princes coming after the greatest warrior the world had ever seen?" Honora moves her king out of check and smirks, resting her chin on one hand and studying the board.

"They tried," she says. "They never got far." Lucky moves a pawn and the goddess retreats. "Besides," she says, picking up her queen and dragging her back to her original position away from the boy's waiting knight, "I'm more of a fan of princesses,

THE LIGHT IS DIMMER

myself." Lucky fights a smile climbing up his lips and a laugh bubbling in his gut.

He stays silent and chases Nora around the board, capturing foot-soldiers along the way. He poises his pieces for attacks around the corner that Honora can just barely see, visualizing positions of the pieces dozens of moves ahead to keep the upper hand.

"Check," he mutters from time to time, keeping score in his head. Maybe if just to add another second to the clock that ticks down slowly above Lucky's head each day he stays with the gods. He's determined to beat the Bleeding One at her own game. For a divine strategist, she's terrible at predicting Lucky's moves.

Honora drops her bishop down to attack Lucky's queen, but seems to realize her mistake as soon as her hand is off the piece. Lucky grins.

"Check," he says, taking the bishop for himself. Nora moves a pawn, Lucky takes her final knight. Nora's rook narrowly escapes capture, and finally, after an hour, Lucky sees his opportunity.

He places his queen opposite Nora's king. "I believe that is check," he says, as the goddess picks up her king to move to the only remaining safe place. Lucky follows her with a knight, and smiles. "And mate." The god huffs.

"Good game. I underestimated you," she says, and Lucky nods.

"A mistake you won't make twice." He stands and exits the room without another word.

"HEY LUCKY, GONNA BE MORE CAREFUL THIS TIME?" LUCKY scowls at the Angel's words, but nods his head all the same. He's never going to get used to the strange feeling of his wings opening up behind him, he thinks, as he can feel each of his vertebrae crack into place to accommodate the silvery cloak.

The wings are made of light. They can't even be touched. Why did they need to hurt so much?

"On your call, then," he says, smiling. Lucky keeps a straight face and doesn't reply, approaching the edge of the balcony, and jumping.

The wind hits his face and ruffles up his hair. He'll also never get used to how familiar the scene is. Elric insists each time upon meeting on the balconies and falling. Because he's ignorant and insensitive, Lucky assumes.

But even still, it's somewhat freeing. As he plummets out of his home in the clouds down, down, down towards the tree line, he smiles. Nikolai wouldn't manage to ruin this for him, he thinks, as he spreads his wings as far as they can go, and is shot back upward by the wind resistance. He cheers as he soars back up into the sky, and hears Elric laughing airily at him. He resents the sound, but can't let it ruin his good time.

He knows what it feels like to hit the ground, but he doesn't have to anymore. He can be reckless and fall towards the earth— he doesn't hit the grass down below, because he's soaring above it all, flying, living.

Though he can't help but hold a grudge or two against the gods for bringing him back, despite it all, he's reclaimed the skies. He may never be able to climb a rooftop and run from merchants again in this life the same way he used to with adrenaline coursing through his veins, always running the risk of being caught, but he can soar.

The first time he came back from practice with Elric, Honora had laughed at him over the pages of a book with glasses perched on her nose, and asked him how he felt. He wanted to stay stoic and angry, but couldn't help a smile climbing up his face.

"*Yeah,*" Nora had said, "*I know what it's like,*" almost genuinely. Then, of course; "*I mean, I was always above everyone else. Now there's just a height difference.*" Lucky scowled and stormed off at the time, but still laughed about it alone in the comfort of his room later.

From his place just below the clouds, he can see his kingdom from above for what it truly is. What used to be his whole life and everyone he'd ever known—miniscule. He wants to be sad. He looks down upon the systems of streets that all lead back to the capital, and a strange feeling like longing curls up in his stomach, but he doesn't shed a tear. Maybe it would be easier if he could cry and let it all out, but it's not sadness that he feels. Familiarity, wistfulness, yearning? Whatever it is, it can't be shaken away by the howling of the wind in his ears.

He shakes his head, and twists to face Elric with an impish smile on his face. At the Angel's confusion, he immediately closes up his wings, back to the ground below, and falls, shooting the god a two-fingered salute on the way down.

He sees Elric stiffen and close his own wings, chasing Lucky down headfirst. He laughs, and curls his wings around himself for the aerodynamics.

When the wings embrace him, he smiles brighter and does a spin in the air. They encase him in a blanket of silver, and despite how cold he and all of his magic will always be, it feels like a warm hug. Like a hug from the very universe itself.

And the universe is saying it's proud, and maybe, despite everything, this is where Lucky was always meant to be.

He cheers loudly as the wind hits him, and just before the trees are below him once again, he opens his wings, and soars away across the treetops with Elric on his tail. The leaves rustle as he passes.

He dives down into the forest, and weaves between the trees with grace, picking up offended twits of birds nearby. He smiles and waves at each one as an apology. Perching orders always give the most attitude.

Slowing to a stop, he lands himself steadily on a branch a meter or two off the ground, and waits for Elric to reprimand him.

The god lands on the ground and stares up to Lucky with a look of amusement. "That was dangerous," he comments, and Lucky smiles.

"Fun, too," he replies, and Elric rolls his eyes. A crow flits down from a nearby elm tree and perches itself on the god's shoulder, and Elric coos. "Bird-brain is at it again already," Lucky says, and Elric laughs.

"Oh, hush. Not my fault I'm the only actual bird between all of you." Lucky perks up, and tilts his head.

"Oh yeah. Why is that?" he asks. It had never really dawned upon him that of the four gods that have existed, three of them have had beams of light somewhere just barely on the visible spectrum, whereas Elric has the only wings with a physical manifestation. Lucky brings his cloak closer to him and tries to touch the cold silver, but his hands phase right through.

"Well, I'm the ancestor," he says, as if that helps Lucky at all. "I came first. I guess that gives me a sort of special privilege. It's nice, in a way. Feels like the universe giving me a connection to my creations." He pets down the crow's back, and it chirps quietly.

"Strange for a God of Death to exist without one of life," Lucky comments, and Elric looks at him with a barely concealed smile.

"Why, they never did consider me as both." Lucky pauses. He looks at Elric. "In the beginning, there was only me. I made—" he gestures out widely to the forest, "—all of this. Eventually I had to stop experimenting, though, and make a real world. That's when I became Death." Lucky looks into his eyes but finds no sign of a joke or lie—not that he expected to. After all, he knows when they lie.

"None of your original creations still exist?" he asks, and Elric shakes his head. He raises a finger.

"One," he says simply. He taps his temples and smiles. "Consciousness. Conscience." His smile widens. "Only my greatest creations."

A pang of sadness hits Lucky's chest, but he smiles all the same. For conscience to be Elric's proudest creation only for his own child to lack it entirely. Divinity has no escape from the ironic plights of mortals.

"Doesn't it make you feel a bit insignificant?" Lucky asks suddenly, and Elric cocks a brow.

"What do you mean?" Lucky thinks for a moment. He doesn't quite know what he means, but it felt right to say. He'd felt it as he soared above the clouds and looked down on his former home and its streets and temples and houses and shops—all the little people that looked like ants from above; all the little people he once was one of.

"Does it feel a bit insignificant?" he asks again, leaning back against the tree. "You know, to look down on everything you've made and all the people that owe their lives to you, but even still, doesn't it feel a bit hollow?" Lucky takes a breath and lets it out. Without his influence, his wings curl around him into a hug and he has half a mind to thank them. "Look at what they've managed to do with this little time they've been given. You've lived for eons and in that time created life, but they can, too. They build and tear down cities and make friends and enemies, and they live their own lives without accordance to any rules you've set. They can create, too, without you. Even if their creations aren't grand and can't stand the test of time..."

There's silence in the forest as the words dissipate into the air. Elric puts his crow down on a small branch, and his footsteps crunch across the floor as he approaches Lucky's tree. He looks up at him, into his green eyes so similar to his own, and he smiles.

"It's never insignificant," he says. "It all stands the test of time." He holds out a hand to Lucky—an olive branch—and hesitantly, the young god takes it. "No life worth living is ever truly over, Lucky."

Lucky scowls and rolls his eyes. "Don't give me the 'live on in their hearts' story—I've heard it all," he says. He opens up his wings, preparing for takeoff, but the Angel stops him, taking his hand, smiling at him.

"No, no, Lucky. You misunderstand. There's something out of all of this that remains, even after the wreckage finally comes. Their lives are never insignificant." He glances to Lucky with fondness in his eyes. "No story worth telling ever ends."

Lucky will pretend he sees nothing in this pronouncement than the ramblings of a god trying to make meaning out of too long a life.

Though he scoffs and flies away off towards the sky once again, he rolls the words over in his mouth again and again, and maybe, just maybe, finds some comfort in the thought.

🐍 17 🐍

Lucky can't help himself.

Even though he knows that Honora and Elric know where he goes every time he runs off to the humans, his heart is still mortal as it always was, and yearns to go back to his home.

So he shows up in the temple again.

It's strange, truly, the types of things he can now see. When he walks to the dais and looks down, he can see tiny specks of silver dotting the floor in several places. He tries not to remember where they came from. The human mind, he knows, can often choose to forget, but does that change in divinity?

There's service today, just like he remembers it. He sits down in the front row, and the grave shoots him a smile, which he returns half-heartedly. This grave, he doesn't remember. It's not the normal man conducting the service, who would have remembered Lucky and asked him where he'd gone. Still, as a precaution, he disguises himself.

He doesn't look like the same boy he used to be. Because of Elric's constant pestering, he dresses like a noble these days, in the same attire that would have caught his eye back in the day when he first met Nikolai, who looked ethereal even when trying to hide amongst humanity. All the diamonds and silver chains and the shimmering aura always about him have been abandoned today. Even still, he's dressed in pure white laced with silver stitching on the seams, and patterning of leaves embroidered onto his chest. He tries not to notice the gazes he draws from the devout. Palace gentry would never be found this far from the capital, but he hopes that can be his excuse if he's asked.

He takes off the white jacket and melts into the familiar warmth of the temple. The air in the temple makes his wings vaguely itch, yearning to break free. He looks around subtly, but doesn't catch Nikolai's eye anywhere. He tends to come to the temple on his own and avoids regular service, so Lucky doesn't know why he'd expected him.

He tunes out the grave's speaking as he looks up to the stained-glass windows, just recently having been replaced, out with the yellow, and in with grey; the grey should shine onto his very own statue each high noon.

He scowls as he looks at his carved countenance. They got it right, sure, but he looks so childish. Why would Elric have called him Innocence in the first place? Or given him the power of forgiveness? It's like he wanted to make a statement. Not that Lucky *was* the god of all forgiveness and rebirth, but that he'd *better* be if he wants to stick around. No matter how much Elric and Honora try to push that they have no malicious intent in bringing him back, Lucky hardly believes it.

"... As our sweetest fruits thrive upon the hand of Death, the Angel's circle of life. One day we, too, shall return to His hands, and from deliverance of soil in Death, nurture the Earth He's grown. In Man's sacred duty to care for His land, we remember that all that we touch is in His protection."

Lucky remembers all this nonsense. The grave would tell them to keep their holy gardens and give back to the soil from whence they came, and just about half of them would go home and forget the advice all over again. In his time with Elric, Lucky had yet to see him damn a soul for improperly growing tomatoes.

"And in our reverence, we honor and respect those relationships we've grown with our brothers and sisters in the Light, for alliance and compromise fly freely in our hearts, and our friendship and love watched over by our Strategist." Lucky raises a brow. Maybe it's this new margrave's own manner of doing things, but his old services never would've recognized Honora as a protector of friendship. Alliance, sure, but not much more.

Despite himself, he smiles, eager to tell her the news once he returns home.

"We keep the Light in our hearts until again we meet, by forgiving and granting kindness to one another as our Innocent would deign," he says finally, setting down the book, and looking out onto the crowd of worshippers with kind eyes. "Blessed be the pious," he finishes, and the believers echo it back. "I'll see you again very soon," he says, smiling, as the people begin to stand and file out the door.

Stragglers stick around and talk to the margrave—ask him about the family, how his cat is doing—about trivial matters. Lucky sticks around, too, sitting in the front simply watching. When the last people finally leave and the margrave meets his eyes, Lucky doesn't shy away.

He's used a bit of magic (Elric has insisted that he *please stop calling his gifts magic*) to cover up the streak in his hair, his most notable feature, aside from the hand. He's confident he won't be recognized.

"Good day," the man greets, approaching to take a seat next to Lucky. Lucky tilts his head slightly in acknowledgement. "You caught only our latter half," he says with humor in his voice, and Lucky smiles.

"Apologies, Margrave. I've been too busy to come to service. I have it in good faith, though, that the gods can forgive me." The man smiles and waves it off.

"Ah, faith, faith! Wouldn't we all like a bit?" he exclaims. Lucky decides he very much prefers the old grave to this man who speaks like an eccentric in a period piece. "There's something that the scripture can't teach, Son, where do we find our faith in purity?" he asks, and Lucky stares at him for a moment before realizing he expects an answer, and he searches his mind.

"There is no pure faith," he responds, "Only those who think theirs more pure than another." A veiled stab at the grave, but he nods in agreement and considers.

"Yes, yes. And what gives you confidence in your faith?" Lucky raises a brow. "Confidence is what the gods give those that are less," he concludes, and Lucky has to stop himself from laughing. Someone's gonna have to tell that to Honora.

"I've been forgiven before," he settles on saying, and the grave smiles. Lucky can't imagine what number of strange thoughts he's thinking. He almost expects the grave to spew nonsense mad as a hatter—telling him all about the windimbles in the wabe, or sprigin trees upon the hill, over the rolling elephant city. Instead, he gets something somehow more puzzling.

"To be forgiven, or perchance, to forgive. That is the price of faith, and aren't we all in debt. Not enough time in the day," he says, "to wait for second chances." The grave pats Lucky's shoulder, then stands and exits out the front door without explanation, and Lucky sits on the bench by himself, staring at the statues.

"What the..."

He watches the sun float higher into the sky momentarily, before he hears the door creak open once again, hinges forever in protest. When will the clergy care to oil it? he wonders.

"Lucky?" He smiles.

"Hey, Nick" he says, turning around to face the man as he walks through the door. He looks as put together as always, with nice brown slacks and a long coat, and his guitar case on his back. It's still unnerving to see him appear so human, but Lucky can't fault him for it. It makes him more approachable than the Siren ever could have been, anyway.

"What brings you?" he asks. He sits down next to Lucky and

sets his guitar on the ground. "It's been a while." Lucky shrugs, and looks up to the statues.

"Service, I suppose?" he responds, and Nikolai simply chuckles.

"I guess. Though, I never do see you here during service."

"I don't tend to come," he says, "It's a bit boring. Plus, margrave's weird," he adds on, and Nikolai nods.

"Yeah, he's a bit much. Good guy, but can't seem to stop talking like a raving madman. He's gone with the fairies, that's for sure." Lucky smiles, and nods lightly.

"You can say that again," he agrees, and Nikolai laughs for a second, before speaking again.

"What did you talk to him about?" he asks.

"Pardon?" Nikolai nods up to the margrave's podium. He stands and grabs the Book off the top and flips through the pages, looking around.

"You know, what crazy things d'he have to say today?" He stops at a certain passage and squints a moment, his brow furrowing in thought, before he moves on.

"Just some old people ravings," Lucky says, leaning back. The contact with the wood fiber of the bench makes his silver cloak sing underneath his skin, and mentally he curses it. He has to admit, he's grown very fond of flying. "Went on about faith and purity," he says. Nikolai nods.

"Tends to do that," he agrees. "He's very passionate, though. I wouldn't say the gods really speak to him, but he sure does believe they do. He's got his heart in it." Lucky laughs a breathy laugh, and Nikolai looks up from the book. "What was that?" he asks, and without thinking, Lucky responds with:

"Gods wouldn't talk to him. He's nuts." Nikolai narrows his eyes in confusion.

"Shouldn't they talk to their speakers on earth?" he asks, and Lucky realizes his mistake, backpedaling.

"Well you know—they would. He's—yeah. I'm just saying

things. Forget it." Nice save. Nikolai still looks suspicious, but he drops it.

"Hm," he lets out simply. He drops the Book back on the pedestal and swivels around to face Lucky, hands clasped behind his back. In this position, in the light of the temple with Nikolai above him on the dais once again, he looks more Siren than ever. "Bakery's doing well," he interrupts Lucky's thoughts. Lucky smiles.

"Not burning things anymore?" he asks, and Nikolai nods, smiling with a fond look in his eyes.

"You'll have to taste my honey rolls now. I've perfected it, I think." Lucky nods and thinks about the honey bread he brought home for tea with Lucky so often. A bit of guilt crawls up his stomach at the thought that he's disappeared without a message on Nikolai again. Had he been expecting Lucky in the bakery, or waiting for him in the square to play him his favorite songs? Had the tea gone cold in his absence?

"I'll take you up on that," he says, and Nikolai smiles. He waves out his long arm and gestures vaguely to the door to the temple.

"Care for a walk?" he asks, and Lucky considers. He hadn't really thought about what to do once he'd gotten to Nick; he just wanted the familiar face again. The last time he'd gone for tea with the man hadn't been optimal, but still, he was trying so hard. And besides, his baking was getting better each and every day. Lucky nods.

"You're on."

They walk to Nikolai's cottage on the edge of town, and he regales Lucky with the tales of the luthier on Sixth who's getting very tired of answering guitar questions nearly every day. Still though, he's patient, Lucky learns, and Nikolai has no shortage of thoughts to give him on music.

The farmer on the outskirts of the village has a new litter of kittens. Lucky beams, and Nikolai says he might adopt one once they're ready to leave their mother. He's already visited them once, and practically claimed a little white and orange puffball as his own. He says he wants to name it Creampuff. Lucky smiles.

Nikolai thinks the bakery regulars are starting to finally warm up to him. He knows he's a bit abrasive, and has a threatening air about him. He says he doesn't quite know why, and Lucky refuses to comment. He's making progress, and the more they taste his cooking, the better his relationships are getting. Lucky's glad he's starting to fit in.

"So anyway, the girl trips over herself, drops a coin in my guitar case and runs off as fast as possible. The mom smiles at me, like, almost apologizing. Made my day," he finishes his story, and they reach his front door. He pulls out his keys and jams them in the lock, and the hinges squeak open much like the unloved temple doors. "I'll have to oil that," he says. "I also need to get a new lock. Blacksmith on Angel's Avenue says he's got plenty, but I can't trust that guy as far as I can throw him." Lucky laughs and nods. "And that isn't more than a couple of yards," Nikolai makes a final amendment, and Lucky laughs harder, while Nick simply smiles.

"I bet you throw like a child," he says, and Nikolai mocks indignance, holding a hand over his heart as he lets the blond inside.

"I am pained, Lucky. How dare you, in my own house," he says. "To be called a child by an actual child. A new low." Lucky laughs loudly and Nikolai joins in, locking the door up behind him. It used to bother Lucky how paranoid Nick was about keeping his doors and windows closed and latched, but he supposed he couldn't fault the man for being protective. Heavens know how many times Lucky went feral protecting his things when he lived on the streets.

"I believe I was promised bread," he comments, and Nikolai rolls his eyes, smiling.

"That's all I am to you. I'm just the bread boy. All Nick is good for is bread," he says, but he moves towards the kitchen anyway, starting up the fire under the kettle and grabbing a basket off his countertop. He stands right in front of the fire, as always.

"Precisely," Lucky agrees, and Nikolai snorts.

"Big word," he says.

"Big words for only the most intelligent man," Lucky retorts. Nikolai drops the basket on the table, and Lucky hangs up his white coat on the doorknob. He settles into a chair and it creaks just slightly. Maybe he'll have to pull some strings to get Nick a better setup. But that's a thought for another time.

"Humble, as well," he comments with a snide smile. "How is whatever it is you do with your day going, Lucky?" Nikolai asks. Lucky laughs, propping his feet up on the chair opposite him.

"Perfectly. Irritating the common folk, disrupting natural order. As I'm meant to," he answers.

"Good to hear," Nikolai says. "Are you ever gonna tell me in what ways you disrupt order?" Lucky pretends to consider, but shakes his head in the end.

"I'm just too cool and mysterious." Nikolai laughs, and sets out cups on the table, dropping sugar cubes into Lucky's. He pours out the tea and Lucky gets a bit too close to it, because it's warmer than the actual house, that's for sure. "Wasting more sugar on me?" he says, and Nick shrugs.

"Children love that, right?" Lucky smiles and shakes his head.

"No, but seriously. That's expensive. It's gotta add up, right? You don't even use it yourself." A soft grin spreads across Nikolai's face and he stirs his tea absently with a small spoon.

"Always worth it for you, Lucky." Lucky's face brightens. "Aww, Lucky's flustered." Lucky shakes his head decisively.

"You can't just say that."

"Say what?" Nikolai asks.

"That—you just say those things sometimes. You can't just do that." *And pretend it doesn't mean everything. It's not the world.*

"Say that you're worth it?" he asks, rubbing salt in the wound, and Lucky looks away. "Lucky, I can always say you're worth it. I mean it, you know. I'd spend my last silver keeping you happy." Lucky shakes his head.

"No. I can take care of myself."

"But should you?" Nikolai asks, and Lucky pauses.

"What?"

"Should you?" he asks again, setting down his spoon. "You don't have to do that. You're young, you've got a life ahead of you. You don't need to fend for yourself." Lucky stares at the man blankly, and he takes in a breath. "All I mean is, I'm here for you. Right? We're here for each other. Friends." *Brothers*, Lucky amends.

"Right," is all he says in return. He raises his tea to his lips, just as he feels something pricking at the corners of his eyes, and turns away slightly.

"Lucky?" Nikolai pipes up with concern lacing his voice. "If I genuinely upset you, I'm sorry," he says, and Lucky shakes his head.

"No. No, it's not you. It's fine," he mutters. When he blinks, he reopens his eyes to see the room darkening, and takes in a deep breath. When he opens them again, it's alright. He takes a sip of his tea to calm himself down. It burns his tongue, but he tries not to flinch.

"Well," Nikolai starts, something cautious in his demeanor— like approaching a caged predator. "I hope you know at least that I appreciate you. You were my first friend here. Maybe my best one," he says, and Lucky presses his lips into a line. "And it might be too soon," *oh no*, "and you don't have to say it back..." *oh gods*, "but I really do love you like family. It's like I've known you forever."

A tear drips off Lucky's cheek onto the table, and everything in the house stills. Lucky doesn't dare to breathe, let alone look Nick in the eyes. He stares at the window, shut over with heavy blinds, and imagines he can see what goes on outside. Nothing stirs inside, and Lucky can feel Nikolai's eyes on him.

The only thing he says is, "What?" Lucky doesn't move.

The first rule of approaching a wounded animal is to make no sudden movements. Nikolai stands up very slowly from his chair with his hands raised in front of him in a placating gesture, keeping his eyes on Lucky the whole time. When he comes to the boy's side of the table, he crouches down, and stares at the little pool of mercury with glassy eyes, inspecting every last drop. Lucky knows he's by his side, but he doesn't take his gaze off the window for a single second.

"... Lucky?" Nikolai says cautiously. Lucky wrings his hands in his lap. "Lucky, what is this?" he asks, and Lucky shakes his head, as if that could stop the questioning. "Look at me," Nikolai demands, and Lucky shakes his head again, refusing to turn around.

Nick grabs his shoulders and spins him around to face him, and Lucky shuts his eyes tight, but Nikolai can already see the drops of silver down his shirt, and falling into the wells on his face.

Lucky searches for an explanation, but can't find anything that could possibly make sense to a human. So instead, he sighs, and opens his eyes, and Nick blanches. He's met with a familiar world of black and grey, but even still, he can see what little color he has left draining from Nick's face as he meets his gaze. And he can recognize something he remembers so clearly—fear. The same visceral fear he'd felt the first time Nikolai himself had stared at him with those spheres of pure gold.

"I can explain," he says in a hushed tone. He drops his gaze to the floor and scuffs his shoes over the wood. Nikolai stands and backs away, and Lucky opens his mouth, holding out his hands in front of him shyly. "Wait, Nikolai, please—" He looks even more terrified.

"Nikolai?" he asks, and Lucky curses himself. Nikolai braces himself, holding onto the kitchen counters for dear life, staring at Lucky.

"Please, Nicky, I can explain, just sit down. Please," he says.

Nikolai shakes his head, and tries to press himself further into the counter.

"What is this?" he asks. "This is a trick. What are you?" A pang of hurt goes through Lucky's chest. He bites his lip, and does something he never wanted to have to do.

"Nikolai, *sit down.*"

He moves to the chair immediately, and Lucky looks at him with an apologetic smile as he seems to process what just happened, gears turning behind his eyes.

"You—"

"Please! Just let me speak!" he exclaims, and Nick shuts his mouth. Lucky searches his mind for a way to begin the conversation, but he's learned over time that actions speak louder than words.

He feels his wings break free from his skin, and the room brightens as they stretch out towards the walls, curling in on themselves to accommodate the small area. Nikolai's mouth drops open, and he mutters one word.

"God..." Lucky smiles uncomfortably.

"Surprise?" he says, and Nikolai is silent for a long moment. His eyes search everything about Lucky—from the white in his hair to the shining threads of his far too pristinely white clothing, and finally circling back to his eyes, now losing their silvery tint and returning Lucky's color vision.

"Holy shit..." he finally says. Lucky can't help it; he laughs. Something seems to dawn on Nick at that moment. "Holy shit," he says again. "Holy shit! Wait—wait, I'm. Oh, I'm sorry."

"Why?" Lucky asks. Nikolai shakes his head in disbelief and his breathing quickens.

"I've been so rude—so informal. I'm sorry, Lord. I didn't know!" he says, and Lucky smiles sadly.

"That was kinda the point," he admits. Nikolai stares at him for another beat of silence.

"I'm sorry."

"Don't be."

"I have to be, right?" Lucky tilts his head.

"Why?" he asks again.

"You're God," he deadpans, and Lucky laughs.

"I'm Lucky," he says, and for the first time, he realizes it might be true. Maybe after everything, "I'm still Lucky."

LUCKY PULLS HIS WINGS BACK IN WHEN HE COMES IN THROUGH his bedroom window. They deserve a bit of rest—as does he.

As he stretches out his arms above his head, he closes his eyes and turns around to face his bed.

"Tired?" He opens his eyes immediately. Elric is sitting on his bed with a cup of tea in his hands, smiling at him. Lucky opens and closes his mouth before choosing to stay silent. Elric extends a wing, which Lucky knows is an invitation to sit by him—he's a very cuddly person—but he stays still. Elric doesn't seem to mind. "How is he?" he asks, and Lucky scowls.

"Go away." Elric frowns and tilts his head to the side, looking at him with pleading eyes. Lucky sighs and crosses his arms across his chest. "He's... different."

"Oh?" Elric replies. Lucky nods.

"Yes. He's like a new person." Elric pats the space next to him on the bed, and this time Lucky gives in. He sits next to him, and the god puts an arm around his shoulder, pulling him in close. It feels a lot like Nikolai's hugs.

Lucky moves away.

"Well, I'd hope so," Elric says with a hint of sadness on his tone, and though Lucky knows that he could never have allowed Nikolai to continue the way he was, the assertion that changing him is for the better still makes Lucky scowl.

Even after everything—all the pain, and the nightmares, and the manipulation, and hurt—Lucky scowls.

"Of course you would," he says. Elric looks at him for a moment, searching his face.

"Not like that, Lucas." Lucky grimaces, and his frown deepens. For once, Elric seems to have the good sense to back off. "Lucky," he amends. He takes a breath. "I just mean that I hope he's happier now." Lucky raises a brow, and Elric presses his lips together into a line, and all at once, he understands. His gaze softens, even if only slightly.

"It's not your fault, you know," he says. Elric looks surprised.

"He said—"

"Yeah," Lucky interrupts, "you think I don't know what he said? I was the first one he said it to. You know it's all lies, right?" Elric doesn't make a sound, and Lucky curses his luck internally that he should be tasked with holding this man's hand. "You'd think you'd develop a hint of common sense after hundreds of thousands of years," he mutters. "Maybe a healthy coping mechanism or two." The scratches on his arms from the nights before and the hunk of metal in place of his hand call him a kettle, but he doesn't acknowledge it.

"I have plenty of common sense," Elric rebuts, and Lucky laughs. He laughs for real, for the first time in a long time.

"Right," he agrees with sarcasm palpable. "Maybe contact that common sense of yours to get it through your thick skull that your kid was a maniac, yeah?" he says. He sees dark splotches of green melting into the god's eyes, but he holds his ground. He won't be intimidated, consciously or otherwise, by another god again. "Come on, Elric, you think he wasn't above lying about his intentions? It's not your fault. It's not anyone's fault but his, and you're gonna get nowhere if you keep pretending it is. Stop living this stupid fantasy."

It's quiet in the room.

Lucky looks around to avoid the god's eyes as his words sink in, and he takes in, not for the first time, the vines climbing up his walls. Elric's own creation, he has to assume—did he think it would be better for Lucky to live in the reclaimed wilderness, or was it always like this?

Had this been the Siren's room before? Would it have been Finnigan's later, or Leo's room years ago?

He feels the god's wing wrap around him, and this time, he doesn't retract. He sits still, waiting.

"I think you just might be right," Elric says, almost too low to be heard, but just enough that Lucky can grant himself a little peace of mind.

"I'm always right," he retorts. Elric's arm comes next, back around his shoulder. He doesn't acknowledge him. He also doesn't leave.

It doesn't matter, he thinks.

He can see traces of each of them scattered around the room —maybe he looks too hard for them, but he can all the same.

It doesn't matter, he thinks, if this world wasn't made for him. If the Angel made this earth for the Siren, and the castle in the sky, and Lucky's own bedroom, alike, it wouldn't matter. It's Lucky's now.

Maybe, for once, he has control of his own fate.

It's wishful thinking, but still, it almost makes him smile.

18

"Stop doing that," Lucky grumbles. Honora keeps picking at her nails idly, a book in hand. "Nora, stop that," he says again, and the goddess looks up.

"I have anxiety," she excuses, and Lucky frowns.

"Gods can have anxiety?" he questions. Nora levels him with a deadpan stare, looking him up and down and raising a brow. Lucky puts two and two together. "Point taken," he mumbles. Nora continues picking at her nails, and the sound very nearly drives Lucky insane. He takes a deep drink of his tea and burns his tongue but can't find it in him to care.

Nora flips a page in her book.

The clock on the wall ticks a mechanical sound.

Lucky throws his head back against the back of his armchair.

"I'm bored," he says to no one in particular. Nora huffs.

"Congratulations," she deadpans. Lucky looks back up at her to see her still staring at the book, concealing a small smirk, and he groans.

"When is Elric coming back?" he asks, and Honora shrugs.

"Don't know. What, you missin' Dad already?" The color drains from Lucky's face and he scowls, looking away. Nora almost seems remorseful. "Wait—or, sorry." Lucky cringes when his voice comes out closer to a whisper.

"It's fine," he says. Honora shakes her head.

"It's not, I should—"

"I said it's *fine*," Lucky interrupts, and Nora shuts up. "Let it go," he says. "You don't get to bring me back here against my will then talk over me for the rest of eternity." Lucky levels him with a glare. "I have the same power as you." As Nikolai. Honora nods quietly, and goes back to her book.

Lucky's won, but the victory feels hollow. He sits back in his chair and counts down the seconds. Nikolai used to lord his power over people's heads, too. The realization brings him no comfort. When he meets Nora's eyes again, he can tell she's figured the same thing, and gives him a sad smile, which Lucky looks away from immediately.

"You didn't try," she says. Lucky scoffs.

"He didn't either." Honora doesn't reply, but Lucky can still feel her eyes on his back. He sighs, and drops his voice low, almost unnoticeable. "Do you ever miss it?" he asks. Nora hears.

"Miss what?" Lucky waves his arm around in a vague circular motion.

"Human. Being human," he says. "Do you ever miss it?" Honora looks at him with an unreadable emotion for a moment, before closing her book, and setting it down on a side table. She gives Lucky her full attention.

"I used to," she says. "A lot. The first couple months I went back down there every day, just to see."

"And now?" Lucky pries. She shrugs.

"And I still do. Not as much, but it's there," she admits. "It's been a couple hundred years since I last knew what it felt like to be mortal. It fades over time." Lucky scowls. "I know what you're thinking—" Honora says before Lucky can let his train of thought run wild, "but it's not that bad. You get used to it. You're always gonna feel that little bit of longing, but it goes."

Nora smiles. "I think it makes us better; to know what it's like, that is. We can care for them more than they can." Despite himself, Lucky smiles.

"You really believe that?" he asks, and Honora nods.

"I am a mortal supremacist," she jokes, "through and through." Lucky laughs at this, and Nora joins him with a small chuckle, which Lucky knows means she's hysterical. It's very hard to gauge the goddess's emotions, but Lucky's learned a few cheat codes. The smallest smile means you've resonated with her, and that's enough. "Can I ask you a question, then?" Lucky nods.

"Shoot."

"Do you forgive him?" Lucky freezes. "You don't have to answer," Honora amends. "Not if you don't want to." Lucky takes in a deep breath and looks around for a moment, maybe for an escape. After a second, he nods.

"I've... accepted he is who he is. I'm fine with what happened. It can't be changed now, I just want to move forward. He would, too," he finishes. Honora looks at him with skepticism, before saying:

"You know, acceptance is not forgiveness." Lucky stares. "I was in your place, too, once. Street kid picked up into divinity— it's hard. I didn't forgive Nikolai and Elric for a while, and I don't ask you to either. Least of all me." When Lucky is quiet, Nora continues with caution. "Lucky, if you let acceptance be equal to forgiveness, you can let people get away with a lot. It's okay to accept something and still wish it hadn't happened."

And there it is. The question.

Honora wants to know if Lucky forgives Nikolai, sure, but most of all, she wants to know if it's possible to forgive them. There's a veiled request under her words that reads *'Please tell me you don't wish you weren't here.'*

And the same way as Lucky could see his opening when he'd first met Honora to get the answers to his questions, he can see it now: Honora's asking if he'd rather be mortal again. She's asking him, dark as it is, if he'd rather die, and doing it in complete sincerity.

Lucky sees his exit—if he wanted to, right now, he could give his answer and let the gods blow him back to kingdom come and never have to deal with this again.

He can almost see it now. He can almost hear his own voice in his mind.

"Do it Nora, Nora—kill me."

He shakes it away.

If he wanted to, he could tell Nora that he wishes he hadn't met Nikolai, and he knows she'll get the message. The goddess is smart enough—she's a damned master strategist and goddess of combat—she'd understand what Lucky really meant to say.

Lucky would like to say he didn't even consider it. Lucky would like to say that he answered without hesitation that *yes, he wanted to live.*

But Lucky knows when he lies.

So he considers.

He thinks about whether it would be easier to abandon this plane and let the broken family deal with their broken son without his intervention. He wonders if maybe he'll be more trouble than he's worth existing in this world, or if maybe the humans could live with two gods instead of three.

He wonders. To die, to sleep, to dream, and to fall away and forget about the past that claws into his mind every waking moment, and the night terrors that plague his sleep.

And that's the question, isn't it? In the eternal sleep of his final death, would Lucky have sweet dreams, finally? Or would he continue to suffer the laughter echoing in the back of his mind each and every night? Would Lucky be able to finally sleep peacefully, or would he drag through the terror inflicted upon him day after day and this time not have Elric's waiting embrace to comfort him when he wakes?

He'd like to say that he didn't even consider the option, just as he'd like to say that never in his life had he stood at the edge of a cliff and wondered what it would be like to jump, and just as he'd like to say that never would he long for eternal sleep—not death nor life, simply ceasing.

But he does. He considers for a longer moment than he wishes he needed to, pondering over every option, because here it is: a choice.

Where Lucky stands, two paths diverge. To tell Honora he cannot forgive, and get his peace once and for all, or to tell her that he's ready to guide humankind from the top.

Lucky chooses his words carefully.

"I... I don't forgive him," he says, "not yet. At the same time, I don't wish I'd never found him." Honora raises a brow, and Lucky looks down sheepishly. "Despite everything, I still love that psychotic mad man," he says. "He won't be absolved any time soon, but... he's still my family." There's silence for a moment in the room as Honora nods, and a meek smile graces her lips which she tries to hide, and Lucky understands she's gotten the message.

After a bit, she stands up, and approaches Lucky's seat, arms stretched out. Lucky flinches away for just a second, but decides against it, allowing the goddess to wrap him in a hug.

It's nothing like Nikolai's hugs.

Lucky thinks that might be fine.

"I'm gonna head off to bed," she lets out in a soft, quiet voice. "Tell Elric goodnight." She's about to let Lucky go before she speaks again. "And thank you," she says. Lucky smiles softly.

"Nora?" he posits.

"Yes?" Lucky burrows his head into her soft cloak, resting against her heart. He knows Honora melts, but she'll never admit it.

"For the record," he says, "I'm going to wake up." He dances around his meaning carefully. "Tomorrow and the next day, and the one after that. For a long while."

Which Nora knows means *I'll stay. I'll live.*

She hugs him tighter. It's nothing like Nikolai's hugs. Lucky thinks that's fine.

❧ 19 ❧

Nikolai watches the months pass by in childish wonder, as if he'd never seen the seasons change from anything other than a bird's-eye-view.

It's strange, he knows, but he can't help himself from rushing to the window every morning to see the progress on the growth of flowers outside. He goes out into the woods occasionally, comparing the blooms on the ground to the ones inked on his arm—maybe if not to identify them, then at least to see the real thing for what feels like the first time.

He knows that it's childish awe that he shouldn't be entertaining, but each time Lucky—apparently Innocence—returns, he encourages him with bright smiles and wide eyes. He takes Nikolai far away from civilization and grows flowers in the woods with the palm of his hand, and makes the birds in the trees sing along to the sound of Nikolai's guitar. (He's not quite sure how he forces them to chirp—if he thinks about it too long, it's rather grotesque, but they never seem to mind.)

Nikolai can tell that ever since the reveal of Lucky's divinity, their relationship has changed—but he can't have expected it not to. After all, once they were adult and child, and now, god and subject. It's certainly something to get used to. But above all else, Nikolai notices that now even more than before, Lucky looks up to him in some strange way.

They visit more often than not in the temple after service; Nikolai brings his guitar to play, and Lucky brings snacks and stories, and those giant silver wings that Nikolai adores. (A strange fascination, not an *obsession* as Lucky had once so kindly put it. He loved trying to touch the feathers and watching his hand fall through the glow, and marvel at the unbelievableness of it all.)

He knows that Lucky holds his breath each time he speaks, and keeps a careful eye on him at all times when he moves. Lucky still flinches away when he reaches out too fast, but he's let Nikolai hug him more and more, which he'll take as a sign.

Nikolai goes back to the temple each day to meet Innocence, and finds comfort in the familiarity of the way the young god leans onto his shoulder and hums along to his songs. His bright green eyes follow his fingers as he picks out a formless melody and he watches quietly when he tunes the instrument, keeping a careful eye on his mouth as he sings as if he expects him to grow fangs.

Nikolai feels something wrong about Lucky. Like in each conversation he's waiting in bated breath for Nikolai to apologize for a past that never happened, and misdeeds he doesn't remember committing. The young god looks at him as if he holds the secrets to the whole world on his mortal shoulders and is waiting for him to finally realize it—as if he were an absolution of the sins of a former life that he just can't pin. Memories are more fallible than fact, and Nikolai's learned never to trust the weaker, so he waits silently. If Innocence has anything to say, he'll hear it eventually.

"And then Dad—or, uh—the Angel, he comes crashing down and his feathers fly everywhere. It was insane. I didn't stop laughing for like, half an hour," Lucky recounts. Nikolai listens quietly, plucking at his strings. Everything Lucky says sounds a lot like a song, and he can't help but add the background music. Nikolai laughs.

"Wonderful," he says, "but you need to sit up." Innocence casts him an indignant glare. His head's been resting in Nikolai's lap for far too long. "Come on, Lucky, I've got pins and needles," he finishes. Lucky scoffs.

"Honestly," he starts, "that doesn't sound like my problem." Nikolai shakes his head and groans.

"Cut me some slack, I am but a fragile human." Lucky makes a face, and when he speaks, Nikolai's voice comes out of Lucky's mouth instead of his own.

"Wah wah, I've got pins and needles." He returns to his own voice, but not before shooting Nikolai a snide smirk at his look of complete befuddlement. "Big deal." Nikolai laughs.

"Where does that come from, anyway?" he asks instead of the several other questions swimming in his mind. "The," he gestures vaguely to his legs, "thing?" Lucky scoffs and sits up.

"Descriptive," he comments, and Nikolai rolls his eyes. "I don't know. Maybe you sat there so long your blood all froze." Lucky gives him a very odd look, slightly raising a brow, as if beckoning Nikolai to respond—like some kind of inside joke he's supposed to understand.

It's uncomfortable.

Nikolai laughs the awkward feeling away. "I don't think that can happen without dying." And as soon as it came, the look melts away, along with the strands of silver that managed to climb up Lucky's eyes (the strangest part of being a god, Nikolai had decided). Lucky smiles without reaching his eyes.

"You'd be surprised," he says grimly. Nikolai can't help but back away just a bit into the wood fiber. He's never scared of Innocence, per se, just unnerved.

"Would I now?" he asks. Lucky nods.

"The human body can withstand a lot of punishment," he continues. "For example..." he trails off, and takes Nikolai's hand.

He presses just his index finger to Nikolai's flesh, and instantly, his palm is alight with pain. He shrieks and pulls away.

"What the—!" he yells, staring at his hand, which dark red spikes have begun to crawl out of. "What was that?" he exclaims, looking back at Lucky, who seems very chuffed with himself.

"Are you dead?" Lucky asks, and Nikolai frantically vacillates his gaze between the young god and his hand, where the spikes have started melting already, streams of blood dripping down his arm.

"What—no?" Lucky nods.

"I told you so!" the boy responds. Nikolai stares at his palm and takes deep breaths. He uses his other hand to cradle it close to his chest. He laughs a hollow airy sound.

"Holy—I would've taken your word for it," he says. He sees Lucky shrug in his periphery.

"I only did it in one place. You're fine." Nikolai cringes. Lucky's index finger isn't that large—only a very small circumference froze up, but even still, Nick could feel his nerves being cut and muscle and tendons being torn through. He can't even begin to imagine the pain that would come with even just the rest of his hand. He lets out an awkward laugh yet again.

"Well, remind me never to get on your bad side," he jokes, and Lucky's face suddenly turns grim.

"Noted."

Nikolai stares at him, and he says no further words. He clutches his hand to his chest and can feel blood seeping into his thin shirt.

Maybe he should've expected Innocence to be just a bit out of touch.

"Right... so, what about the Angel being bad at flying?" Lucky smiles a bright smile and falls back onto Nick's lap with an unceremonious huff.

"You should've seen it, Nick! He refused to walk for a week!" Nikolai laughs along and smiles.

Noted.

❧ 20 ❧

"To my worst nightmare,

Elric said it's easier to speak your mind when there are no witnesses. At least, that's what he'll have me believe. He says it should be therapeutic for me to talk to you without actually... you know... talking to you?

It's stupid, but he says he won't let me out of my room until I have some pages to show for it. I think he was joking, but you can never really tell with him. So, here I am.

Where do I begin?

You've changed a lot since I first met you. Even only after these few years since you've been revived, I can see the weathering of age gracing your features. Subtleties of human nature I never would've noticed that seem so unnerving on your face. In the time I knew you as the Siren—it already feels so many immensities away—I'd watched each day in wonder as you'd return without a pockmark or grey hair to be spoken of. I suppose that can only be on me and my naivety, which I did have a lot of.

I still do, you should be happy to know. Though you won't be. You're not the same man as before.

In some way, I've begun to think you smaller than before. Not physically, of course, you'll always be taller than should be natural, but in a way, you don't take up the same space you used to occupy.

Maybe my mental real estate is no longer plagued by your constant digging around in my brain, but that doesn't feel true.

No, there's something different about your energy. The same dark smile, with sharpened teeth foreboding of something terrible to come, doesn't strike me in the same way as it used to. And your laugh and your voice which used to send shivers down my spine and seem to shake the very earth to its core... it's smaller now. Like something about you has shrunk back.

It's hard to get used to. It's been years now, I know—you think you're twenty-six now, if only you knew—but still, each time I visit, I find myself tensing up when you smile, expecting to see your razor teeth and sinister grin, and the darkness that once lurked behind it all that promised me that you could tear me apart for one step out of line. But you don't. Not anymore. I still try to feud with that fact.

There's a certain nostalgia that comes with hitting rock bottom, I've realized.

The cold, crushing weight of the depths of the sea floor feels safe though you know it's always been anything but.

It drags you in and urges you to pick up a boulder to toss to the side, and swim deeper at the cost of crushing yourself, but you don't care—you never have. There's only the sand at the bottom, and then the rocks below, and then magma and flame that eats you alive but despite everything I need to swim further. I've not met bedrock yet, and the little demon at the back of my mind tells me that I can go past what I've already known.

There's a certain safety that I feel wanting to return to you every single day, and yet, when I reach you finally, it fades away. It's replaced by real safety. Because my brain wants to convince me that familiarity is equal to safety, and what I know of you from my past is the most comfort-able I can ever be. And I know it's a terrible thought to want to return to the worst times of my life, but I know nothing else other than the cold embrace of the stones at the bottom of this ocean of misery that's always been my life—such that I don't know who I am if I'm not suffering anymore.

So every time I see you I hope, distantly, that you'll remember what I am and what you used to be, and we can fall back into the rhythm of old times. And I'll come back to you day after day because it's far from comfortable and so far from safe and endangers my life at every turn, but hell, it's familiar. It's all I can understand.

And I hope that you'll look into my eyes and not see the god you know me to be now but instead the scared child I was those years ago and I still am. Because despite the powers, the mind control, the freezing and boiling, and wrapping up whoever's vocal cords I please into a knot—I'm still Lucky. I'm still the terrified kid that came into your temple ages ago and begged at your feet for forgiveness and in the end? I'm the one that must be forgiving you.

I watch you play your guitar and remember the days where you laced your words with saccharine promises that you'd never fulfill—that you'd love me, that you'd protect me, that I'd always be safe with you. I wish with all I am that I could feel the same hope that I did each time you made one of your terrible vows, because if nothing else, it was something to believe in.

I've run out of things to believe in, now.

Elric's working with me. It's hard. It's the hardest shit I've ever done but he says it gets easier every day.

He's trying to help me, I know he is, but I just can't let him. Something in me wants to hold onto this nostalgia for a past that he says I never should've been made to go through because it's mine. It's the only one of these lifeless things that truly is.

I don't own the Voice, I don't own the powers. I don't own this earth and I certainly don't own the virtues they've ascribed to me—kindness, revival, the Spring. What hogwash.

But my life? My past, my hurt? My 'trauma,' as Elric calls it? That's mine. No one else gets to have that. Especially now that you're not here to remember it.

I suppose it's worse because I know that you, like I once was, are running out of time. It won't wait for you to finish your story. The Storyteller doesn't put down their pen until they say you're ready, and that could be tomorrow, for all we know.

So I watch, and I wait. And I can't quite explain the feeling that comes with waiting for you to remember what I'm truly worth, and waiting for you to understand that this crumbling vignette of peace we've finally reached is fragile.

All it would take is one conversation for you to realize what you used to be, and what my mind still thinks you are. And then we could go back to normal, and you'd shatter fragile things around me but still hold me like I'm porcelain, and one wrong move will break your pretty possession.

All it would take is one little push closer to the edge.

I don't know what I want more.

Anyway, you'll never see this. Gods know I'll never give it to you nor read it nor voice even a fraction of what I've claimed here, so I suppose Elric was right. I guess I do feel a bit better, but the bar is very low, you understand.

I look forward to tea tomorrow. Don't burn the bottoms of the cookies again.

-Lucky."

⚜

"Duel me."

Nikolai stares at Innocence completely dumbfounded as he produces two identical rapiers out of thin air, and tosses one to the mortal, who lets it fall on the grass before him.

"Excuse me?" he responds, bending down to pick up the sword. The weight of it in his hand feels unfamiliar. He twists the hilt around to get a feel for the grip, looking Lucky up and down with suspicion.

"You heard me. Let's duel." He swings his own blade around with agility, his dexterous hands winding around the hilt as it flips around in the air. Nikolai scoffs.

"There is a very clear skill differential here," he says. Lucky shrugs.

"I don't know what that means. Blades up." He raises his sword, but Nikolai shakes his head.

"See, here lies the problem, Lucky—you are a god. There is

no way I am beating you." Lucky presses a hand to his chest in mock offense.

"So just because I'm a god, you think I must be strong? What a stereotype." Nikolai laughs.

"It's a very easy assumption to make," he shoots back, and Lucky slouches, his posture going from battle-ready to slighted child.

"Come on Nikolai, just fight me!" Nikolai groans, adjusting his grip on the handle of the blade.

"If I do, will it shut you up?" Lucky holds his hand to his heart.

"For the rest of eternity," he swears. Nikolai doubts that very much, knowing Lucky, but he capitulates anyway, sighing and raising his blade to meet Lucky's in the middle.

"Fine," he relents. "En garde." Lucky smiles.

"How dare you speak French to me." He swats Nikolai's sword down out of the air, breaking their pre-round truce, and the fight begins. Lucky thrusts the tip of his blade towards Nikolai's now-exposed chest, and is parried away at the very last second before impact as Nikolai scoffs in indignance.

"You want to kill me?" he asks, sidestepping to avoid another blow from the god.

"Of course," he says. Nikolai can't tell if he's joking. "And yet you agreed. What do you get out of this?" Lucky asks, making Nikolai take pause. "I could cast you aside. What do you earn from this unorthodox alliance of doves and crows?" Nikolai scrunches up his nose in thought. He strikes out toward Lucky, who blocks his attack with practiced agility, and a mocking smile on his face.

"Time," he responds finally. Innocence seems thrown off, and hesitates for a moment—just long enough for Nikolai to slide in close and hold his sword to the god's neck with a smile. Lucky pushes him away with a hand to his chest, and brings up his rapier to clash with the mortal's again.

"And what does that mean?" he asks. Nikolai parries his blow away with a sickening metal screech, and he cringes, ready for a long night of sharpening in his cottage.

"The longer I stay," he says, striking out. "The more you complain." Lucky shoves his sword away, dancing around his blows fluidly. Lucky laughs.

"What does that earn you?" he asks with sarcasm on every syllable.

"Your companionship," is Nikolai's first answer. He strikes away Lucky's rapier. "Kindness, when there isn't much in this world to go around." Lucky beats him away. He retreats before reaching out again, and nearly brushing Lucky's arm before he's parried. He smiles, and grabs onto Lucky's outstretched arm, knocking his blade to the ground with a clatter, and pulling the boy in close to look him in the eyes. "A brother," he finishes. Lucky's face goes red. "Do I hear a yield?" Nikolai asks with a smug smile on his face. Lucky grimaces, looking down to the ground.

"I..." Nikolai thinks he's about to capitulate, when: "Never yield." He puts on an impish expression and knees Nikolai in the crotch, laughing and jumping away to pick up his abandoned saber in the dirt.

"Foul play!" Nikolai wheezes, bending over himself. Lucky only cackles louder.

"This is war," he responds in a sing-song voice. Nikolai groans, and stands straight up, albeit with some pain, to see Lucky standing above him with the tip of his foil pointing straight at his head.

Nikolai grabs the end of the rapier, feeling it cut slightly into his palm, and warm blood starts to drip out of his hand. He shoves it away, and straightens his arm to block a coming attack. A metallic clang sounds in the air, and Lucky staggers backward. Nikolai laughs. He must make quite a sight; sword in hand, slightly bent in pain with blood dropping from his hand to the ground.

"Are you okay?" Lucky calls suddenly, his eyes drifting between the mortal's face and his hand. Nikolai laughs.

"The question is," he says. He sweeps out a leg to wrap behind Lucky's knees, sending him falling over onto his back on the grass. Nikolai points his saber to Lucky's neck. "Are you?" Nikolai accidentally touches Lucky's flesh just the slightest bit, seeing silvery ichor beads of blood come out of his throat. He expects it to be handwaved, and pulls his blade away muttering an apology.

Then there's a sudden blinding flash of light like the glow of Betelegeuse, and a swift kick to Nikolai's shin. He drops to the ground and hears heavy, thundering footsteps on the dirt as he looks up to the sky.

"I'm fine!" Lucky says. Nikolai can hear him shuffling around, sitting up. "Really! It was all in good fun!" Nikolai wrinkles his brow in confusion, and sits up, propping himself up on his elbows.

And then he sees it.

Or rather, Her. The goddess, Lady Retribution herself, kneeling beside Lucky and staring at the small drips of silver on his neck with a gaze of pure fire. She reaches up to unclasp a gold hook at her neck, pulling off her blood-red cape and holding it out to Lucky, who stops her with a hand.

"Do not clean up blood with your cloak, I swear," he warns. The goddess sighs with an undertone of anger in the sound, and re-clips it. "I promise," Lucky continues, "I'm fine. He did nothing." Nikolai shrinks back slightly at being addressed, and the goddess snaps her head to him, pinning him with a crimson stare.

"You did this?" she asks Nikolai. The mortal can feel anxiety gripping at his chest, and he sucks in a deep breath between his teeth. He feels like he's going to die. No, he knows he's going to die. He shuts his eyes as the tightness swells in his stomach. He hears a sound of skin on skin, and immediately, the feeling dissipates.

"Don't do that!" Lucky shrieks, pulling his hand away. The goddess sighs. Nikolai almost wants to laugh. *Lucky slapped her.*

"Sorry," she says. "Got carried away."

"It's... alright," Nikolai says in a small voice, the overwhelming aura of doom falling away and allowing him to breathe. "And sorry, Lucky," he amends. Lucky looks caught off guard for a second, before rolling his eyes.

"Don't be. You did nothing." Nikolai nods, swallowing his fear down in his throat. "As I guess you've gathered," he continues, "this is Honora Wood, Lady Retribution," Lucky says in a mocking voice. The goddess scoffs.

"Nora," she directs at Nikolai. "Don't be pretentious." Nikolai nods, a half-smile gracing his lips.

"Pleasure to meet you," he says, and Honora stares at him for a moment, looking him up and down with wary eyes, as if waiting for something. Searching.

"You as well," she says finally. As soon as she arrived, she disappears entirely, leaving only the slightest impression in the dirt from her boot to prove she ever was really there. Lucky lets out a deep breath and shakes his head, crawling to where Nikolai sits on the grass.

"Are you alright?" he asks again, quieter. He takes Nikolai's bleeding hand without waiting for an answer, and studies the red.

"I'm fine," he replies, but Lucky shakes his head. He clasps his hand tightly, and Nikolai whimpers as a silver light encases their hands. When Innocence lets go, the flesh of Nikolai's shallow cuts reaches across and sews itself back up. Nikolai stares at it in awe.

"Thank you," he says, and Lucky nods quietly.

"You ought to be careful," he says, with suddenly glassy eyes. "It heals," he continues, then, softer, "but if it can bleed, it can die."

⚜

"*Nikolai,*

I'd forgotten how fast time moves for mortals. Although, I suppose I never really knew. I've never had this bird's-eye view, and it really does change your perspective.

It's... sad. That's all I can think to write. It's sad. I watch day by day as you grow older and greyer, and your skin begins to wrinkle, and hairs whiten (further than they already have), and I can't help but feel saddened.

It was different, you see, when I was the mortal and you were ever-lasting, because I knew you'd be there my whole life. Now I watch each and every day as you wither away, piece by piece. Though you're still quite young to humans, to me, every step you take feels like it could be your last, and I watch in bated breath on every birthday that passes, waiting for the final cord to be cut.

It goes by too fast. I never realized it when I was in your place, but it's so, so terribly short. It feels not a year has gone by since you were revived in my place, but here you are—what do you think, 30 years old, now? I guess I shouldn't have blinked. Just like that, six years have passed. I've suddenly woken up and you're now nothing like the man you used to be. It's a strange, fickle mistress, time is. It waits for no one.

Elric and Nora—they like to think it pauses for them, but I can see it. I can see in their eyes the slightest indications that they've lived as long a life as they have. When they walk by the mirror and grimace as if they can't recognize themselves, or when the light hits their eyes just right and you can see the little spots of darkness dancing in their irises. They'll swear nothing's changed, but time waits for no one. Not even gods. Every new scar on their skin bears the marks of too long a life, and every little imperfection branded onto their countenance sends something akin to pride blooming in my chest. It's almost as if I can say 'Look, look, you're fallible, too!'

They forget that sometimes.

Well, Elric forgets it. Honora understands. She wears the slight greying of her eyes like a badge of honor.

Sometimes it feels wrong that I can't age. At least not at the same rate. I'll have hundreds of years before I have a wrinkled lip or cold outlook on the world to show for it, or even nearly half as many scars as Nora can boast.

From time to time, accidents happen, and I'll stare at the shards of broken glass on the floor as if they hold the secrets to the world.

If the marks on our flesh are all we can ever earn to show we've truly lived a life and not been trapped in a protective bubble, then it shouldn't be too much to ask... To pick up the shards, one by one, and to cut the marks of time out of myself. It wouldn't hurt too much, right?

Nora catches me in those moments. She pretends she doesn't know what I'd considered, but I can see it in her saddened eyes each time that she understands—that, hell, maybe she'd thought about it herself.

I know she's not as weak as I am but it soothes the hurt.

In any case, uh, this isn't about me. It's about you. You're finally aging. Time's caught up with you. I'll visit later today with some honey and a fruit basket in hand, I think. You never did care for material possessions so much as experiences. I'll show you what I learned on the guitar. I'm sure you'll be proud.

The old you might've been, too.

Happy birthday, Nick.

-Lucky"

"LUCKY, YOU CAME!" LUCKY SMILES A BRIGHT SMILE AND shoves a box into Nikolai's hands, pushing past him into the much warmer cottage.

"'Course. Anything for big brother Nicky," he mocks. Nikolai crosses his arms over his chest and huffs.

"Don't say that, I will cry," he says, wrapping the god into a hug regardless. Lucky melts into his arms, and he smiles. His hair smells like vanilla. The scent would be pleasant if it weren't for the fact... "That's my soap." Lucky wriggles out of his grasp.

"Oops, can't hear you," he says, dropping himself onto a kitchen chair dramatically. Nikolai rolls his eyes and goes to sit with him. "Open it," he insists, gesturing at the box in Nikolai's hands. "You wouldn't reject a Triad's Day gift from your own god, would you?" he says with a mock pout on his face. Nikolai laughs.

"Of course not." He pulls at the brown paper wrapped around the box and rips it off easily. He pulls off the lid of the box to find "Rocks?" Lucky nods.

"You were bad this year. We can't reward that behavior." Nikolai scoffs and Lucky lets out his signature cackling laugh before pulling a smaller, more neatly wrapped rectangle shape out of his pocket, and passing it to Nikolai, who sighs. "Kidding. Take this."

Nikolai repeats the process. Only this time when he takes off the top, he sees something different. A golden chain with a bright sapphire pendant, glimmering in the low candlelight of his kitchen. He stares at it blankly, and sucks in a sharp breath through his teeth. He looks up to Lucky, whose face has gone a dusty pink.

"Lucky..." he mutters under his breath. Lucky shakes his head.

"Don't use that tone with me." Nikolai smiles brightly, with the slightest feeling of a tear on his cheek. He wipes it away.

"Aw, Lucky!" he exclaims, rounding the table to hug the boy again. Lucky pushes him away, face now thoroughly red. "That's so cute, Lucky!"

"I'm not cute!" Lucky shrieks, and Nikolai laughs.

"Fine, fine," he says. He clasps the pendant around his neck and smiles at the weight. Like a physical reminder he is loved.

Or at least, he hopes Lucky loves him the same way he does.

"I had something for you, too," he says lowly. Lucky looks up.

"You don't need to do that," he says, and Nikolai waves his hand.

"Sure I do," he says. He turns away and walks into his room, hearing the god's sounds of protest behind him. He grabs the fabric off his bed, and holds it behind his back as he comes back out into the kitchen. "It's far less extravagant," he says, "but it's something." Lucky's eyes widen as he presents a fuzzy brown cloak like his own. "We can match," he says.

Silver liquid drops off Lucky's face, and Nikolai smiles.

ॐ

"NICK,

Another year, another letter. I don't know when it started to feel like a sin to not write to you, even if you'll never see it. Regardless, here I am.

You're, what, 36? Give or take a couple millennia? It's been a long time since your revival. Or, I suppose, your fall from grace and outcasting from the heavens.

Sorry about that. I can't help but feel a little sense of responsibility. Maybe if you'd never met me, you'd still have your life now, and your family, and your powers... Elric says it's not my fault at all. He says it was fated.

I don't believe in fate, because if it was real, why would it do this to us? Just to watch us get attached, to keep seeing us feeding our little delusions that we can love, and be regarded as flawed as we are but be loved regardless? That's the dream, isn't it?

You asked me once, as I stared up at the sky, what I was thinking, and I couldn't give you a real answer. Shooting stars dashed across the expanse of empty space, and in their sparkling trails, I could see your old eyes staring down at me asking me the real questions of this life.

Who are you? Who are we? Why does it have to be this way? What have we done to each other?

I know I should stop dwelling on it, because the god I used to know is gone, and he can't hurt me anymore—but there you are with your arms open wide, wearing his face and his same smile and those brown eyes speckled with gold that I used to fear, and I just have to believe you're him, even if you never will be again.

Somehow I always manage to make these letters depressing. I don't know why. I've been doing fairly well these days, I think. Ordinary things have begun to make me so happy, just lately. They're... good distractions, if nothing else. Elric takes me out flying a lot. Honora never comes with—she seems more preoccupied with scanning through every last inch of the library archives for the millionth time over. I don't know why she does it anymore.

Healing isn't a linear process—that's what Elric says. He says I need to be less hard on myself, but there's a little voice at the back of my head that keeps telling me that it was all my fault, and maybe I'd deserved it. He tells me that your 'abuse' wasn't love, but if it wasn't, then what is?

You said you loved me. I didn't think you could lie.

I don't have much left to convince me that love was real, but there are some things. I have the scars from those... blades of blood that you always gave me. My arms are pocked and peppered with them, and now that my blood is the same shade of mercury as my tears, the skin around the wounds has greyed.

I have the gashes and cuts from all the times I'd do something wrong, and you'd break glass and shatter windows and not care if I was in the path of the shards.

And this stupid fucking hand.

The metal taunts me. I shouldn't have this. I should have a stub of an arm with no dexterity because I'm the one that did this to myself. Why did they replace it? It's one of the only things I have. I deserved this—this is because you loved me.

Yesterday I considered it again. Honora walked in on me pulling at it, and digging my nails into the metal vines plunged into my flesh, trying to tear the prosthetic away. I didn't get very close. It barely even started bleeding before she came into my room and caught me. I only got one wire out. It hurt like hell, but I wanted it gone, so, so bad. It was like a piece of me was a mirage. It's not like how the Voices were when you were still the Siren—this voice I know is entirely my own. I just don't know why it tells me to do this.

I pick up glass, and I stare at fire, and I pull at the prosthetic trying to rip it off myself and see my mangled, bloody flesh for what it is instead of the pretty picture Elric's painted.

He calls them intrusive thoughts.

He told me the first time when I was cutting apples for lunch. I said,

"Ever just have that little urge to cut your finger off?" and he stared at me like I'd said something crazy.

I guess I had.

So I try to keep that in mind.

I've picked up some hobbies to distract myself. Sewing, crochet, painting. I'm not good at it, but Elric taught me impressionism.

It never stops that little voice from saying 'Hey, that needle would fit perfectly in your eye socket!' but it's a start.

I guess above everything else, I should say that I miss you. A lot. I see you nearly every day, and we sit down and have tea and talk about life, and you tell me little stories, and your captivating words make perfect vivid images. But you're not the same. You can't be. Something in me is still trying to believe that, you know?

Elric says the Siren was bad for me. I believe him. I know I believe him because what he calls nightmares I call 'memories,' but I can't help myself from missing you as you once were. I know you loved me. You were bad for me. You never thought I could do anything right. You were violent and you were manipulative and you hurt me and broke things and took out your anger on whatever living thing was closest, but you loved me. It was you and me, until the end.

Wasn't it?

Happy twelve years.

-Lucky"

⚜

NIKOLAI WATCHES LUCKY WITH WARY EYES AS HE SWIRLS HIS tea around the cup with a grim expression plastered on his face. He stares.

Lucky's been different lately. He hasn't changed at all—he's young and vibrant as ever. Each year while Nikolai's skin grows pocked and his face wrinkled, laden with the struggles of life, Lucky only becomes more youthful, and, lately, his smile, more dark.

He pulls at his sleeves—a nervous tic he's developed over the past years—and watches the god like a hawk. Innocence says nothing, gears turning behind those bright eyes of his.

Nikolai takes notice of a small cut on his cheek, just below his eye. It's healed over and will disappear soon enough, his silvery blood bringing a grey flush to the wound. It looks unnervingly straight and precise. Nikolai wants to know where it came from, but he holds his tongue.

"Do you want more sugar?" he asks. Lucky shakes his head, and Nikolai narrows his eyes, looking the boy over. "What's going on?"

"It's nothing," Lucky bites out with a particularly sharp, scathing tone. Nick frowns and opens his mouth to ask again, but is cut off before he can even form a single syllable. "It's fine. Stop prying," Lucky says. Nikolai sits back in his chair and nods, taking a long drink from his tea.

He looks around. It doesn't feel right for the cottage to have become dusty with time, and his face wrinkled and hair greyed, then to look at Lucky and still see a young teen in place of a man.

Then Nikolai spots it.

A slight flickering on the wall drags his attention away from the worn paint of the house, back behind him towards the kitchen counter.

There, out of the way and almost unnoticeable to anyone who wouldn't care to look, sits a small flickering candle, burning low but bright. Nikolai blanches. In twenty years, he's never forgotten to blow out his candles before Lucky came. He's been diligent, standing in front of the fire, blocking the god's view when he cooks. He's put out all the fire in the house and sat with only the natural light of the windows in every conversation—he's never slipped up.

He stands quickly.

He approaches the flame, licks his finger, and is about to snuff it out, when:

"Don't," Lucky snaps. Nikolai stares at him.

"If it's the fire, I can—"

"I said, *don't*." Nikolai feels the loss of control take him over and moves to sit back down at the table. Lucky never gives him commands. He must be serious.

"Okay, okay—I won't. But's if it's really bothering you..." He doesn't finish his sentence. When he turns back to meet Lucky's eyes, the god's irises are a pool of pure silver and his pupils have faded away. Nikolai takes in a sharp breath and nods resolutely. "Right."

Lucky stands. Nikolai stares.

Lucky walks to the candle and picks it up, staring at the flame with such intensity Nikolai would think it killed his whole family and then some.

"You always loved fire," Lucky says. Nikolai tilts his head, as if beckoning him to continue, but he doesn't say another word.

"I... not especially, I don't," he mutters. Lucky doesn't look at him.

"You loved it—you loved it, you thought it could solve your problems. Nikolai, can it solve your problems?"

"I don't know what you mean Lucky, are you alright?" Nikolai tries, and Lucky chuckles.

"It's the only thing you never used against me," he says with a hint of sadness tainting his voice. "It's the only one that didn't leave a mark." Lucky stares down at his exposed arm, and Nikolai's face pales.

"Lucky, what are you doing?" he asks. He wants to stand up and pull him away but Lucky's command is still in control. "Lucky—Lucky, stop, what's going on?" Lucky smiles a wry smile and presses the flame to his skin, and Nikolai shrieks. "Lucky!" he yells, trying to will himself to stand. "Lucky, stop!"

Lucky continues to smile, though silver hits his cheeks. Nikolai can only hope that a drop will fall from his eye and kill the flame for him.

He never wondered what burning flesh smells like, nor did he ever want to find out.

There's a bright, blinding flash of green in Nikolai's vision, and he shuts his eyes tight.

"Lucky!" a voice yells. It sounds familiar. So familiar—like he'd known this voice all his life—he just can't place it. He can almost hear something in the back of his head.

Just remember that.

What is he supposed to know?

"Lucky, what are you doing?" the voice yells. Nikolai opens his eyes to find not one, but two gods standing in his kitchen. Clad in dark robes with giant feathered wings curled up behind him is the figure of the Angel of Dawn.

In Nikolai's house.

He just can't catch a break.

"Go away!" Lucky shoots back. His voice wavers as he raises it. The familiar voice returns—why does the Angel sound so much like home?

"Lucky, put it down!" The Angel rips the candle out of Innocence's hands and blows it out. He takes the god's arm and studies it intently, and from the little opening Nikolai has to see from where he sits, the sight is grim. There's no better way to put it—Lucky's melted. "What were you thinking?" the Angel practically yells. Lucky flinches, and Nikolai has to fight the urge to stand and hug him and comfort him and push the Angel away for scaring him, because isn't that his dad? The Angel sees his mistake and wraps his arms around Lucky, who relaxes just a bit. "Don't ever do that again, what the hell was that?" Silver tears stain the Angel's robe.

"It's the only thing I have Elric," Lucky cries. Elric? "It's all I have left of him, please," he mutters. *"Please."*

Nikolai starts to connect dots.

He remembers from thirteen years ago when he first became friends with Innocence that he'd picked up the telltale signs of abuse. Lucky said it was his brother. His brother is gone.

It's all I have left of him.

"Lucky, Lucky, honey—we've talked about these thoughts.

Please, don't scare me like that." Lucky breaks down sobbing, burying his face in the Angel's robes, head on his shoulder, gripping the fabric on his back with a clutch like steel.

He looks more human than ever.

It makes Nikolai sick.

He looks like a terrified child. Not the same kind of terrified that was scared to hug Nikolai a decade ago, or the terrified that didn't say a word when he first saw him play guitar—this terrified child meant something. Something Nikolai couldn't possibly dream of understanding. It speaks of a lifetime of abuse and pain that Nikolai can't stand to see. Heavens help Lucky's brother if he's still alive—he won't be for long once Nikolai gets to him.

"I just can't do it, Elric," Lucky says, voice watery. Nikolai's heart aches. "They just keep talking."

"It's okay. It's okay, Honey. It's alright, Sunshine. We can work through it," the Angel continues. "They'll get quieter. With time." Innocence shakes his head. Nikolai suddenly realizes he hasn't been breathing for a few seconds watching the interaction.

"They won't," he denies. The Angel pats his hair.

"There's a light at the end of the tunnel. I know you can't see it yet, but there is." Lucky's quiet for a moment, and his next sentence breaks Nikolai's heart into thousands more pieces. He can't put them back together.

"And what if the light at the end is dimmer than the one I entered through?"

Everyone is silent.

"Lucky..." Nikolai finally speaks. The Angel seems to only register his existence at that moment. He shoots him a wry smile that doesn't meet his eyes.

"It will be alright, Nicky."

"Is he...?" Lucky doesn't say a word. He cries quietly into the Angel's shoulder. The Angel looks down at the god, who looks more like a boy than a deity, and nods.

"He will be," he says.

There's another bright flash, and the goddess appears in the room, stoic and stony, taking in her surroundings. The Angel nods at her, speaking silently, and a grim look passes through their eyes. The Angel looks at him, and, with a soft, kind smile on his face, says:

"Nikolai, I think we need to have a conversation."

❧

"*NICKY,*

So.

They told you.

They told you everything.

I didn't get to be there. It's... understandable. I freaked out enough already—Elric says I've earned a bit of rest, for my mind more than my body. He's practically quarantined me in my room so that I can't harm myself again.

It also means I can't come visit you, but I guess that's the price to pay for safety.

So, they told you everything, I guess. It's all out in the open.

They say you didn't take it too kindly. I don't blame you. Just days ago you had a kid you loved like a brother that you'd never harm, and then the very next day...

They found you on the roofs earlier. That's what Honora says.

They found you on the roof, doing what I did too many times when you were the Siren.

Every man who's ever looked off the edge of a building has felt that strange instinct, and just wondered what it would be like to jump.

People like me and you think about it a lot more.

Honora says they found you on the roof looking out at the sunset and thinking hard. I'm trying to pretend I don't know why you were there.

Nikolai—I don't need any more blood on my hands. Neither of us do. I don't want yours on my hands, and I can't let you go back to who you once were. I know I'll never say it to you when I finally get to see you again, but I need to say it now. It's been tearing me apart against every-thing else because I know how it feels, Nicky.

Don't jump.

You can't.

I know, I know, which one of us wants to be the pot, and which, the kettle? but I need you to understand—you can't leave me. We can't leave each other.

Against all odds, we found each other. You're my brother, Nicky. You always were. Even when you were the Siren, you still were, you just lost your way.

That's what we've all done, isn't it? All these tragic missteps and bumps along the way—we're all fucking lost. None of us know what we're doing and we pretend we do because it makes us feel powerful, but Nikolai, I think you've always known that you're lost. Before Finny, before Serena, before Leo and Honora, and before me, you knew it all along. This has all been your sick and twisted way of giving yourself purpose, and you know what? I can't forgive you for all you did to me, but I can't blame you either, because I know how it feels.

I know exactly what went through your head looking at that drop from the roof to the ground, Nicky. I know because I've thought about it, too.

I have this feeling that even if Nora hadn't found you, you'd still have come down. Because we're saps. We're sorry saps that need each other, and you know that. We have to make a choice, Nikolai. We've both made the choice at least once, and we're gonna keep doing it again and again and again because that's how we are.

It doesn't get easier. It never gets easier, and when that voice at the back of your head asks if you're finally ready to die, there's a part of you that's always going to say yes. It doesn't get easier, but it gets quieter.

There's gonna be a part of you that will never stop saying yes. It'll never stop telling you that a needle will fit perfectly in your eye socket, and it will hope and pray against you every time, but I know how you are. You're a stubborn bastard. You're single-minded and dedicated to your goals, and I only have one request—make it your goal to live. Don't go.

The light at the end is dimmer, Nicky, but hell, it's worth it. It's better than running blind in the dark. It's a promise of something new.

Every cloudy sky makes the world dark, but it promises that the sun waits somewhere underneath. Every cloudy sky still has light somewhere behind it—we just need to find it. I know we can.

Because one day, Nikolai, both of us are gonna wake up in the morning, and instead of counting down the hours aimlessly until it's time to go back to sleep, we'll wish there was more time in the day. We'll see everything we once used to use against ourselves and each other and we'll never want to look at it again. We'll see each other and instead of seeing in our eyes the broken people we used to be, and all the pain we've caused each other, we'll just see each other. It'll feel like the first time.

That's my dream.

Because when I hear 'do you want to touch the fire' in the back of my head, what I know it's really saying is 'do you want to die?'

No, Nikolai.

I don't want to die

anymore.

Please tell me you feel the same.

-Sunshine"

NIKOLAI WAKES UP.

He's sitting in his bed alone, and the room is dark.

It's nothing like the first time he woke up in this house. The dusty mirror has been replaced, and his floors are swept. He's made it his own, with paintings hung up on every wall, and books scattered about in corners, on desks, and crowding his bedside table.

Somewhere under this mattress, there's a guitar pick he still hasn't found.

And he can't breathe.

No—scratch that, he can breathe. He just... can't.

His brain is fighting him. He can't breathe. It just won't let him.

He sits up straight on the mattress, and makes a conscious

effort to breathe—in and out, one breath at a time, stabilizing himself. As soon as he stops thinking about it, his brain won't let him anymore, and he goes back to making himself take a breath in and out. Manually. It's uncomfortable, but he does it. It feels so hard. It feels like so much effort that he can't give, but he keeps going.

While he makes himself breathe, he takes a second to think.

Lucky hasn't come to see him in weeks.

He can't blame him. He wouldn't want to see himself either.

When he'd learned that he was the Siren in the temple, the Mad Leviathan in the Book of the Triad, but more importantly, Lucky's dead brother, he didn't know what to think. He barely knows what to think now, as he sits in bed, forcing himself to breathe in and out consciously because his body won't allow him to.

And it hits him.

He stares out at the sky. The moon is bright. He'd miss it a lot if he left.

It hits him.

He's being given a choice.

He's being given a choice to take the easy way out and never worry about hurting Lucky again. He can lay down and let his mind take over for him, and not make himself inhale, and simply wait for the tides to take him. He can take the easy way out. He'd never feel a thing. He'd never hurt anyone again.

But then... there's Innocence. Somewhere in that night sky, there's his brother that he hasn't made it up to. Somewhere out there, his family is waiting for him. Somewhere in the night sky, there's a trio of gods that outcasted him for his own good, and that want only to see him get better and be better.

He hopes that they can see he's trying.

It would be so easy to lay back down and let his subconscious take over and finally give him peace. It would be so easy to not have to battle with his own mind ever again, and never cause

Lucky any more harm. It would be so simple to say goodbye—
that he wouldn't even know he'd done it.

It would be easy to see his son again.

But...

Nikolai lays down. It's not an easy choice. It's the hardest
choice he's ever made.

He breathes.

He doesn't remember it in the morning.

❧

"*NIKOLAI,*

Happy 60, you old man.

Wow. Forty years and I'm still writing you these stupid letters.

*It doesn't make sense, honestly. When we go out together, people
assume I'm your grandson. Ew. I would not want to be your grandson in
a million years. You'd probably kill me for attention.*

*I shouldn't make those jokes, but you've gotten so much more comfort-
able in the past years since you learned about your past. You even joke
about it to me, sometimes. Sure, you don't really say much about what you
did to me personally, but I didn't expect that.*

*Still though, the sadness and reticence hasn't quite left you. Earlier
this year, when we were out on a walk, you saw a little girl with red hair,
and I could see the tears in your eyes. I tried to pretend I didn't notice, but
I think you could tell that I saw.*

*You tell me sometimes that you feel terrible that you can't remember
their faces or names. It must hurt a lot. You were a father once.*

You'll never see his face again.

*I drew Serena and Leo for you once. You said you wanted to see them,
and you knew I could show you.*

You keep those portraits on your bedside table.

*It... it makes me proud. The Siren would never have done that. The
Siren didn't love them like you do. Which is what makes it so terrible
you'll never meet them.*

I can see it, you know? I can see when you look at Serena's portrait and stare into her eyes and study every feature, trying to see what you'd lost. I can see you struggle to imagine the graphite as her bright emerald green eyes or copper hair. I can see it when you study the white streak in Leo's orange hair, and tug at your own strands, as if imagining that he got it from you.

He didn't.

I can't bring myself to tell you that.

I see it when you stare at your wife's eyes and smile and imagine that she were smiling at you, and that she knew you for who you are now instead of the man you were when she died. I see it all.

I wish I could do something to help. I wish I could ease the pain of you loving so deeply these people you never truly knew but planned to spend eternity with so long ago—lives ago, eons ago. I wish I could bring them to you, if only to let them know that you're sorry.

You miss them. You miss them, and you need them, but you never knew them. I know how it feels.

When you're with them, you seem the happiest you've ever been, and the most miserable you ever can be at the same time. Siren didn't deserve them—you deserve them. You deserve your wife and son, and they deserve you.

I would've loved to see Leonato grow up.

I think Fin and I would've been friends.

I'll never know, either.

I can hear it, you know?

I took your epithet as god of music and literature. I can hear your music, Nikolai, even when you think I can't.

I heard the love song you wrote to your son. I think he would've cherished it. I do, at the very least. He never can, but I do. I remember how he used to laugh when you played the piano, and I saw how he'd dance around in clumsy circles to the sound of your guitar, and I think he would've liked this one.

Serena would've accepted your apology, too. You have a way with words.

'I was a fool, seeking attention,

facing flaws of my own invention,
made more than a few mistakes.
I wish you were awake,
I'd say it to your face,
ask you for your grace,
though mere tolerance is my fate.'

I think you've earned quite a bit more, you know?

Siren never would have spent sleepless nights pacing tracks into his floors worrying over whether or not Serena could forgive him—he wouldn't want to be forgiven. He thought he already was.

I never thought I'd say this when I was still young and left out on the streets hiding from your former self, but you know what?

You've done well.

I forgive you.

It's been a long and horrible process. It's taken me forty years to realize it—forty years where the man I'd known was gone and done with, and a doppelgänger left in his place, but I've understood now. It was never you. Nikolai as I know him never would have hurt me the way the Siren did. I won't blame it on his madness. I won't blame it on Elric or Nora or Fin—it was all him.

It wasn't you, though.

So, after all this time you've worried and wondered what you could do to finally be absolved, I want you to know, simply being was all you ever needed. You're not the Siren I used to know, and one day, I know I'll believe that that's okay.

After everything that's happened, and even if you'll never read this, it's important for me to finally say; I forgive you.

Happy birthday, Old Man.

-Sunshine"

TIME WAITS FOR NO ONE.

That, Lucky knows.

Lucky also knows that it unwinds like a tangled cord in everyone's mind—tripping over knots and bumps along the way, and smoothing itself into something fathomable as it goes to try to soothe the hurt.

Lucky knows that Nikolai wouldn't have wanted a large event.

He was content to spend the most of his time cooking, baking, singing, and living a quiet, peaceful life. He didn't care for material things, and only ever wanted to be with his family —both the one that he left, and the one that needed to leave him.

He wouldn't have wanted an extravagant ceremony.

These are all things Lucky knows.

So why does it not feel real until the casket is lowered into the ground? Why does it only feel true when shovels of earth are tipped in over the top? Why does it only feel real when he glances behind him and sees emerald tears dripping down Elric's cheek, and beads of crimson pooling in Honora's eyes?

Nikolai will forgive him for all the tears he's forgotten to shed in his absence. His mind wishes to convince him he's not yet gone—that any minute he'll come into the cemetery with a tray of cookies, wondering where his brother had gone. He'll forgive him for the fact that, in his denial, he's forgotten to grieve the way he should, because it hasn't yet sunk in that he'll never again throw flour in his brother's face, or hear his music, or comfort him as he cries. Lucky waits to wake up and see it's all been a dream—from the very start of a winter long ago all the way to the far colder realization it all has to end. Lucky waits to wake up for too long, and before he knows it, days have passed as he forgets to shed a tear, and his denial convinces him he's not gone. It's hard to consolidate the many conflicting ideas of the man inside his mind. The murderer, the Siren, the loving and carefree mortal Nikolai, the father who never met his son, the brother that loved and protected boundlessly—they feel like different people in Lucky's head, but he knows they have to be the same.

A different man wouldn't have heard the stories of the Leviathan and beaten himself up over it tirelessly, apologizing to his brother day after day and spending his lifetime making it up to him. A different man wouldn't have spent his decades atoning for sins he didn't know he'd committed—but Nikolai did.

Lucky can't imagine the idea of the man he loved being gone now, forever, but he knows it has to be true.

Because time waits for no one, and it certainly never would've waited for Nikolai.

When Honora and Elric leave after the burial, Lucky goes with them.

It's a grim sight to see his brother's headstone placed in the ground. "*Nikolai Wood,*" it'll read. "*Friend, son, brother, father.*"

Maybe that last one can be true for Nikolai when it never was for the Siren.

He hopes Leo and Serena have been waiting on the other side.

21

Lucky doesn't visit Nikolai's grave.

There's a certain finality to seeing the stone resting under the weeping willow that he's not sure he would be able to stomach if he finally took the plunge. One singular gravestone below the crying limbs of a beautiful waterfall of a tree, on a hill overlooking a grassy valley—under that grave, an olden god sleeps. He rejoins the earth as his penance, and one day soon, nature will retake his soul as She was always meant to.

Lucky doesn't want to see it.

He keeps himself occupied for the first few weeks. He sews himself pillows and embroiders his shirts with flowers and leaves far too reminiscent of the forest of tattoos on Nikolai's arms. He doesn't embroider much after that.

Then he picks up cooking. He makes Elric scour the globe for the finest ingredients, and makes feasts each night that the two gods praise him for to the ends of the earth. He still can't shake the memories of Nikolai's pastries from his mind whenever he sprinkles cinnamon into a dish, or salts a pan of potatoes. Nora loves his potatoes, but he can't bring himself to make them.

Lucky doesn't take up the same space that he used to.

SAMARA KATHARINE

Rooms that once could be filled by his chaotic and energetic presence feel empty and lonely, even with all three of the gods inside them. There's an empty space in the gods' palace that Nikolai used to occupy. Even if he was never there, they always had the promise that one day he could be.

That's not true.

Lucky starts gardening.

He goes out with Elric during the day and waters his vegetables. Elric talks to the flowers as he pulls weeds, comforting them.

"*I know,*" he says, "*I know it hurts. It'll make you feel so much better, though.*"

There have been times Elric stops pulling weeds. He says some of the younger flowers refuse, and he doesn't want to hurt them, especially if they can't understand how it helps them. Lucky listens to their conversations, and wonders how Elric can understand them. They never speak a word.

He asked once, and Elric gave him a sad smile, and told him that only he could ever understand.

So Lucky pretends.

I water my flowers every day,
they tell me stories as I go.
The dandelions dream of floating away,
every time the wind blows.

They don't respond to him. Sometimes Elric catches him outside talking to them and telling them stories while he draws pictures in a weathered brown journal. He knows Elric can see, and he's sure Elric knows what he's doing, but he never does comment. He simply observes, and sometimes, he smiles.

Lucky learns about the early days when he tends the garden with Elric. They talk about everything and nothing, and Elric tells him about the first days he made the earth, and all of the wonderful things he put on it.

The first plant Elric made was grass.

Later that day, Lucky flies out to the forest alone without shoes on his feet, and feels the soil under his toes. Bees buzz past him and butterflies perch on his fingers. He returned that day to tell the flowers all about the forest far away that they will never see. They don't say anything, but something tells him they truly do listen.

The tulips tell me stories of home,
and the little rock where they grew up.
If you see a tulip under a stone,
bring some sugar, offer it a cup.

But Lucky can't fill up his whole day with plants the way Elric can.

Months following his brother's death, he finds himself all alone in the library archives. He looks up to the perfectly preserved, varnished portrait of Nikolai on the wall, tall and imposing. It must be from before Krista—Nick is smiling.

Lucky tries to think of something to say, but nothing comes out.

He takes a random old leather-bound book off a shelf, and walks away.

It's about music.

He puts it back.

If you see a lily growing in a pond,
call out from your place on the bay.
Do not step in, it's a sin,
they don't teach magic to those who wade.

Elric and Nora leave him alone for the most part as he goes about his days. He shows up to breakfast and dinner, and secludes himself away for the rest of the time. The vines creeping into his room begin to grow fruits on each stem, and he laughs to himself. He doesn't doubt it's Elric's doing. He eats lunch in his room and throws apple cores and mango skins out the window to fertilize the grass below.

When he's alone, his eyes drift to Nikolai's guitar in the corner. He kept it for himself. Mortal Nicky spent quite a bit of time trying to teach him how to play, and Lucky just couldn't bear the thought of giving it away or leaving it in his cottage to rot; least of all Honora's suggestion: burning it.

Sometimes he plays it.

Most times he tears his gaze away with moisture gathering in his eyes.

But there's nothing he can do to stop it; he misses Nicky. He can't keep himself entertained during the day without his mind drifting back to his dead brother, who currently decomposes under the earth, feeding the worms in the dirt.

So even though he's tried so hard to avoid it, on the third month after his brother's death, he gathers up the courage. He goes to the garden and cuts violets and peace lilies, and in the dead of the night, with a box in hand, he flies away.

> *If you see a flower washed up ashore,*
> *run, and do not look back.*
> *The ocean loves you, the petals, too,*
> *but the flowers warn you only once.*

HONORA AND ELRIC KNOW THAT LUCKY FLIES BACK HOME. They each lay awake in their own beds, staring at the ceiling, pondering their new addition to a broken and disheveled family. Quietly, Nora stands up out of bed, and walks the dark and silent halls to Elric's room, footsteps pattering on the floor.

She slides the door open to find her father sitting up straight already. He turns his head and gives her a warm smile.

"Hey Nora," he says, his voice strained.

"Hey Dad," she responds, closing the door behind him. Elric's expression softens.

"Dad?" he parrots. "You haven't called me that in a while. Something's wrong." Nora chuckles, and sits down on her father's bed, crossing her legs, and avoiding eye contact.

"Astute observation," she mocks. Elric laughs a little, but quickly sobers, looking at her with fond eyes.

"What's going on?" he asks. Nora nods, and lets out a heavy breath.

"Lucky left," she says.

"I know," Elric responds. She shakes her head in consideration, huffing.

"I just wish we could help him," she says. "He's struggling. He hasn't even visited." Elric nods, and reaches over to tug his daughter closer to him. Honora rolls her eyes and shuffles over begrudgingly, resting her head on the Angel's shoulder.

"We're all struggling," he says. "We all have our different ways of getting through it. Lucky's smart. He'll be alright, I promise." Nora nods and doesn't say anything. Elric sighs. "But that's not all that's on your mind," he prompts. Nora doesn't speak, trying to bury herself in the crook of her father's neck as if she can avoid it. "Honey, what are you really thinking about?" he asks.

Nora stares across the room at the portrait of Krista and Finnigan on Elric's dresser.

"It's nothing," she settles on. Elric shakes his head.

"Not true, what is it?"

She looks into Fin's hazel eyes—bright and full of life—and Krista flashing a fond smile.

"I don't need to be the literal god bemoaning her struggles when it's all negligible," she says. "Other people have it worse." Elric follows his gaze to the painting, and frowns.

"Nora, we've talked about this." Honora sighs.

"Right, right," she capitulates. "'If you use other people as a yardstick, you'll always come up short,' I know." Elric smiles and rubs his daughter's back.

"So what is it?" he asks. Honora fiddles with the fabric of her shirt.

"I was just thinking..." she starts. The Voices get loud, and she shakes her head angrily.

I wish you'd drop dead!

You took everything.

"You and Lucky," she tries again, "you guys know he loved you." Elric opens his mouth but Nora cuts him off. "In his own twisted way, he showed you guys," she says. She feels something prick at the corner of her eye. "Do you remember the last thing he said to me?" she asks. "When he was still..." Elric thinks for a second, and tries to speak, but it doesn't come out. Honora nods. "He said he wished I'd die."

"Nora..." Elric tries to console. The goddess blinks tears away.

"And you know, I try to think like, 'Yeah, I wouldn't want that guy's love anyway,' but... The last thing my brother ever said to me, Dad. 'You took everything.'" Honora laughs at herself. "It's stupid because I shouldn't want a child murderer to like me, but he was my brother." *Was.* What a terrible word. "I just can't shake this feeling lately that I should've stayed mortal."

"Nora, no, don't think like that." Nora laughs.

"But it's true, isn't it? Your grandson would still be here. You'd still have your daughter-in-law if it weren't for me. I just think maybe th—" Elric smacks her head. "Ow."

"We don't think like that around here," he says. Honora reaches up to rub the back of her head.

"You didn't have to hit me," Nora mutters. Elric smiles.

"We don't do things halfway around here either."

"Point taken," she grumbles.

"Don't think like that, Nora. I know it's easier said than done, but I can't say this enough—I chose you. All of you. I wouldn't give any of you up for the world. All of," Elric gestures wildly, "this is not because of you. It's because of him and his madness. Don't take any responsibility. You showed compassion and you tried your best." Elric smiles, and pulls Nora closer, hugging her. "If anything, you're the most innocent one of all of us." Honora chuckles.

"And Lucky?" she asks.

"Okay, second place to Lucky." The two of them laugh together while Elric runs his fingers through Honora's tangled blonde hair, pulling out loose strands, and smoothing it down. Elric's voice is soft and quiet when he next speaks. "But really, Nora. Don't worry about it. The Nikolai who said that wasn't your brother." She scoffs, but he lets Elric continue. "He was sick, and he was out of his mind, and you shouldn't believe anything he said that day. Nikolai? Nikolai Wood, after his revival? That was my son."

Was.

"What a terrible word," Honora mumbles. Elric laughs, and Nora's not quite sure if he understands what she means to say, but she laughs all the same.

He leans back on his pillows, and pats the empty space next to him with a smile. Just like her childhood, Nora curls up beside her father and pulls the blankets over herself.

"I blamed myself, too," the Angel whispers. "Even we are not infallible."

And just like her childhood, she waits for her brother to come home.

LUCKY SETTLES DOWN ON HIS KNEES BEFORE THE STONE, AND keeps his gaze to the ground.

He can't quite bring himself to look up and see the name carved into the grave, because that would make it real.

He puts the flowers on the soil along with the small box, and tries to waste time picking at his nails to avoid the inevitable. But if Lucky's learned anything in his years on earth—time waits for no one. He doesn't have time to waste or give away.

"Hey," he says finally. He chuckles to himself, looking up to finally see the grave. Nikolai Wood, friend, brother, son, father. "Lame greeting," he continues, "but I don't know what to say."

Nikolai, being months dead, doesn't respond. Lucky sighs.

"I'm sorry I haven't visited," he says. "I've tried to convince myself you're still alive and you won't mind. Maybe I could go back to your cottage for tea, and there you'd be standing by the stove, humming a formless tune to yourself. It's not true, I know. But I've gotten very good at playing pretend." There's silence. Aside from the whispering wind that ruffles the leaves of the willow, there is no sound. "I pretended the Siren loved me. I pretended I deserved everything he did. I played make-believe that it could last forever and I'd always be safe with his arms around me."

It feels all too familiar for Lucky to be sitting on his knees speaking to someone who could never answer back.

"You know, Honora told me this story," he continues, trying to ignore the feeling of pain in his chest. "She overuses her powers. Like, a lot. When we first met, she didn't even walk. She only teleported. Anyway, she told me about it a couple days ago." Lucky smiles remembering it. "She was once like me. She thought you guys would take it all away, so she started abusing the power she had while he had it, because she was sure it couldn't last forever. Then it did." His smile falls slightly, and he picks at his nails again. "That's what it feels like coming back to you, I think. It couldn't last forever, so I tried to get all the hugs and all the kisses and all the love I could squeeze out of the Siren before he took it away from me. You're not like that though. I know you're not him."

By his feet, the wind makes the head of a dandelion bob up and down, and his mind drifts to images of Finnigan speaking to the flowers, and their little movements he took as affirmations. He smiles.

"And you know, I realized something the other day." He gathers his confidence, biting at his lips and wringing his hands.

It's not an easy thing to admit. He opens his mouth and lets it fall out before he can think about it. "I love you," he says. "That's it. I've always known, but—" he cuts himself off, and mercury tears gather at his waterline. He blinks them away. "I never said it," he finishes. "I always assumed you knew," he says, "but I never told you. You told me every day. You punctuated sentences not with periods but with 'I love you's, and I never said it back."

The tears come faster now, climbing up Lucky's throat trying to make themselves known. He can't quite hold them back anymore. Silver paints the ground, and as it evaporates, it leaves layers of frost on each blade of grass.

"I'm sorry," he says. "I'm sorry that I never did. I don't—" he takes a watery breath. "I don't like the fact that I can't tell you now. I should've said it before, I—I was scared, you know? The last time I loved someone..." he trails off, looking up to the leaves of the willow. "But that wasn't you," he says. "So I'm sorry."

A warm breeze tickles his cheek, and for a moment, he almost understands how Fin felt. He laughs.

"Oh, right," he says, reaching into his pocket. "I brought you something." He sets a guitar pick gingerly down in the grass beside his peace lilies. "Just thought you'd want to have it. You know, figuratively. I found it in the library. Of course you were the type to specifically go to a quiet place to play." He chuckles. "All you know is disrupting the peace. Can't blame you though, it is pretty fun. Nora the other day was trying to wash some dishes from dinner, and I just came up behind her and scared the immortal life out of her!"

Honora had dropped the plate into the sink. It shattered, and she had stared at Lucky like she'd seen a ghost, trying to block his view of the glass pieces. Lucky lets out a breath, and smiles at Nikolai's grave.

"I didn't pick up the glass," he says. "Dad and Nora tried to hide it from me, but I didn't even want to." For once, that isn't a lie. "I haven't thought about it in so long. You know they're finally gonna replace my windows? They had some stupid mechanism that stopped them from opening. It was so I couldn't jump out, but they never said that. But they're getting rid of them now."

The willow sways. Lucky looks around, down the hill towards the grassy valley where dandelions and daisies bloom, where one day, his body, too, may lay, and give back to the earth from whence he came.

Somewhere, in that grassy valley deep that Lucky was always meant to see, an innocent soul sleeps. Six feet deep in a five-foot coffin at no more than four tall. Three gods keep him in their thoughts until two can finally join him where one already has.

Lucky smiles. A small, sad thing, but a real one. He hopes Fin is happy, wherever he really is.

"Anyway," Lucky says, looking back at Nikolai's stone. "I miss you," he admits, "a lot. But Elric... Elric said something to me a while ago. He said that 'No story worth telling ever really ends.' I guess it means something to me. At least to just think that you're not truly gone—though thank the stars above, I don't think anyone would've been able to handle a thousand more years of you." He laughs and drops his gaze back down to the flowers. "In any case, I hope Death treats you well. Even after all you've done, I think you deserve it to have some peace now. And your storyteller, too; they can finally put down their pen. There are more stories to be told around here."

Lucky crosses his legs and settles down on the soil. He takes a piece of paper out of his pocket, and shows it to the grave.

"Like this kid in the village," he says. "He reminds me a lot of myself." He studies the portrait he drew of the boy—fluffy dirty-blond hair and piercing eyes, each with a different color, a wide smile on his face, and a butterfly perched on his nose. He smiles. "He's an orphan, too, and really resourceful. I've been leaving him things, but I'm not gonna make your same mistakes." Lucky takes in a breath of the fresh spring air, and looks up to see the moon bright in the sky. It smiles at him, he thinks. "I named him after Fin's best friend. The one that died in the fire. I never did get to know much about Archer, but I think he deserves a second chance." Lucky nods resolutely and stares back at the grave with passion in his eyes. "He'll have a better life than the first. I promise."

It's not like the Siren's old promises; Lucky can feel it in his heart that he won't find it in himself to break it.

"So yeah," he breathes out. "That's what's been going on. I hope you're happy. I hope you have in Death what this life couldn't give you. I hope one day soon that flowers will spring from this soil and have your spirit in them." He reaches out for the small box, and finally opens it. "And I hope at the very least," he pulls out the papers, "if you can't read these letters yourself, you can at least know that, once, someone loved you and didn't know how to say it." He reads the opening line of the first paper. *To my worst nightmare.*

He clutches the letters in his hands, and feels them turn ice cold and brittle in his grip. One by one, he crumbles them up into frozen, icy fibers, and scatters them in the dirt around the grave, watching them melt and dissolve away into nothing in the earth's warming touch. A wistful smile graces his lips as he closes the box, and curls his wings around himself. They're cold as always, but bring a sense of comfort that's been foreign to the young god for years.

"I'll visit again soon," Lucky says. The wind kisses his cheeks, and he shakes his head, laughing an airy laugh. "I'll bring snacks, maybe. We'll have tea, just like old times."

He extends his wings to their full expansive length, and can almost feel the breeze in his intangible silvery feathers. He stands, and looks up to the sky, and almost hears Nikolai's voice on the wind. He's saying he's proud.

"Until then," he says. With a two-fingered salute, he smiles, and takes off towards the clouds.

And there are many more tales to be told in an infinite life beyond what mortals can comprehend. There's the story of the kitten named Creampuff who lived her years by a god's side. There's the story of a boy with two different colored eyes, chosen by the gods and given the name of one whose story was never told. There's the long story of a young warrior hundreds of years ago who earned the favor of a god and said goodbye to the world she'd known.

There's the story still yet to be told of a margrave in a lonely temple thinking up riddles in his free time, and doling out advice that falls off the surface of his listeners' minds like water off a duck's back.

There's the story of two loving parents of a golden-haired boy, whose faces are obscured in the folds of the fabric of time, who didn't live to see their son's seventh birthday, and who will never know how far he went, and of that same boy's baby sister who he's sure he used to hold.

In the end, there is only so much time in the day to listen to tall tales, and one day, each of them will have their moment.

As Lucky soars, not for the first time, he looks at the fall, as the still-sleeping village falls away into obscurity beneath the clouds.

Lucky smiles.

ACKNOWLEDGMENTS

Where do I begin? First, of course, thank you to you, the reader, for coming on this journey with me and Lucky until the very end. I can't express how honored I am to have captivated your attention for this long, and I thank you sincerely. This silly aspiration of mine is coming to life because of you, and I will forever be grateful.

Thank you to the entire team at Bow's Bookshelf for extraordinary patience with me through this process, and for coaching me through my inexperience; you guys rock. To Anna Stileski, thank you for taking a chance on me and helping this dream come true.

Thank you, as always, to some of my best friends: Holly Kringler, Liliana Becker (and the whole "Nerm Family"), Maddie Panaiia, Peyton McCauley, Alex Sasyniuk, Abbie Wagstaff, and Charlie Blue. For forcing me to close my laptop from time to time to drink water, and for being my first team of (slightly unwilling) beta readers. Thanks, of course, to Nicholette, for being my very first die-hard fan and for pushing me through the editing process, and to many other friends along the way I could name for hours. I have no words to describe how wonderful you all are, so can I offer you photos of my cat instead? He's in my lap as I write this.

To a few people who don't know me but contributed to my storytelling style all the same, J.R.R Tolkein, Michael Ende, Kendare Blake, Suzanne Collins, Donna Tartt, and strangely enough, Madam Secretary of State, Madeleine Albright.

Zero thanks to my cats for sitting on my keyboard and very frequently deleting important passages. I love you, but I owe you nothing.

Thank you to Madonna Arnold for fostering creativity, and for out-of-focus pictures of the moon at nine at night.

To Ray, thank you for being yourself unapologetically, and inspiring me to do the same, and also you're welcome, for providing you a synopsis of TLID so you could lie to your English teacher that you read it.

Thank you to my father for signing the contract with me. You're a real one.

To my grandmother, Susan, I hope you would have been proud. Rest easy, and thank you for the memories.

Thank you to Terra for many long nights awake talking, for buying me too much coffee, for your vibrant spirit and quick wit, but mostly, for everything.

ABOUT THE AUTHOR

Samara Katharine lives and writes in Minnesota and is finishing her senior year in high school. She is moving on to university to study criminology fall of 2023. The Light is Dimmer is her debut novel.

Ingram Content Group UK Ltd.
Milton Keynes UK
UKHW012339260723
425847UK00003B/20

9 798887 160221